Tabloid Star

One hot night, one freeze frame...and one shocking surprise.

As a bartender at the Lucky Seven club, Josh Bauer could take a different guy home every night...if he wanted to. Working three jobs, however, makes it hard to connect with anyone. One man, though, is too much temptation to resist. A steamy encounter in a back alley leads to an explosive night of sex in Josh's bed—a bed he isn't surprised to find empty the next morning.

What does surprise him, though, is the front page of a tabloid. Apparently his one-night stand isn't as anonymous as he thought it was.

Ryan Kellar's career is taking off. Advance buzz about his movie says it's a blockbuster, and going home with the gorgeous bartender is the perfect way to celebrate. And he thought he'd gotten away clean—until the picture in the paper shocks him into reality. Was Josh really just playing...or playing him for a fool?

Trust isn't big on their list right now, but as their worlds fall apart, it's all they have. At least until they figure out who took the picture. And why...

Warning: Hot manlove, gratuitous licking of tattoos and dealing with stalking paparazzi.

With This Ring

The end of the year is the start of a whole new beginning...

Josh Bauer and Ryan Kellar sweated through a turbulent start to their relationship. Now that they've embarked on a life together, filled with family friends—and each other—Ryan's suffering sweaty palms again. For an entirely different reason.

It's not the heat they generate every time they're alone together. It's not even the crush of people at Josh's jam-packed birthday party. It's the birthday present Ryan's carrying in his jeans pocket. The one that could make him the happiest man in the world, come New Year's Eve.

If Josh says "yes"...

Warning: Hot guy on guy sex. A happily married couple and a rocking New Year's Eve party guaranteed to keep you up all night.

Look for these titles by
T.A. Chase

Now Available:

Love of Sports Series
Out of Bounds
High Line

Bound by Love
Tabloid Star
With This Ring

Print Anthologies
Playing the Game
A Tabloid Love

A Tabloid Love

T.A. Chase

A Samhain Publishing, Ltd. publication.

Samhain Publishing, Ltd.
577 Mulberry Street, Suite 1520
Macon, GA 31201
www.samhainpublishing.com

A Tabloid Love
Print ISBN: 978-1-60504-776-8
Tabloid Star Copyright © 2010 by T.A. Chase
With This Ring Copyright © 2010 by T.A. Chase

Editing by Tera Kleinfelter
Cover by Anne Cain

Tabloid Star, ISBN 978-1-60504-662-4
First Samhain Publishing, Ltd. electronic publication: September 2009
With This Ring, ISBN 978-1-60504-856-7
First Samhain Publishing, Ltd. electronic publication: December 2009
First Samhain Publishing, Ltd. print publication: November 2010

Contents

Tabloid Star

Dedication

Tabloid Star is dedicated to Jambrea, who with her pictures and her support, helped bring Josh and Ryan to life. Thank you for all you have done. Also, to my marvelous editor who manages to clear up my errors and make my story sparkle. C., you are the love of my life.

Chapter One

Josh tossed his backpack in Rachel's office, checked his clothes in the mirror next to the door and headed out to the front. Sliding behind the bar, he smiled at Tammy, the bartender he was replacing.

"How's it been tonight?" He grabbed a bottle of Jameson and poured out a shot for the guy closest to him.

"Just starting to pick up. It should be a busy one for you. Thanks, hon." She winked at the man leaving her a tip. "Hey, thanks for getting here early. Maria's picking me up here and we're going to hit the new club that opened down the street."

"You and Maria still pretty hot and heavy, huh?" He didn't skip a beat as he drew two pints of Guinness and mixed a screwdriver.

"God, that girl can kiss. I've never had a lover who loves kissing like her and what she can do with her tongue."

"Whoa there...TMI, Tammy. If I wanted to hear about chicks having sex, I'd be straight." He chuckled as she flipped him off. "Go on, get out of here. I've got this covered and Pete's coming in at twelve."

Tammy squealed and hugged him. "You're the best, Josh. I take back all those nasty things I told Simpson about you."

"No wonder the newbie was looking at me weird the other

night."

He spent the next half-hour getting into the swing of serving drinks, flirting with the customers and keeping the bar clean. He was grateful he only had to work his morning job before coming to the Lucky Seven, where he'd work until three in the morning. The days he had to work all three of his jobs were hell, but he did what he had to do to survive.

The Lucky Seven was one of the best kept secrets in West Hollywood, which was saying something, considering nothing stayed a secret in any part of Hollywood for long. Soon the club was packed, bodies grinding on the dance floor to the driving beat of the music. The drink orders were coming fast and furious, but Josh was an expert on crazy nights and kept up easily.

He acknowledged Pete's arrival with a nod, not breaking stride as he mixed martinis and cosmos for the waitresses.

"Good-looking crowd tonight," Pete commented as he passed by, heading for the ice chest.

A quick glance around and Josh agreed. "It is, but then again when isn't it? I don't think ugly people are allowed in WeHo, Pete."

Grabbing a towel, he dried the sweat off his head before tossing it on the shelf behind him. A commotion at the other end of the bar caught his attention and he moved toward the two men standing there. He didn't usually break up fights, but since the place was crowded and it would take a few minutes for the bouncers to get there, he'd see if he could defuse the situation first.

"You're a jackass, Bill." The taller of the two men growled, a frown marring his face.

"Maybe so, Ry, but at least I'm not a chicken shit." Bill slugged Ry's arm.

"Don't hit me." Ry shoved the other man away. "A chicken shit? What the fuck are you talking about?"

Bill grabbed the edge of the bar before he could slam into the girl standing behind him. "Yes, a chicken shit. You always look, but you never touch. You're too scared of the consequences to do anything you really want to do." Bill waved his hand, seeming to encompass the entire club. "So many choices, yet you'll go home alone. At least I won't."

Josh got there before Ry could land the punch he was swinging. "Hey, guys, can I get you something to drink?"

Bill's hazy blue eyes met his with a smirk. "Yeah, liquid courage might help my friend get lucky tonight."

Ignoring the sarcastic tone in Bill's voice, Josh made a point of checking Ry out. He admitted to himself he liked what he saw. Ry was tall with a lean muscular build, more like a runner than a weight lifter. The baseball cap Ry wore made it hard to tell what color his hair was and the sunglasses hid the color of his eyes, but his tight black jeans and dark blue T-shirt gave Josh a hint at Ry's body. Josh's cock twitched, interested even though Josh didn't tend to take customers home.

"Well, I don't know about needing any liquid courage. If your friend's looking for something, I'm sure he could find it quite easily here."

Josh winked at Ry and a surprised grin crossed the man's face. Shaking his head, Bill nudged Ry with his shoulder.

"See, I said you could have anyone you wanted in this club. Why not live a little and celebrate?" Bill picked up his beer and gestured into the crowd. "I'm going over to talk to that curvy redhead. I hope you brought cab fare, buddy, because we won't be leaving together."

Ry scowled, but mumbled, "Go get her, stud, and don't worry. I have money."

They watched Bill weave his way through the crush of people until he disappeared. Josh looked back at Ry to find the man studying him. Ry slid his sunglasses down and looked over them, tracing the length of Josh's body. Josh swore he felt heat from each part of his skin those dark brown eyes touched. The desire blazing in that glance told Josh Ry was looking for someone different than Bill was.

"You want something to drink?" His question came out husky and he swallowed, trying to wet his suddenly dry throat.

"Drink? Sure, I'll take a whiskey, neat."

Josh forced himself to walk away and grab a glass. He could feel Ry's gaze burning into his back as the man eyed his ass. Taking a bottle of the top-shelf whiskey, he filled a high ball glass and handed it to Ry, who slid his fingers along Josh's as he took the drink, shooting lust and blood to Josh's groin.

"Fuck," Josh whispered.

"Thanks." Ry's pink tongue peeked out, wetting his plump bottom lip and drawing Josh's attention to it.

Josh groaned and adjusted his cock, searching for room in his too-tight jeans. "What exactly are you looking for, honey? I'll be happy to accommodate you, but you have to be sure."

Ry checked him out again, his eyes lingering at the growing bulge at Josh's groin. Hesitation colored Ry's words when he leaned forward and whispered, "I think you know what I'm looking for."

He could tell Ry didn't pick up men often, or probably not at all by the way the man's gaze darted away from him the moment he uttered that statement.

"Pete, can you handle it for ten minutes while I take my break?" Josh didn't look away from Ry, shouting his question over his shoulder toward the other bartender.

"Sure, Josh. I've got it." The smile in Pete's voice told Josh his friend knew what was going on between him and Ry.

He moved from behind the bar, gestured for Ry to follow him and made his way through the crowd toward the back of the club. Josh hit the back exit door at almost a run, letting the metal door slam open as he yanked Ry through the doorway. As the door shut, he pinned the man to the brick wall and kissed him.

Chapter Two

"Omphf..."

The air in Ryan's lungs rushed out as he hit the brick wall and the burly bartender attacked his mouth like the army running a frontal assault on the enemy. Opening, he allowed the man to sweep in and stroke his tongue. He curled his hands in the fabric at the man's sides, tugging the guy's T-shirt up over his head. Ryan purred at the sight of the bartender's lightly furred chest covered with tattoos that Ryan wanted to taste.

He closed his eyes and his head spun as what little oxygen he had was used up. There was a flash of light and he needed air before he passed out. Finally, he broke the kiss, panting and staring in shock at the man pressing against him.

"I don't know your name," he murmured.

A dark eyebrow shot up and the bartender grinned. "My name? Do you always ask the name of the guy you're about to blow in an alley?"

"I'm about to blow? Aren't you assuming something?"

He shivered at the arrogant smile the man gave him.

"You'll be assuming the position in a moment." The man stepped back and held out his hand politely. "I'm Josh."

Fuck. Something about the assurance in the man's voice made all the blood in Ryan's body rush to his groin.

"I'm Ry." Feeling silly, he shook Josh's hand.

"With the introductions out of the way, are you ready? I don't have much time left before I have to get behind the bar and I really want to see your mouth wrapped around my cock."

Shit. No one had ever talked to him like that. As much as he seemed to like having a man order him around, he wasn't going to be a push-over.

"What do I get out of it?"

Josh's gaze wandered down Ryan's body, stopping at his groin before coming back up to meet his eyes. "You get me coming in your mouth and then when I'm done working at three, you get me in your ass."

The X-rated images Josh's words conjured up made Ryan's cock ache even more and almost drove him to his knees. His indecision and nervousness must have showed on his face because Josh cupped his cheek and gave him a quick peck on the nose.

"We don't have to do any of it. I thought you were looking for what I could give you." Josh shrugged. "If I'm wrong, no hard feelings."

An easy out and Ryan should take it. There was too much at risk if he got caught. He opened his mouth to call off whatever was happening between them, but Bill's voice echoed through his head.

You always look, but you never touch. You're too scared of the consequences to do anything you really want to do.

Bill was right, and oh how he wanted to do Josh. Hell, it was a quick suck in an alley and then a quick fuck at Josh's place. No one would be the wiser about what he'd done. Not even Bill, though he knew he could trust his friend if the man ever found out.

Digging in his front pocket, he slowly sank to his knees. He held up the rubber.

"Hold this until I'm ready."

"So sure you were going to get lucky or were you a Boy Scout?" Josh took the foil wrapper from his hands and knocked the cap from his head. "I want to be able to bury my fingers in your hair."

Ryan grunted. He didn't care what Josh wanted or did. He focused intently on the growing bulge in Josh's pants. With shaking hands, he fumbled with the buttons of Josh's fly. He swore softly.

Josh smoothed a hand over Ryan's curls. "Easy, baby. I've got time. We'll take it at your pace. You need me to undo those?"

Ryan shook his head. No, he would do it on his own. It was a minor achievement, but what the hell. He was stepping over the lines he'd drawn a long time ago and he would accept responsibility for it all.

He gave a sigh of relief when he got Josh's pants open and he pushed the sides apart to reveal Josh's large prick. Why wasn't he surprised that Josh wasn't wearing any underwear? His mouth watered and he longed to taste him. Wetting his lips, he leaned forward.

"You get one lick, before we put the rubber on. I'm clean, but there's no point in starting bad habits." Josh braced both hands on the wall above Ryan, blocking Ryan from sight should anyone look down the alley.

Okay. One lick. He could do that. He flicked out his tongue and caught the single drop hanging at the slit in Josh's flared head. Though he was tempted to take another taste, he knew Josh was right. No point in risking anything for a moment of pleasure.

Josh tapped his shoulder and he caught the condom Josh dropped into his hand. He tore it open with his teeth, nuzzling the soft area where Josh's torso and thigh met while he unwrapped it. He nibbled a little, causing Josh to draw in a breath. Scraping his teeth over that spot, he worried the piece of flesh until a nice dark mark blossomed.

"None of that. You can explore later. I want your mouth." Josh tugged on his hair gently.

With a quick wink up at the man, Ryan rolled the rubber down over Josh's thick shaft. Filling his lungs with air, he swallowed Josh down until he had his nose buried in the curls at the base of Josh's cock. He hated the taste of the rubber, but loved the way Josh smelled of sweat and man.

"Shit. You look just as good as I thought you would."

He managed to look up and meet Josh's heated gaze. Ryan blushed. It was silly, really, to be embarrassed because the man he was sucking off thought he looked good with his cock in his mouth.

Josh caressed Ryan's cheek and smiled. "Do you want me to do the work?"

God, Josh must think he was an idiot. He placed his hands on the man's hips and slid back until only the tip of Josh's cock stayed in his mouth. He teased it through the latex while tapping Josh on the hip bone, letting the man know he could move if he wanted to.

Josh took his hands off the wall and threaded his fingers through Ryan's hair. "You ready?"

Ryan barely nodded before Josh started thrusting, each stroke hitting the back of Ryan's throat. He took it, keeping the suction hard. Sliding his hand over, he cupped Josh's balls and rolled them in his palm.

Grunting, Josh sped up and lost his rhythm. He shoved

into Ryan's mouth, claiming him in a way Ryan had not been subjected to in a long time.

He hummed, wanting to feel Josh come, even if he couldn't taste him. Ryan scraped a nail over the soft patch of skin behind Josh's balls.

"Fuck," Josh shouted, filling the condom as his hips jerked and his fingers dug into Ryan's head.

Ryan continued working Josh's cock with his mouth until he stopped moving. Pulling off with a soft pop, he rested his head back on the brick and looked up at the man towering over him.

Josh carded his fingers through Ryan's hair with a soft smile on his chiseled face before running his tumb over Ryan's swollen lips.

"I knew you would be good."

Ryan ducked his head at the praise coming from this stranger. Josh took care of the condom, tossing it in the dumpster before tucking his limp cock back into his jeans and buttoning up. Reaching down, he put his hands under Ryan's arms and lifted him to his feet, which was no mean feat. Ryan wasn't skinny or short. He only stood an inch or two shorter than Josh, but he definitely didn't have the bulk the bartender had.

He gasped as Josh undid his jeans and slid a rough hand over his cock. Arching his hips, he grasped Josh's shoulders and moaned.

Josh nibbled along his chin and sucked on his earlobe. "Thought I'd get you off because there's nothing worse than sitting around a club with a boner all night."

"Who said anything about sitting around?" he managed to stutter out before all his brain cells found better uses of their time like enjoying the strength of the fingers wrapped around his prick.

"Must be wishful thinking on my part. I was really looking forward to pounding this ass later on tonight."

"Oh, okay."

What else could he say at the moment? His balls drew tight to his body and he came, spilling his spunk all over Josh's hand. Ryan rocked until his cock grew soft. He slumped against the wall and Josh held his hand up to his lips.

"Clean me," Josh ordered softly.

Holding Josh's gaze, he took his time licking his come off the bartender's hand, sucking each finger clean and making sure every inch of Josh's palm was free of come.

"God, you get to me quick." Josh adjusted himself with his other hand. "Let's get inside before Pete comes looking for me. I've got a clean shirt you can borrow."

Ryan looked down and saw the stains on the front of his shirt. A noise came from the entrance of the alley. He glanced around wildly. Had someone been watching them? God, he hoped not.

"Easy. It was just a cat. No one's out here with us." Josh smoothed his hand down Ryan's arm to take his hand. "Let's go in and get a drink, huh?"

"Okay."

He had a few more hours before he had to come back to reality. His body decided it wanted to spend that time with Josh, so he'd follow where the man led him.

Chapter Three

Picking his T-shirt up off the ground, Josh strolled in from the alley, his walk loose, smiling to himself. Ry just might be the best cocksucker Josh had ever gotten busy with. He couldn't wait to see what it felt like to be buried balls-deep in the man. Ry's grip tightened and relaxed around Josh's hand as they made their way to Rachel's office, letting Josh know the man was there, but also clueing him into the fact that Ry seemed a little nervous now that the sex was over. Good thing they could get to his boss's office without going out into the club where others might see them.

Stepping into the office, he tugged Ry in behind him and shut the door. He went over to the couch and sat, pulling Ry down onto his lap. Pretty brown eyes blinked back at him, still hazy from Ry's climax. Josh nuzzled his throat, nibbling a little, and Ry shivered.

"You okay," he murmured, trailing kisses along Ry's chin.

"Yeah. It's just been a while since I've done something like that." Ry rested his hands on Josh's shoulders and leaned into him slightly.

Josh took Ry's weight easily. "Done what? A hand job? A blow job? Or doing it in an alley?"

Ry chuckled. "All of it really, but mostly in the alley. I try not to do stuff like that where I can get caught or be seen."

"Don't worry. If someone looked down the alley, we were just two bodies. No one would have been able to figure out who we were or see our faces. Besides, I was standing in front of you."

He sighed and stood, setting Ry on the couch before moving to his backpack. Crouching, he tugged a shirt out and shook it out before tossing it over to Ry.

"Here, you can wear this. You can either stuff your shirt in my bag and we'll wash it at my apartment or you can throw it out."

Ry caught the shirt and turned it around in his hands for a moment.

"It's clean." Josh stood and leaned against the door.

"Oh, I know. I've never borrowed a shirt from someone before." Ry smiled.

"You've never done a lot of stuff, have you?"

He shrugged. "I might be slightly in the closet."

Josh shook his head. "You need to get out more, man. Change your shirt. I have to get back behind the bar."

Ry stripped his T-shirt off and Josh admired his ripped abs. As much as he wanted to, he didn't touch Ry's skin to see if it was as smooth as it looked. He really did need to get back or Pete would throw a fit. He took it as a good sign when Ry shoved his shirt into Josh's backpack while Josh pulled his shirt back on.

He brushed a kiss over Ry's nose and grinned. "Come on. You can sit at the end of the bar or go and dance. Do whatever you want. I've got three more hours before I can take off."

Josh decided he was going to call in another favor from Pete and get the man to clean up without him. His bed was calling him and he really wanted to see what Ry looked like spread out over his black sheets.

Ry stiffened when they entered the main floor of the club and the noise rolled over them like thunder. Josh let Ry yank his hand free and out of the corner of his eyes, Josh saw Ry pull the brim of his hat down to cover his face.

"You should probably sit in the corner if you don't want anyone to see you." He'd dealt with closet cases before, though why Ry went with him out into the alley if he didn't want anyone to recognize him didn't make sense to Josh. Yet he'd learned not to ask too many questions of one-night stands.

Ry ducked his head, but gave Josh a shy smile. "Thanks."

"No problem." He gestured to a stool at the end of the bar. "You can sit here and relax while I work."

Ry didn't say anything, just sat. Josh slipped behind the bar, washed his hands and poured Ry another whiskey. Glancing up, Pete winked, but didn't comment until they were both at the other end away from Ry.

"By the smile on your face, I'm thinking you figured out if pretty boy there sucks as good as he looks." Pete's grin was wicked.

Josh shook his head. "If I did or didn't, I wouldn't be telling you."

"You're actually going to take him home with you, huh?" Pete popped the tops off three bottles of beer and set them out for one of the waitresses. "I thought you didn't do that anymore."

Smiling, Josh took an order and started mixing drinks. He didn't have time to reply until about ten minutes later. He kept an eye on Ry, making sure he had enough to drink, but not get drunk. Ry seemed to stay relaxed, though Josh did notice the man tense when people got too close to him.

Josh didn't care that Ry seemed to be hiding from something or someone. He didn't talk about his bed partners, not even to his closest friends, and everyone deserved privacy as far as he was concerned.

"Why him?" Pete stood next to him while they poured some beer off the tap.

"Don't know. Maybe I'm just lonely."

"You wouldn't be if you tried a little harder." Pete bumped him with a hip. "There are a ton of people who would kill to go home with you."

He looked up to see interest shining in Pete's eyes. The man's attraction to Josh had never been a secret, but Josh didn't play where he worked. Being more into casual encounters than long-term relationships at the moment could make Josh's job difficult if the other person wanted more.

"I know. Just been too busy lately."

Josh set the glasses down in front of three men and winked at them. They all handed over big tips. Tucking them in the tip jar, he chuckled softly. He knew how to work the men and women who came to the Lucky Seven. A little flirting and some smiles always got him more tips. One of the men slipped him more than a five-dollar bill. He checked the piece of paper, knowing it was a phone number. Tucking it in his pocket, he made his way back down to where Ry sat.

"How about something else to drink?" He leaned on the bar, invading Ry's space. "I don't want you too drunk to not thoroughly enjoy my reaming your ass later."

Ry blinked and blushed again. Josh didn't fight the urge to reach out and stroke a finger over those flaming cheeks.

"You are the prettiest thing I've seen here in a long time," he murmured.

"I bet you say that to all the guys you take home." Ry's teasing words held a hint of insecurity.

Josh tilted his head and frowned. "Now that you've got me pegged as an insincere flatterer who'll say anything to get a guy in my bed, how are you ever going to believe that I don't do this very often?"

"But you've done it?"

He waved a hand vaguely at the dance floor. "It's a fucking buffet here. Who wouldn't be tempted to sample? I work three jobs and it takes a toll on me, but I'll be honest and say even if I were wiped from working tonight, I'd still be trying to drag your sweet ass home."

Ry seemed to think about it for a moment before nodding. "At least you're honest."

"Lying might get me fucked, but it doesn't cure what ails me, you know? I'd like to think I'm a better man than lying to get some ass." Josh heard Pete shout his name and he stood. "I'll get you a soda."

"How about water? I try to stay away from caffeine as much as possible."

"Water it is. You do drink coffee though? I mean who doesn't like hot black coffee in the morning?" Josh served Ry the water.

"Sure I do. The best way to drink it is naked in someone else's bed." Ry leered at him.

Josh threw his head back and laughed. "I knew you had it in you. I'll stop back by later."

He wandered off to help Pete out with a smile on his face. Yep, tonight was the first night in a long time he was really looking forward to going home and climbing into bed.

Chapter Four

Ryan sat at the end of the bar, watching Josh work the crowd surrounding them. Sinking deeper into the shadows, he kept his head down and didn't meet anyone's gaze.

He played in the water ring left by his glass. What the hell was he doing? Going off into a back alley and giving some guy a blow job wasn't him. He avoided any situation where a scandal could ensue. His agent would have a cow if he knew what Ryan was contemplating doing next.

Josh's gruff laugh broke out over the music and Ryan's eyes wandered along the tattoos gracing Josh's arms. God, he wanted to lick each one of them and follow the light treasure trail of hair leading over Josh's six-pack abs to where it disappeared under the waist of his tight blue jeans.

Ryan wet his lips and saw the bulge in Josh's jeans swell a little more. Surprised, he glanced up to see Josh staring at him with a knowing look. His cheeks warmed and he dropped his gaze to the scarred wood of the bar.

Damn, he felt like a virgin about to get his cherry popped. He'd had his share of lovers, most before he came out to Hollywood, but still, he wasn't a neophyte to the whole hooking-up thing.

Yet, his eyes went back to Josh like a moth hunting for the flame that would kill it. What was it about Josh that short-circuited Ryan's brain and made him throw away the caution he'd learned to cultivate? He got another wink from the bartender before Josh turned to answer a question that someone yelled at him.

Could it be the bald head with just a hint of five o'clock shadow on that square jaw? Or the well-muscled chest and arms? Ryan shook his head. It couldn't be just those things because he saw gorgeous men all the time on the streets of Hollywood.

Pete, the bartender Josh worked with, squeaked as Josh pinched his ass and Ryan smiled. No, looks only got a person so far with him. Josh's supreme confidence and slight arrogance was what made Ryan's ass clench and his throat dry. God, he was going to feel Josh for at least a week, he was sure, and he would end up screaming the man's name by the end of the night.

Ryan had always been attracted to self-assured men. He wanted someone as strong as he was because he didn't have time to coddle anyone. He wasn't a selfish lover, or he didn't think he was. He just had too many other things to worry about at the moment to have time to take care of someone else.

Josh said he worked three jobs. There was a man who understood the value of work and also didn't play games. Of course, when a man looked like Josh did, he didn't need to play games. The man had to have a flock of potential lovers around him every day. Ryan caught the glances Pete threw at Josh when he thought Josh wasn't looking. Oh yeah, that man wanted Josh like a bear wanted honey, but Josh wasn't looking back.

"Can I buy you a beer?"

Startled, Ryan knocked over his glass. He turned to see a large middle-aged man standing behind him. Ryan checked his hat and shrank further into the shadows. He hoped no one would recognize him, though it wouldn't matter right then because he was just sitting at a bar having a drink.

"Ummm...thanks, but I've reached my limit for the night." He gave the man a smile and turned away, hoping the man got the hint.

An enormous hand landed on his shoulder and he grimaced as the stranger squeezed. He didn't want to get into anything at the Lucky Seven, but if the guy didn't stop touching him, he'd be taking a swing.

"I said I'd like to buy you a beer."

"And he said he didn't want one, Thompson." Josh knocked Thompson's hand off Ryan's shoulder. "What did I tell you about manhandling the customers?"

Out of the corner of his eye, Ryan caught Thompson's sneer.

"You said you'd kick my ass, but I don't think you have it in you. I saw this pretty boy come in from out back with you. Thought I'd offer him a chance to see what a real stud looks like."

Josh's eyebrow shot up, but he didn't take the bait. Ryan snorted and both men turned to look at him.

"I've been up close and personal with one stud. I don't think you could live up to my expectations now."

Thompson glared at him and Josh gave him a pleased look. Ryan smiled at Josh without Thompson seeing him.

"Go on, Thompson, bother some other guy. This one is taken." Josh laid his hands flat on the bar and met Thompson's narrow-eyed stare.

"One of these days, you're going to bite off more than you can chew, Bauer, and you won't have any of your friends

31

around to protect you." Thompson spun on his heel and stalked off.

"To protect you?" Ryan laughed. "Does he really think you'd need help taking care of him?"

Josh shrugged. "Some guys have an over-inflated opinion of themselves." He rubbed his thumb over Ryan's bottom lip. "So you think I'm a stud, huh?"

Ryan stuck out his tongue. "Don't get too puffed up there. I might have just been saying that to get the guy to leave."

"You're the one making me puffy. And don't wag that thing at me unless you mean to use it." Josh caught the tip of Ryan's tongue between his thumb and finger, giving it a little tug.

Without thinking or worrying about anyone watching, Ryan leaned forward slightly and wrapped his lips around Josh's finger. Sucking, he drew it in and scraped Josh's skin with his teeth. Salt, lime and lemon mingled on his tongue, making Josh a flavor he'd love to taste more of.

"Much more of that, you'll be on the bar and I'll be doing body shots off your abs...among other places," Josh growled.

Ryan shivered, and hell if his cock didn't stiffen to press against his zipper hard enough to leave marks. He eased back and let Josh's finger go with a grin.

Josh shook his head. "Who knew there was such a tease under that mysterious exterior?"

Before Ryan could answer, a tall blonde woman came from the hallway to sit next to him. He gave her a smile and Josh leaned over the bar to kiss her cheek.

"Rachel, love, what can I get you?"

"You know what I like, Josh." Rachel's voice held the clipped accents of upper crust Britain. "How's business going?"

Rachel must be Josh's boss. Ryan touched the brim of his

hat. Had she seen him flirting with Josh? He didn't want to get him in trouble.

"It's been steady. Pretty good for a Thursday night." Josh set a martini in front of her. "Dirty, with three olives."

Rachel sipped and sighed. "You make the best martinis."

"That's why you hired me." Josh strolled away to mix two drinks and came back. "How are you doing, boss lady?"

Her gaze wandered over the crowd. "I'm doing fine, Josh." Her blue eyes landed on Ryan and she smiled. "Why don't you take off early tonight? I'll finish up your shift and help Pete clean up."

Surprise crossed Josh's face and Ryan figured Rachel didn't tend bar very often. Something seemed to be bothering her, but it wasn't his place to ask.

"Are you sure? I don't mind staying." Josh rested his arms on the bar and shot Ryan a glance.

"I don't have anywhere else to go," Ryan commented. And he really didn't. He didn't have anything to do until later tomorrow afternoon.

"Go on. You've been here late every night this week. I don't want my best bartender getting sick because he doesn't get enough sleep. I can handle the bar for a couple of hours."

Josh came from behind the bar and gave Rachel a hug. "I'm not going to argue anymore. Thanks."

Ryan fought to keep from laughing as Josh dragged him back to the office where they grabbed Josh's backpack before heading out through the back exit.

"I live just a couple of blocks down. We can walk or we can catch a cab."

"I'd like to walk, if that's okay with you."

The urge to jerk his hand away from Josh almost

overwhelmed him, but he beat it back. He tightened his fingers and tried not to think about how good it felt holding on to him. No one would expect to see him out walking the sidewalks like normal people.

"Walking's good with me." Josh slung the pack over one broad shoulder and swung their hands as they made their way down the sidewalk.

Ryan let his mind empty as they wandered, ignoring the crowd of people around him. The nice thing about Hollywood was he never felt like he stood out. No one stared or pointed at him, whispering behind hands. No one looked twice at two men holding hands.

He did notice how Josh blocked people from bumping into him or bothering him in any way. Ryan wasn't a small guy, but somehow Josh made him feel taken care of and cherished. Shaking his head, he gave a silent chuckle. Now if that wasn't the silliest thing he'd thought in a long time.

God, they needed to get to Josh's apartment so Josh could fuck all the sappiness out of him.

Chapter Five

Josh opened his apartment and reached in, flicking on a light and gesturing for Ry to go in. He dropped his backpack by the closet door and waited until they got into the living room before he grabbed Ry by the hips and dragged the man to him. He took those plump lips he'd been staring at all night, wanting another taste. He didn't ask for Ry to open for him, he demanded it. No holds barred this time.

Ry encircled Josh's shoulders, running his hands over Josh's bald head and neck. He groaned and allowed Josh to sweep his tongue in to play with Ry's. Arching his hips, he rubbed against Josh, showing that he was more than willing to follow Josh's lead.

He broke the kiss when his head started spinning and his lungs protested their lack of air. Stepping back, he tugged off his vest and nodded at Ry.

"I want you naked now."

The man laughed but didn't hesitate reaching for his belt. "What? No tour?"

"You can get that after I fuck you over the back of my couch," he growled, kicking off his boots and stripping off his jeans without looking away from Ry.

Still wearing his T-shirt, Ry reached out to Josh and grasped his cock, pumping it with slow easy strokes. Josh let him do it for a minute before easing Ry's hand away and leading the man to the couch.

"Bend over."

He placed Ry's hands on the back of the couch, humming in appreciation as Ry did as he was told plus spreading his legs slightly. Josh trailed his fingers over Ry's balls and cock from behind.

"Oh." Ry arched and widened his stance a little more, offering all of his body to Josh.

"Beautiful," Josh murmured, pushing Ry's shirt up with his free hand before caressing the soft skin at the top of his crease.

"Are you just going to stare at my ass all night or are you actually going to fuck it?"

Josh jerked his head up to meet Ry's teasing gaze. He grinned and popped the man's ass, hard. Ry moaned and pushed back. Oh, someone liked that. And Josh had to admit, he liked the look of his red hand print on Ry's tanned skin.

"I'm in charge here, honey. Don't get pushy or you won't be getting any." He winked to temper his growl.

"We can't have that because I really do want something." Ry directed his eyes toward Josh's cock and wet his lips.

"Stay right there. I mean it, no moving or else I'll have to punish you." Josh paused to think about where he'd left the lube he kept in the living room.

"That's the best threat you could come up with?"

He narrowed his eyes and stared at Ry for a second before the innocent look on the man's face caused him to break into a smile.

"Just stay there. I want you over the couch and I need to grab the lube and a condom." He stalked to his bathroom where he found the necessary items.

When Josh got back to the living room, Ry was draped over the back of the furniture with one hand wrapped around his cock and the other playing with his nipples.

He swatted Ry's hands away. "Those are mine."

A full-body shiver rocked Ry and Josh could tell the man got off on his possessive attitude, which was good because Josh wanted to ensure Ry remembered him for the next week or so. And while he didn't tend to be scary stalker possessive, in the bedroom, he liked to be in control.

After turning Ry back around, he popped open the lube and got his fingers slick. "Here, hold on to these." Josh handed him both the lube and the condom.

Ry took them and braced his hands on the couch in front of him. Josh ran one finger down Ry's crease, pausing to tease his puckered rosette before continuing on to scrape a nail over the soft skin right behind Ry's balls.

Ry's indrawn breath rushed out as Josh went back to his hole and pressed one finger in up to the knuckle. He didn't give the man time to adjust before pulling out and adding a second finger.

"God," Ry moaned, the muscles in his back flexing as he rode Josh's fingers.

"That's it. Take them." Josh leaned down and bit the firm ass cheek in front of him as he worked on stretching Ry.

Ry jumped but didn't pull away. Actually he whimpered and his skin flushed as he rocked faster, fucking himself on Josh's fingers. Josh let him get away with it for a few seconds before he put a stop to it by easing his fingers out.

"No," Ry protested.

Josh blew a quick puff of air over Ry's opening and he smiled at Ry's half-strangled squeak. Fucking him was going to be so much fun.

"Ready for three?" He didn't wait for an answer. He breached Ry as far as he could and stilled.

"Oh fuck."

Ry's head dropped and his inner muscles clenched tight around Josh's fingers. He fondled Ry's balls and cock, helping the man relax. When the vise around his fingers loosened, Josh began pumping in and out, hitting Ry's gland with each thrust.

He fisted Ry's shaft, letting the man fuck his hand while he prepared him. Soft groans and gasps filled Josh's apartment. Josh licked the sweat from Ry's back, savoring the taste of salt and man.

"Please, Josh. I need you in me."

Ry's pleas grew in volume until he was practically shouting them. It was only then that Josh removed his fingers and tapped Ry on the shoulder.

"Give me the slick and condom."

Ry's hand shook as he held them back for Josh to take. Josh had the feeling this man was going to be the sweetest fuck he had in a long time. Tearing open the foil packet with his teeth, he kept one of his hands on Ry, not wanting to break their connection. He rested the tube on Ry's back for a moment while he rolled the rubber over his prick.

Ry groaned and Josh ran his fingers through the man's dark brown curls. "Hush. It'll only be a minute."

He squirted some lube in the palm of his hand and then tossed the tube over his shoulder, not caring where it landed. After coating it, Josh positioned his prick at Ry's opening and gripped the man's hips.

"Push back, and don't forget to breathe."

Flexing his hips, Josh started to push in, invading Ry's ass and causing him to sigh.

"So full," Ry muttered.

"You're so tight. Haven't done this in a while, huh?" Josh surged and buried himself deep into Ry.

"Ah" was all Ry said. He trembled, every inch of his body begging Josh to use him.

Josh couldn't ignore his body's demand to move, so he planted his feet and thrust, reaming Ry with each hard, deep stroke.

"Josh, please. Harder."

Skin slapping skin overwhelmed their harsh breathing as Josh put all of his strength behind driving Ry over the cliff and into his climax. Prying his hand off the other man's hip, he reached around and gripped Ry's cock, pumping it in time with his thrusts. Josh flexed his fingers, tightening his touch to be almost too much for Ry.

"Josh," Ry cried, his liquid heat spilling over Josh's hand and his ass clenching around Josh's cock like a vise.

The smell of Ry's come and the feel of his muscles milking his prick threw Josh over the edge as well. He drove into Ry and froze, filling the condom with every drop of come he had in him.

Ry's arms gave out and he slumped onto the couch. Josh stood firm, not allowing his legs to give out. When the tremors stopped, he eased out, encircling the bottom of the condom so it didn't come off. He grabbed some Kleenex and took care of the rubber. Grabbing one of their T-shirts from the floor, he cleaned off his hand and Ry as well.

Hauling the man upright, he chuckled as Ry melted against him and embraced him. Ry licked a line over the wing on Josh's chest.

"I want to lick all of your tattoos," Ry whispered, his tone sleepy.

"You are more than welcome to do that, but wait until we're in bed. I don't think I'd be able to hold us both up."

Josh crouched and swept Ry up in his arms, Ry's head resting on his shoulder.

"Good idea."

Ry's words were slurred. Shrugging, he continued on to his bedroom. It didn't matter what Ry called him as long as it wasn't some other guy's name.

He got them into bed and under the covers without dropping or injuring either of them in some way. He threw his arm over his face and sighed as Ry snuggled close to him, laying his head on his shoulder.

"Let's take a little nap, and then you can lick to your heart's content."

A low snore greeted his comment.

Chapter Six

Wrinkling his nose, Ryan mumbled and rubbed his cheek against something warm, slightly furry and very firm. Frowning, he reached out to touch the pillow he was using. None of his pillows at home were this firm, or this warm for that matter.

A hand landed on his hand and a rumbling sound came from his pillow. What the hell? Ryan froze, really awake now, his eyes wide and heart beating. Where was he?

"Hush, honey," his pillow growled.

Growled? What the fucking hell happened last night?

Ryan opened his eyes cautiously, wondering what he would see, hoping it wouldn't end up being a "coyote ugly" moment. He really didn't want to have to chew off his arm. He took a deep breath and steadied himself.

The sight that greeted his gaze was enough to make a nun give up her vows of celibacy. Stretched out before his eyes in all his naked glory was Josh, the bartender from the Lucky Seven.

He wiped his face, hoping he wasn't drooling like an idiot because, damn, that was one fine body beside him. Josh had the build of a serious gym rat, ripped abs and chiseled biceps. His chest hair was thicker than Ryan's, but not so thick that he looked like a bear rug.

And all those tattoos were fucking hot. His fingers twitched along with his cock at the thought of tracing them. Reaching out, he ran a finger lightly over the wolf on Josh's hip. He shifted closer to see some of the others etched into Josh's tanned skin. Oh, there was a matching wolf on the other hip.

Ryan ran his tongue over his lips, trying to fight the urge to stick it in the middle of the star tattooed around Josh's belly button.

"You're practically vibrating." Josh cupped the back of Ryan's head and encouraged him to lean forward. "Go ahead. I promised you could lick to your heart's content later."

He blushed, but didn't resist the firm grip on his head. Pressing his face into the soft skin above Josh's hip bone, Ryan took a deep breath. God, he smelled great. Sweat, sex and kind of spicy scent which must have been his soap. Ryan licked and Josh shivered.

Oh yeah, this was going to be fun. He pushed back against Josh's hand and the man let him go. At least he wasn't going to be forced into anything. Ryan laughed silently as he sat back to plan his attack. No force needed. He'd decided the first moment he laid eyes on Josh, he would go anywhere the man led him.

Daylight and reality would arrive soon enough. Right now he was safe inside Josh's apartment with the world locked out and he could indulge all his secret fantasies, even some he never knew he had.

He'd start with the intriguing design spread over Josh's chest. It was wings done in reds and blues. Trailing his finger tips over the edges, he smiled as Josh moaned.

"You're going to torture me, aren't you?" Amusement danced among Josh's words.

"Me?" he asked. "You're the one who spanked me."

Josh grinned and tapped Ryan's ass lightly. "You deserved it, and be honest, you liked it."

Oh, he did like it, but he wasn't about to admit that little kink to a stranger. Well, not a complete stranger. Josh had fucked him and even knew his name, but that still didn't mean he should spill all his secrets to the man.

Capturing one of Josh's nipples in his teeth, he tugged. The man under him arched, his hands fisting the sheets around them, and Ryan appreciated the fact Josh was letting him have control, for a little while at least.

He played with the little nub of flesh, flicking it with his tongue and nibbling on it with sharp teasing bites. Letting the abused nipple go, he moved up an inch and sucked up a dark mark. For some reason he didn't want to think about, he wanted Josh to have a reminder of the night they spent together.

"Fuck. Your mouth should be declared illegal."

Ryan snorted softly. How weird was it to finally hear a man say that after all the women he'd kissed the past couple of years? Yet the fact this particular man said it made his pride swell. Silly really, but he didn't want to be just another fuck for Josh. He wanted there to be some kind of connection between them.

Hell, he was starting to sound like a girl again. Sex was sex and there didn't need to be anything deeper going on.

Letting his mind go blank, Ry slid his hand down Josh's rippling abs to cup the man's balls and squeeze while he laid a trail with his tongue down Josh's chest to trace the star around his belly button.

Josh gave a harsh laugh mixed with a moan as Ry blew a puff of air over his wet skin. The wet tip of Josh's prick bumped Ryan's chin, reminding him that there was something better to suck on than Josh's tattoos.

Pulling back, he studied Josh's cock. It was thicker than

his own, but not as long. His asshole clenched as he remembered how it felt to have Josh inside him. He started to settle between Josh's spread legs, but a light slap to his head made him look up.

"Why are you always hitting me?"

Josh ran a thumb over Ryan's lip before dipping the digit into his mouth. Ryan allowed it in, sucking on the rough skin, tasting salt and man.

"That was just a tap, and if you don't want me to suggest what I was going to suggest, then go right ahead and suck me. Here's a condom."

He followed the gesture Josh made with his free hand to Josh's cock and swallowed. Nipping hard, he let Josh jerk his thumb out of his mouth before asking, "What's your suggestion?"

He took the condom from Josh and rolled it on the man's cock.

"That you put another condom on your prick, wiggle your sweet ass over here and I let you test my mouth out while you prove to me that the first time you blew me wasn't a fluke."

"A fluke?"

Ryan spun around, placed his knees on either side of Josh's head and shuddered as Josh's hot breath washed over his cock. What the hell was it about this man that fired Ryan up so much that a gentle taunt could make him race closer to the edge than if he'd touched him?

Josh's chuckle caused more warm air to dance around Ryan's throbbing shaft. He whimpered, rocking his hips and brushing Josh's lips with his wet head.

He jumped when two large hot hands landed on his hips and gripped tight.

"Easy. Let me get the rubber on first." Josh sheathed Ryan in latex. "I was kidding because no way was what you did to me in the alley a fluke. You practically sucked my brains out my cock and that hasn't happened in a long time." Josh pinched his thigh and commented, "I thought you wanted to lick my tats."

Ryan hummed and bit his bottom lip to keep from begging Josh to do it again. When he was sure he could control his inner slut, he said, "I found something else I'd rather lick more."

"Then have at it. Far be it from me to keep you from something you want." With that bold statement ringing in Ryan's ear, Josh swallowed Ryan to the root.

"Oh my fucking God," Ryan shouted, glad he hadn't taken Josh's prick in his mouth or he might have bitten it off.

He froze, his head swimming and completely forgetting what he was supposed to do until Josh flicked his ass with his fingers.

"Sorry," Ryan muttered, relaxing his throat and sucking Josh down until his nose was buried in Josh's nest of curls.

Shit, Josh worked his cock like he'd reamed his ass. Tongue, teeth and suction all served to drive Ryan closer and closer to the edge. And he thought he was the one in control.

Ryan did his best to keep up, using every trick he'd learned to bring Josh along with him. He slipped his hand between Josh's legs and grabbed the man's balls, squeezing and fondling them with a firm touch.

They rocked together, finding a rhythm they both liked. His balls drew tight to his body and the small of his back tingled.

Ryan touched Josh's side, trying to warn the man that he was about to come. He didn't want to take his mouth away from Josh's prick.

Josh pulled off him, tilted his hips and spread his ass cheeks. When Josh's tongue plunged into his ass, Ryan couldn't keep from screaming.

"Josh!" He lifted his head away from Josh's groin and filled the rubber around his cock.

The man's tongue fucked him until he was empty of any come. Ryan managed to get his lips back around Josh and it was only a second or two before Josh grunted. He wished he could taste Josh's come, but it wasn't safe.

Ryan waited until Josh stopped moving before he rolled to the side. His eyes closed and his body sank into the mattress under him. He was as limp as a wet noodle everywhere.

The bed tilted and he peeked out from under his eye lids to see Josh climb out of it. His gaze stayed stuck on the man's ass as he left the bedroom and disappeared into the hallway.

When he could no longer see Josh's firm ass, he looked up at the ceiling and thought about moving. He needed to get rid of the condom and leave. Spending the rest of the night wasn't an option.

Josh came back with a washcloth and some toilet paper. Ryan blushed as the man took care of him, cleaning him up and disposing of the rubber. Afterward, Josh slid back under the covers and pulled Ryan close.

"We still have a few more hours before I have to be up," Josh murmured, minty breath warming Ryan's ear.

"Okay."

Ryan held still and kept his breathing steady until Josh's soft snore filled the room. He snuck out from under Josh's arm and quietly made his way out to the living room where he got dressed. Tugging on his baseball cap and Josh's sunglasses, he opened the apartment door and checked out the entranceway before he left.

He walked outside and pulled out his cell phone. He'd call for a cab to take him home. The city lights made the night as bright as day and Ryan glanced back toward Josh's place.

The night had been incredible, but reality insisted it didn't happen again, and he could never go back to the Lucky Seven again. He couldn't run the risk of seeing Josh and having his body betray him like it did tonight.

Chapter Seven

Beep! Beep!

Josh swore he'd break his fucking alarm clock someday. As he stretched, his hand landed in the empty space beside him. He opened his eyes to double check. Ry wasn't there. Sighing, he rolled out of bed and headed for the shower.

There were no unusual sounds in his apartment, so he knew Ry had left. It must have been some time shortly after their mutual blow jobs. Josh always slept the hardest after sex. It would have been easy for Ry to slip out without waking him up.

He turned on the water, letting it heat up while he brushed his teeth. Straightening, he caught sight of a dark bruise right above his left nipple and one on his hip. The bastard had marked him. Shit. He should have done more than just spanked Ry's ass.

Climbing in, Josh let the hot water roll over his neck and shoulders. His muscles were loose and he felt more energized than he had in a while. He'd have to get laid more often. Good sex always brightened his outlook.

After drying off, Josh dressed in jeans, a T-shirt and work boots. He poured a mug of coffee that had brewed while he showered, and grabbed his tool belt and hard hat as he left his apartment.

"Hurry up, Sleeping Beauty," Antonio called from the truck as he waited for Josh.

"Fuck me, asshole." Josh climbed in and slammed the door shut. "We've got plenty of time."

Antonio glanced at him before pulling out into traffic. "Oh ho, did you finally get some ass last night?"

His eyebrows raised, he looked at his best friend and asked, "Do you really want to know?"

He laughed as Antonio turned slightly green and shook his head.

"Forget I asked," Antonio muttered.

"I thought so." Josh settled in the seat and sipped his coffee.

Antonio had been his best friend since they were fifteen and living in the *barrio* on the bad side of L.A. They both could have fallen into one of the many gangs that populated the area, but their friendship gave both of them strength to fight the pressure.

Josh came out to Antonio when he was twenty-one. While he didn't understand and didn't want to talk about it, Antonio never turned his back on Josh.

"Let's just say I slept well last night." He winked.

Antonio rolled his eyes and changed the subject. "Reese says we have about five more weeks at this site. He's already got us another job lined up after this one's finished."

"Cool."

One thing Josh liked about Southern California was there really wasn't an off-season for construction.

Throughout the day as Josh worked, his mind wandered back to Ry, the man's mouth and his ass. Yep, good sex always made the day better.

Later, after working ten hours at the construction site and six at the restaurant, Josh strolled into the Lucky Seven at a few minutes before eleven. He set his bag in Rachel's office, nodding at the boss lady, and took his place behind the bar.

Pete leered at him. "I see you let pretty boy mark you."

Josh glanced down at his chest, bared by the open shirt he wore, and his eyes crossed. "I saw that this morning. I should've spanked the guy harder." He finished buttoning it.

Simpson, the new bartender, squeaked, but Pete didn't react except for a shake of his head. Josh winked at both men and went to work.

He was closing in on the end of another long day when Rachel sat at the end of the bar. He mixed her usual dirty martini and handed it to her.

"Thanks for covering me last night." He rested his elbows on the edge of the bar.

"You're welcome. I figured you'd want to get an early start on the rest of the evening." Her smile was bright; whatever had bothered her last night was gone.

"I did."

Rachel didn't push for details and simply nodded. "Are you going to see him again?"

"Probably not. He was gone when I woke up this morning. Guess that tells me about my status right there."

Josh wasn't hurt that Ry had left without telling him. He was simply disappointed because he would have loved another go at Ry's ass before they went their separate ways.

"Sometimes one-night stands are perfect because of what they are. You don't have to worry about them hanging around and bugging you when all you want to see is their ass heading out the door."

"Sounds like you're talking from experience?" He laughed. "Male or female?"

"That time it was male, though some of the women I've been with have been just as bad." Rachel shook her head. "Why don't people have more self-respect?"

Josh grabbed a towel and wiped down the top of the bar. "I don't think it has anything to do with self-respect. More than likely, it's just wanting to be with someone. You're a beautiful lady, Rachel. I can see everyone flocking around you."

"Really? And you're a flirt, Josh, but that's what I like about you. I can flirt back and you won't be getting any ideas."

He tossed the towel back on the shelf behind him and grinned. "No, I won't, though if I liked girls in that way, I'd be doing everything in my power to get you in my bed."

Blushing, Rachel finished her drink. "You know, that guy you left with last night looked familiar. Did you get his last name?"

"Darling, he was a one-night stand. I was lucky to get his first name and I can't be positive *that* was real."

"True. I was curious is all. I'm going to take a walk around the club. Page me if you need me." Rachel stood and walked away.

Josh watched the heads turning in her wake. If she would only look around, Rachel could find any number of men and women who would love to warm her bed. Shaking his head, Josh took an order from one of the wait staff. It wasn't any of his business what Rachel did in her private time. He just didn't like the sad expression she got once in a while when no one was looking.

"Hey, Josh, are you going to catch that new action movie coming out this weekend?" Simpson brushed past him as the kid went to grab some ice.

"What's the name?" He winked as he handed the waiter his drinks and the waiter blew him a kiss.

"Something weird like *Luther is King*, I think. It's a sci-fi fantasy combo, but it's supposed to have some kick-ass fight scenes." Simpson ducked his head slightly and blushed. "Plus that new actor, Ryan Kellar, is fucking hot and he's starring in it."

Josh shook his head. "Sorry, kid. I don't have time to go to the movies. When I have free time, I go to the gym."

Simpson eyed Josh's body. "That would explain it."

He reached out and patted Simpson's ass. "Thanks, sweetheart."

The kid blushed again. Had Josh ever been that young?

"Quit flirting with the youngsters, Josh."

Pete pushed by him, but shot a grin his way to let him know the guy was teasing.

"I can't help it, Pete. All that blushing is cute."

Before Simpson could protest being called cute, Josh moved down the bar to fill orders as they came in. Things were heating up at the club and he'd be busy for the rest of the night.

Josh liked to keep busy and if he searched the crowd for a certain baseball cap and sunglass-wearing man, he never let himself admit it.

Chapter Eight

Shit. Ryan's nose itched and he fidgeted.

"Don't move." The makeup artist popped him on the ass. "I don't have time to re-do this if we smudge it."

"Sorry," he muttered and wrinkled his nose.

"Kellar."

He glanced up to see Raz, his agent, standing in front of him. "Hey, Raz."

"Where the hell were you last night? I tried calling you and couldn't get through." Raz glared at him over thick black-framed glasses.

"My battery died and I went out to celebrate with Bill."

Actually he had turned his cell off the minute he stepped out of his apartment. He didn't want Raz bugging him.

"You're done, Mr. Kellar. Don't lean or brush up against anything for ten minutes. The paint has to dry."

"Thanks, Bertie."

Bertie flashed him a bright flirtatious smile and Ryan grinned back as he stood. Oh, he knew he shouldn't be flirting with the cute little twink, but he was still feeling good from the night before.

Raz grabbed his arm and dragged him from the makeup room. "You didn't go out with that redneck, did you?"

He shook his arm free. "Yes, and Bill isn't a redneck. He's in town visiting me for a couple weeks."

"I bet he dragged you off to some second-rate club where you'd never be seen by the right people." Raz groaned and shook his head. "I'm going to have to give you a list of all the right clubs to go to. You need to start hanging out with the other A-list actors, Kellar, if you want to become a star in this town."

"I thought you said I was a star already." He rubbed his itching nose and rolled his eyes. "Give me the list. I'll look it over."

And shove it in the closest trash can. Ryan understood the need to keep up appearances, but too many people had come to Hollywood looking for their one shot and ended up losing themselves along the way. He'd given up a lot to get as far as he was. He didn't know if he was willing to give up any more.

Nodding, Raz looked him over with a practiced eye. "I see you went and got waxed again."

He touched his chest where it still tingled a little from getting the hair ripped from his skin. "Yeah. I still don't understand why these photo shoots can't happen while the movie's being shot. It makes more sense since I was already made up like Luther."

"That's not how the industry works, Kellar. Get used to it. Oh, by the way, I booked you on the Taylor Show early Tuesday morning. It'll be great publicity."

"Not that gossip queen?" He groaned. The woman did her level best to make every person who went on her show look like a complete ass or an idiot. He didn't want to know which one she'd decide he needed to be.

"She's good for your career. Just go along with whatever she talks about. Luther is your first big starring role and people need to get familiar with your face."

Ryan heard giggling and looked to his left. Three women were standing there, staring at his chest and abs with hungry eyes. Shuddering, he hurried away from them toward the studio where the shoot was taking place.

It wasn't that he didn't like women. On the contrary, he loved women. He liked how they smelled and their curves along with the way they dressed, but that didn't mean he wanted to sleep with any of them, especially those back there.

They looked like predators out searching for their next meal and he didn't want to get eaten by them. There were men and women who knew how to play the game better than he did, and to be honest, he didn't want to learn. He never wanted to use someone to get ahead.

"You must have gotten in early enough last night. You don't look like you lost any sleep." Raz assessed him quickly, no doubt looking for bags under his eyes.

"Early enough," he said vaguely.

He wasn't sure if getting into his own bed at six that morning would be considered early by Raz's standards, but he didn't think the agent needed to know what time Ryan had gotten home.

Bill hadn't gotten in until right before Ryan had to leave to get his chest waxed. He promised his best friend they'd hook up after the shoot and he'd take Bill sightseeing. Of course, maybe Bill had other plans with the little redhead he picked up at the club.

His cell buzzed and he tugged it out of the front pocket of the tight leather pants they'd dressed him in. Stupid wardrobe people. Did people really wear lace up black leather pants with combat boots? Checking the caller ID, he chuckled.

"Hey, man, I was just wondering if you made plans with

that pretty redhead I left you dancing with at the club." He held up a hand at Raz's impatient sigh.

"Nah, dude. She was good for one night, but I can't see hanging out with her for any length of time...unless it was in bed." Bill's laugh crashed over the phone.

He joined in. "You really are an asshole."

"So we still hooking up for some sightseeing? I want to check out that Chinese Theater place and the Walk of Fame thing we're always hearing shit about." A sly tone came into Bill's voice. "And you can tell me all about that fucking amazing bartender you picked up last night."

Ryan's cheeks heated and he ducked his head, turning away from Raz. "I'll give you a call when I'm done here and we can meet up somewhere."

"Gotcha. You're not alone or not with someone you can talk in front. That's cool, man. I'll catch you later, but you will be spilling all the nasty details."

"Bastard."

He hung up and sighed, putting his phone in Raz's outstretched hand.

"Okay, just listen to what the photographer is saying. Let him direct how you pose. He's the professional and you are just a body to him."

Raz pushed open the door to the photo studio and Ryan rolled his eyes.

"I feel the same way."

The low voice made him jump and he flushed at getting caught acting like a teenager. He turned to see a tall blond man with amazing green eyes smiling at him. A slightly shorter dark-haired man stood next to him.

Ryan's gaze skipped down to where the men's hands were

clasped together. His surprise must have shown in his eyes as he looked back up at the blond.

"Don't worry. It gets easier."

What would get easier? Did the blond know he was gay and how hard it was getting to hide it? Or did he mean the whole celebrity thing?

"Garrett, we're done here. Thanks for stopping by," one of the photographer's assistants called out.

"You're welcome, Connie." Garrett turned to leave, but stopped and turned back to say, "You've got talent. Don't let the rest of the bullshit get to you."

"Ummm...thanks." Ryan couldn't help but be proud, even though he wasn't sure who Garrett was. It was obvious the man was someone important in the movie industry or the other people wouldn't be rushing around him, opening doors and holding out pieces of paper for him to sign.

The dark-haired man with Garrett stood, relaxed and grinning, as Garrett signed autographs and got pictures taken with fans. Ryan noticed how the man's hand never left Garrett's body, whether it was holding his hand or touching his back while Garrett talked to a young girl.

"Holy fuck, do you realize who that is?" Raz trembled with excitement.

"Not really. He looks familiar." He nodded at the prop guy who handed him two large, very futuristic looking automatic hand guns. Lifting them, he tried to balance their weight and look less awkward than he felt.

"That was Garrett Johnson. He was nominated for a Best Actor Oscar for his role in *Racing the Past*."

Ryan glanced over at Garrett, his eyebrows raised. An Oscar-nominated actor had told him he had talent? Maybe he had chosen the right profession after all.

"Mr. Kellar, we're ready for you."

Sighing, he headed toward the backdrop where the photographer and his crowd of assistants stood. The acting part he liked. It was all the publicity shit that came after the movie was done and in the can that drove him crazy.

Chapter Nine

Cursing his stiff muscles, Josh straightened. He'd strained his back at the construction site earlier in the day and bending over to re-stock the coolers behind the bar was murder. He should have waited until Simpson got there and made the younger guy do it.

He rested his hands on his hips and twisted, trying to loosen up. He jumped when warm hands settled on his shoulders and started rubbing.

"What's up, old man? I've never seen you move so slowly." Pete's teasing words flowed over Josh.

Biting back a groan at how good Pete's massage felt, he leaned back against the other bartender. "Strained my back at the construction job this morning. Things are starting to tighten."

"Shit, Josh. You work too hard. You need to take care of yourself once in a while."

He didn't want to think about why he needed to work. "I have bills to pay, Pete."

Pete grunted, but didn't push the subject. His thumbs dug into the length of Josh's muscles along his spine and drew a low moan from him.

"You know...I could go home with you after work and give

you a true massage," Pete offered, his warm breath bathing Josh's ear.

Josh reached back and patted Pete's hip. "Thanks for the offer, but I don't fuck people I work with."

Pete's disappointed sigh flowed around him. "I know, but it never hurts to ask."

"Hey, you two," Tammy called as she walked behind the bar. She pinched Pete's ass and kissed Josh. "You hurting, Josh?"

"It's nothing." Turning, he hugged Pete. "Thanks, man."

Tammy eyed him for a second before she said, "It's a Monday night. We won't be that busy, plus Simpson's coming in later. Pete and I can handle it. Go home and soak, Josh."

"Thanks. I'll go tell Rachel."

Usually he wouldn't have taken her up on her offer, but his back hurt just enough to convince him it was a good idea. He knocked on the office door and waited until he heard Rachel say "Come in".

"Hey, boss lady," he said as he pushed the door open. "I wanted to let you know I'm going to head home. I twisted my back this morning and the damn thing's as tight as a drum."

Rachel looked up from whatever she was reading. "Evening, Josh, I was about to come and get you. I think you need to see this."

He sat in the chair she pointed to and took the paper she handed to him. It was one of those tabloid rags, *The Hollywood Enterprise.*

"I didn't know you read this shit. Did they find Marilyn Monroe living in a nursing home in Mexico again? Or is Elvis working at a fast food place in Ohio?" He grinned, but Rachel's expression never changed.

"Look at the front cover."

Frowning, he did what she said and glanced at the cover. He took a moment to comprehend what he was looking at.

"Holy fuck! That's me."

He stared at the blurry picture. It was him, or technically, it was his back, but he'd recognize the dragon tattoo anywhere. Josh's gaze went to the blurred face of the man he was kissing.

"Jesus fucking Christ." He slammed his fist against his thigh.

Someone had taken a picture of Josh and Ry kissing in the back alley of the club. He read the headline.

"Kiss and Tell Us."

"Who is he?" He shot a glare at Rachel. "He has to be someone famous if the *Enterprise* is putting us on their cover."

"The man you took home on Thursday turns out to be Hollywood's newest heartthrob. He's on all the magazines and talk shows. His name is Ryan Kellar and this is why I thought he looked familiar."

She tossed him another magazine and he grinned through his anger.

Ry glared back at him from the glossy cover, brows lowered over cold dark chocolate eyes. Some kind of futuristic-looking semi-automatic gun rested on one tanned shoulder while Ry's other hand gripped the butt of a larger than normal hand gun. His long legs were encased in lace-up black leather pants and black combat boots. This headline read, "Kellar is King."

"Shit, this was the actor Simpson was drooling over the other night. The one whose movie is like a box office hit or something."

"Kellar's the newest sensation to hit Hollywood and this picture could either destroy his career or make it. Depends on what he does, I guess." Rachel's sympathetic gaze met his. "You'll have to be ready for some publicity yourself. It's not going to be hard for reporters to find you."

Fuck. He didn't need this right now. He was barely keeping up with his bills as it was. He couldn't afford to get fired if one of his bosses took exception to the photos or the publicity.

Josh scrubbed his hand over his head, absently noting the stubble. He'd have to shave soon. God, what was he going to do? How nervous Ry had been and how he'd worn sunglasses in the middle of the night should have been a clue that Ry was worried about being seen.

How was he to know that the man who practically sucked his brains through his cock wasn't just a closet case? Oh, he would never have done anything to "out" the man, even if he knew who Ry really was. Josh didn't play those games.

"Do you think I should try to get a hold of him? Maybe tell him I didn't have anything to do with this." He gestured to the tabloid.

Rachel shook her head. "I doubt you'd be able to get a hold of him and besides, I don't think he'd believe you anyway."

Josh slumped and his back protested. "You're probably right."

There was no "probably" about it. Rachel was right and Josh had to think about what he would say or do in case some ambitious reporter found him and started asking questions.

"Go home, Josh. You're tired and hurting. Get some sleep and stretch your back. Tomorrow will be soon enough to think about all of this."

Rachel stood and walked around her desk, stopping in front of him to offer her hand. He took it and let her help him get to his feet. After hugging him, she walked him to the office door.

"Get out of here. Hopefully no one's found out who you are yet and you won't get molested on your way home."

He grabbed his pack, slung it over his shoulder and kissed Rachel's cheek. "Thanks. I'll be back tomorrow night for my usual shift."

"Just make sure you take care of your back. I don't want you further injuring yourself. Simpson can take your hours if you need another day."

As much as he would have loved to take a day off, his responsibilities wouldn't let him. "I'll be fine, boss lady. See you tomorrow."

Josh slipped from the club and wandered down the sidewalk toward his apartment building. His entire body ached, but in a weird way, it was his heart that hurt the most. He hoped those pictures didn't ruin Ry's career. It didn't seem fair that actresses could be caught on film doing shit like that and get away with it or at least without any damage to their career. Let an actor have that happen to him and he was blacklisted the minute the picture hit the streets or the internet.

He got home, went in and locked his door, dropping his bag as he made his way to the bedroom. Flopping down on the bed, Josh buried his face in a pillow. He'd take a nap and go back to the club afterward. Being alone and having to think about all of this was going to drive him crazy.

God, he should have known that no place was private, not in Hollywood. Sometimes living here sucked.

Chapter Ten

"Joining us right now is Ryan Kellar, the hot new star of *Luther is King*. Put your hands together."

Taylor's bright smile was all teeth and Ryan had the strangest feeling she was going to take a bite out of him in some way. He tugged on the cuffs of his shirt and took a deep breath before stepping out under the lights to wave to the audience.

He took Taylor's hand and kissed her cheek like Raz told him to do. The bleached blonde squeezed his hand with her cold fingers. Ryan fought back a shiver and sat where she pointed.

She eyed him for a moment before looking down at her notes. "So *Luther* is your first starring role?"

Relaxing, Ryan answered her question. The feeling of a shoe about to drop somewhere didn't go away, but anticipating it could make him stiff and ruin the interview. Raz would cut his balls off if he screwed this up.

Taylor's questions were light and only slightly personal. Soon enough his ten minutes were coming to a close and Ryan hadn't done anything to embarrass himself.

"We're almost out of time with Ryan Kellar, but I have one more question to ask."

She pinned him with her laser gaze and he tensed, knowing she was about to drop something on him he wasn't going to like.

"I must say I was surprised when my copy of *The Hollywood Enterprise* arrived on my desk this morning." A slight smirk tilted the corners of her lips. "Is there something you're not telling your adoring fans, Ryan?"

His gaze hit the cover of the tabloid she held up and his heart stopped. Fuck. Who had taken that picture? Josh told him no one saw them and yet there they were, in all their horny glory, making out in the alley.

His face was blurry, so any one who didn't know him wouldn't have been a hundred percent sure it was him. Yet anyone who knew Josh would recognize that tattoo.

Ryan's hands shook as anger welled in him. Smarmy bitch. She'd been setting him up the entire interview for this one moment. His cheeks heated and he knew he was blushing. No, he wouldn't give her the satisfaction of knowing she surprised him.

Plastering a smile on his face, he shrugged. "You know those tabloids, Taylor. They'll do anything to make money. What makes you think it's me? I can't tell what those guys look like."

"Really?" The tone of her voice said she didn't believe him.

He grinned and the producer called for a commercial break. Standing, Ryan waited until the grip had taken off his microphone before storming out of the studio.

His cell phone started buzzing as soon as he made it to his car. Sliding into the back seat, he let the driver close the door and yanked out his phone. The caller ID said it was Raz. Great, the man must be having fits.

"Yeah?"

"What the fuck was that, Kellar? What the hell did you do last Thursday?" Raz's shrill voice shrieked over the phone and

Ryan held it away from his ear.

"What does that picture look like I did last Thursday?" He shoved his hand through his hair and swore. "Fuck. He told me no one would see us."

"And you believed some fag?"

Was Raz's contempt for him or for Josh? Ryan shook his head. At the moment, that wasn't the important issue.

"I want you in my office ASAP. We have to figure out damage control and I want to know more about this asshole you kissed."

They'd done more than kissed, but Ryan wasn't about to tell Raz that.

"Fine, I'll be there as soon as my driver can get me there."

He hung up on Raz's continued diatribe and tossed the phone on the seat next to him. "We have to go to Raz's office," he told the driver before settling back to look out the window.

Who could have taken the picture? He swore there hadn't been anyone else out there besides the two of them. He rubbed his chest as it tightened from stress and worry. What was he going to do? Should he admit it was him and come out? Or should he deny everything and find a good-looking girlfriend to cover his ass?

Resting his head against the cool glass, he shut his eyes and took deep breaths. He had to remain calm or he'd never be able to make a rational decision about this whole issue.

Ryan strolled into Raz's office twenty minutes later to find his agent speaking softly into the phone, anger lacing every word.

"We have no statements to make at this time." Raz slammed the receiver down into the cradle and glared at Ryan. "Were you drunk or high?"

"What?" Ryan dropped into one of the chairs facing Raz's desk. That wasn't the first question he expected to hear from Raz.

"Come on, you had to be high or drunk to do something like that. They say every man is a six-pack away from bisexuality. So which one was it?"

"I had a few drinks," he admitted.

"Good." Raz shuffled some papers on his desk. "I got one of my assistants to do some research on this guy in the picture. He has to be the one who set up the opportunity for the photograph. What's his name and where does he work?"

His chance to tell Raz that the alcohol had nothing to do with the kiss slipped past him and he was distracted by Raz's comment about Josh.

"He works at the Lucky Seven Club. Do you believe Josh set the whole thing up? Like he had someone waiting in the alley and that he might have known who I was from the beginning?"

He didn't want to believe that. For some reason he didn't want to think about, he wanted to believe Josh was innocent.

Raz's snort said the man thought Ryan terribly naïve for making that statement. He buzzed his assistant, passing on Josh's name and the club he worked at. "Tabloids like *The Hollywood Enterprise* pay good money for pictures like this."

Leaning forward, he rested his elbows on his knees and let his hands dangle between his legs. "He didn't know who I was. I never told him my full name. How many pictures are there?"

"The fuckers at that rag say they had a ton more, but they've only printed four of them so far." Raz tossed the tabloid at him. "Page five."

He let it fall to his feet, reluctant to touch it like he'd be tainted in some way. Nudging it with his boot, he managed to get it open to page five without having to use his hands.

Jesus fucking Christ on a stick! He groaned silently and squeezed his eyes closed. More shots of him sticking his tongue down Josh's throat and gripping the man's ass as they ground together. He could almost feel the heat and passion between them. Josh couldn't have been faking all that need and desire. No matter how good an actor he might be, Ryan knew Josh wanted him as much as Ryan had wanted the bartender.

Several minutes of silence passed as he dealt with the feelings of betrayal and hurt threatening to overwhelm him. Shit, things like this happened to other people, not him. He'd tried hard to keep out of the tabloids while building his career.

Raz's assistant bustled in, holding several papers and handing them to him. She didn't even glance at Ryan before she left.

"It looks like your kissing partner there needs some serious cash."

Raz's statement registered in Ryan's mind and he looked up. "Josh needs money?"

"Yes. It seems Josh Bauer makes a substantial payment every month to a woman up north. Just two days ago, a payment of four thousand dollars was sent to them."

"Four thousand dollars?" Ryan blinked. Was that how much Josh got for the pictures?

"I'll try to find out who she is, but we haven't had enough time to dig that out yet." Raz frowned.

Ryan ducked his head and pushed the paper out of his sight. So Josh had sold him out for money. Best fucking night of his life and he got screwed by a con artist. God, he was an idiot.

Raz stood and walked around the desk. "I'm going to write up a statement and release it to the press. I don't want you doing any impromptu interviews or anything like that. Let me handle this. Done in the right way, we can actually use this to further your career. Scandal's always good for publicity."

He wanted to shout at Raz and tell him no that he wasn't going to use this trash to help his career. Ryan didn't want to be one of those tabloid stars who became famous because of the stupid shit they did. He couldn't find the words to say it and his mind was numb. All he really wanted to do was go home and drink himself unconscious.

He climbed to his feet and stared at Raz for a moment, trying to think of what he wanted to say. "I'm going home."

"Good idea." Raz escorted him out of the office, talking the entire time. "Get some rest, but don't drink. Drinking is what got you into this mess."

They made it to the sidewalk where Ryan's driver had the car parked. Climbing in the back seat, he ignored whatever Raz said to the other man. He just wanted to get home and lick his wounds.

"Where is the bastard?"

Ryan shoved his way through the crowd at the Lucky Seven, heading toward the bar. A bottle of Jameson provided him with liquid courage and he'd decided to confront Josh in person.

He saw one of the bouncers making his way toward him and he detoured slightly. He didn't want to get dragged out of the club just yet.

"There he is," he muttered, spotting Josh as the man stepped from the hallway where that woman's office was.

Ryan forced his way there in enough time to swing and catch Josh on the chin as the bartender turned.

"Fuck me." Josh stumbled and grabbed his chin.

Shit. Of course, the man would have an iron jaw. Ryan cupped his own abused knuckles in his other hand.

"No, that's what you did to me, you fucking bastard." He poked Josh in the chest, ignoring how his chest hair teased his fingers. "Four thousand dollars for pictures? How dare you lie to me and make me think you wanted me? All you really wanted was money to send to some whore up north."

Ryan yanked his arm back, ready to hit Josh again, but one of the bouncers got to him first. He found himself surrounded by two beefy arms and lifted an inch or two off the ground. He wiggled and swore.

"Put me the fuck down, Fatso. I have every right to beat the shit out of that motherfucker."

He tried slamming the back of his head into the bouncer's face, but ended up nailing his head on an iron chest. Stars swam before his eyes.

"Jesus, are you made of steel or something?"

"Put him down, Micah. I'll deal with him, but we're not doing it here where everyone can see. You don't need any more press."

Ryan staggered as he was suddenly dropped to his feet. The liquor made his vision blur and his stomach roil. He swallowed quickly while the whiskey tried to come back up.

Josh grabbed his hand and dragged him to the bathroom where he pushed him to his knees right before he vomited. He hadn't eaten anything all day, so nothing came up but the alcohol and stomach acid, causing his throat to burn.

When he was finished, he sat back and hung his head, wondering what the hell had gotten into him? He'd been so hurt and angry that coming to see Josh face-to-face seemed like the only way to ease the pain. Now he looked like a jilted lover.

"Come on, Ry. Let's go talk about this." Josh offered a hand.

He stared at it for a moment. Scarred and rough, it was the hand of a working man. Josh's grip was firm as he took Ryan's hand and helped him to his feet. As he swayed, Josh encircled his waist and let him lean on one of his broad shoulders while they went to the office.

"I shouldn't be here," he murmured.

"No, you probably shouldn't be, but now that you are, we're going to talk."

Ryan didn't like the sound of that.

Chapter Eleven

Josh wiggled his jaw from left to right, wincing at the ache it caused. "You've got a mean right hook there, Ry."

"It's Ryan and the least you could have done was fall down." Ry pouted as he listed to the left slightly.

"Ryan. Fine. I could have fallen over, but I've been hit by meaner, bigger guys than you. It'd take more than you've got to knock me down."

Ryan still looked a little green around the edges, so Josh went to Rachel's mini-fridge and pulled out a bottle of water.

"Here, drink this and rinse out your mouth. It might help you feel better." After tossing it to the other man, Josh went back to leaning on the desk where he picked up a peppermint candy from Rachel's dish and handed that to Ryan as well.

"I'm not sure anything would make me feel better," Ryan muttered, but opened the bottle and sipped. After he got the cap back on the water, he popped the mint in his mouth and looked at Josh. "How could you do this to me?"

"Do what?"

Ryan shot him an incredulous look. "You've got to be kidding, right? You set me up, took me out to that alley where your partner in crime snapped those pictures of us. Was the four thousand dollars you got for them worth it?"

Sighing, Josh rubbed the back of his neck and grimaced. His back throbbed along with his jaw. He didn't have any idea what the hell Ryan was talking about and he couldn't get past the hurt shining in the man's dark brown eyes.

"Explain this to me like I don't have a clue what you're talking about." *Because I don't*, he added silently.

"My agent did a little digging into your background after that bitch of a talk show hostess dropped the tabloid cover in my lap. He says that you need a lot of money and that you sent some woman up north four thousand dollars the other day. That's a hell of a lot of money for a bartender unless you're doing stuff on the side."

Ryan's bitter smile cut into Josh and he had to fight the urge to hug the man. That gesture wouldn't be welcomed at this point. Wait...did he just say that a check had been sent to a woman up north?

Josh went to his backpack and pulled out his phone. Hitting the number already programmed in, he fidgeted until someone answered.

"What are you doing?" Ryan shot him a look over his shoulder.

"Just a second." He heard the phone click.

"Hello?"

"Erin?"

"Yes. Josh, is that you? I didn't expect to hear from you. It's not your normal day to call."

He smiled at Erin's cheerful voice. "I know, but I need to ask you some questions. Did you receive a check for four thousand dollars in the past two days?"

"Yeah. It was a money order. You should know, you sent it to me."

Josh heard papers shuffling in the background.

"Here it is. I haven't deposited it yet. I have to admit I was surprised to see it. Your next check isn't supposed to be until next month."

Damn. He nodded, even though he knew Erin couldn't see him. "I know, sweetheart. I'm afraid that money didn't come from me."

"Who would have sent it then?"

"That's the sixty-four thousand dollar question. Can you scan it and email it to me? And don't deposit it. Someone used it to make me look guilty."

"Guilty of what?"

Meeting Ryan's gaze, he said, "Of hurting someone I'd never want to in a million years."

Ryan's stare dropped to the floor.

"You'd never hurt anyone unless they did something to someone you cared for, Josh."

Erin's defense of him made his heart swell a little.

"Thanks. Take care of Pedro for me and I'll be up in a week to visit."

"I hope everything works out."

He hung up and stuck his phone back in an outside pocket of his pack. Moving back to stand in front of Ryan, he closed his eyes and took a deep breath.

"I don't know what happened or who took those pictures, but I promise you, I had nothing to do with it. I didn't even know who the hell you were until Rachel told me today."

Ryan's disbelieving snort filled the room. "Yeah right. Not to be egotistical here, but how could you not know who I was? My face has been plastered all over magazines, the TV and billboards for the last couple of months."

"You must have left my apartment in a hurry Friday morning if you didn't notice that I don't own a TV. I work three jobs, usually every day, and I don't have time to read magazines, watch TV or go to the movies." Josh's chuckle was weak. "I'm sorry and I'm sure you wouldn't believe this, but not everyone who lives in Hollywood is obsessed with movies and actors."

He wasn't sure if Ryan's blush was because of how arrogant the man's statement suddenly seemed to him or if he was embarrassed by Josh's words.

"If you didn't know who I was, why did you hit on me then?"

Josh stared at Ryan. "You're kidding, right? Fuck, you are the sexiest thing I've seen in a long time and my cock thought so as well. If I had known who you were, I probably wouldn't have asked you out back or to my place. I don't need the publicity being with someone like you brings."

Josh thought about Erin and Pedro. God, he hoped the reporters wouldn't find out about them. They didn't need to be bothered by his screw-ups.

Ryan's expression turned thoughtful. "Who are Erin and Pedro?"

"No one you need to concern yourself with."

They weren't going there. Ryan was someone Josh fucked, not someone he was going to have a relationship with. He didn't talk about them to anyone except Rachel and Antonio, but only because he'd been friends with both of them for years.

Ryan nodded, but Josh could still see curiosity in his eyes. He walked over and leaned over, placing his hands on either side of Ryan. He stared into Ryan's eyes and made sure the man understood he wasn't joking.

"Don't get a bug up your pretty ass and go looking for

them. If I hear anyone's been bothering them, I'll come looking for you and your face might not be so pretty when I'm done."

A brief flash of fear shot through Ryan's eyes and the actor nodded. Hating that he had to threaten Ryan, Josh backed off and went to sit behind Rachel's desk. He wanted to put his arms around Ryan and promise to help him find out who did this to him, but Josh knew Ryan still didn't believe or trust him.

"What's your official stance on the pictures going to be?" He wanted to get back to the original problem.

Ryan shrugged. "Not sure. My agent told me to go home and he'd take care of it, though he might pull the whole 'he was drunk' explanation."

Josh curled his lip in disgust. What a fucking cop out. Hell, he hated when men couldn't be man enough to admit they liked males instead of females. *Wait a minute*, the voice in his head spoke up. *This is Ryan's career. He's probably worked for years to get to this point. He should risk all of it because you think he's a pussy for not coming out?*

He rubbed his temples. The voice sounded remarkably like his mother, God rest her soul, and it really irritated him when she, or it, was correct. He had no right to judge Ryan for his actions when it could mean the end of what looked to be a promising career.

"I know you don't think much of me because I'm in the closet, but it never came up before and now I don't know what to do." Ryan clasped his hands together and rested them in his lap.

"Ignore me. What you do is your business. I just got caught up in it. I guess you could consider me collateral damage. Whatever your agent comes up with, I'll play along and if I get asked by any reporter, I tell him whatever you want me to. I'm not out to ruin your career or profit off you either."

Ryan stayed silent and Josh knew the jury was still out on that one for the other man.

"You know what I'd really like is to find out who took those pictures. I wonder if it was simply a matter of being at the right place at the right time or if he knew who you were."

The dejected look on Ryan's face brightened and Josh realized that action might take the actor's mind off the scandal for a little while. Josh had no doubt that the whole thing would blow over in a day or two, considering how many other stars got their faces splashed all over the tabloids every day. It would be a one-day wonder and then some other star would have an embarrassing moment caught on someone's camera.

What he said to Ryan was true though. Josh did want to find out who took those pictures and if there was someone else behind them, because it didn't seem like the usual paparazzi move to send the money to Erin and implicate Josh for the whole thing.

It was too elaborate a scheme for the jerks who usually took pictures to think up.

He stood and strolled to the door. Gesturing to Ryan to follow him, he opened it and stepped out into the hallway.

"Go home and don't drink anymore. I'll see what I can find and get back to you about it. Keep your head down and try not to get caught in any alleys."

"Jackass," Ryan snarled. "I managed to stay out of alleys for several years and when I finally break my one rule, pictures pop up in magazines I swore I would never be in. You're the only one who has ever tempted me, so don't give me that bullshit."

Josh's cock twitched at Ryan's confession and his control broke. He was about to do something colossally stupid, but he couldn't help it. He wasn't going to let Ryan leave the club without tasting his lips once more.

He gripped Ryan's shoulders and shoved him back against the wall next to the office door. He smashed his mouth down on Ryan's and the man's gasp allowed him entrance. He swept his tongue in, tasting the peppermint Ryan had earlier. For a second, Ryan responded, his hands flexing at Josh's waist, and he sucked on his tongue.

A soft moan ripped from Josh's throat and he ground his body closer to Ryan's. When their jean-covered erections brushed, Ryan tensed and shoved Josh away.

"God damn, I can't think when you kiss me and that's not something I wanted you to know." Ryan ran a hand over his mouth. "I need to stay away from you. You're no good for my career and I could get into more trouble with you than I need right now."

Josh let Ryan leave, watching that firm ass as Ryan pushed his way through the crowd. Rachel joined Josh as the actor went out the front door.

"How did it go?" Rachel's voice was dry like she hadn't seen the punch thrown by Ryan earlier.

"Amazingly well. After he punched me and threw up, he was at least willing to listen to me. Or maybe he was just too sick to argue." He cupped Rachel's elbow and drew his boss into her office. "I need some help."

"Anything you need. I'm here for you and Erin."

Erin and Pedro were the two most important people in Josh's life and he needed to remember that. No matter how much he loved having Ryan in his arms or bed, he had to stay focused on the honest truth. Ryan would never give up his career for a blue collar guy like Josh.

Chapter Twelve

The door ricocheted back at Ryan as he slammed it open. He dodged out of the way and groaned as his head protested the move. After closing the door with less force, he staggered to the couch where he fell onto it face first.

"Shit, buddy. You didn't wait for me before you tied one on."

Bill strolled in from the hallway, toweling his hair dry. Ryan closed his eyes and hoped the world would stop spinning. He never should have stopped at that bar after leaving the Lucky Seven.

"I'm not going out with you tonight," he muttered.

His friend laughed. "Of course not. One more drink and you might die of alcohol poisoning."

Bill sat in the chair next to the couch.

"What brought this binge on?"

"You haven't turned the TV on?"

"Nope. You know I hate TV. It's mind numbing and totally boring unless it's some kind of sporting event."

He did know that, but he'd been so traumatized by the revelation of the tabloid cover, he figured everyone had seen it.

"Pictures of me and the bartender from the Lucky Seven appeared in *The Hollywood Enterprise*."

"You're kidding?"

Rotating his head took some thought, but he managed to do it and shot Bill a one-eyed glare. "Do you really think I'd joke about something like this?"

"What were you doing?" Bill's voice held concern.

"Just kissing, but still there's no way anyone could mistake Josh for a girl."

His cock stiffened, even through the alcoholic haze, at the memory of the last kiss they shared.

Bill grinned. "That's the truth. Not even the butchest dyke has a body like that guy's."

Ryan grunted and closed his eye again. *What a body though.*

"You've got it bad." His friend punched his arm.

Fuck, he'd said that out loud.

"Doesn't matter. Raz thinks Josh set me up and sold the photos to that rag. He sends money to some woman up North."

He heard the squeak of the chair as Bill leaned back in it.

"You know how much I *love* your agent, Ry. Are you sure he's telling the truth?"

"About the woman or Josh taking the pictures? And why would Raz lie?" He pushed himself up, setting his heels on the edge of the cushion and resting his forehead against his knees.

"Both, and let's face it, no matter what you do with this scandal, it's good for your career."

"I went to see Josh after drinking some whiskey."

His friend nudged the empty bottle on the floor between them with his foot and Ryan sighed.

"Okay, so I pretty much drank the whole thing. Fuck you. I had a bit of a shock today."

"Poor baby. If this is the biggest scandal of your career, you can consider yourself lucky. Trust me, there'll be more the longer you keep working in this industry."

Ryan nodded. Some would say being a tabloid star meant he'd made it to the A-list of actors. The paparazzi didn't waste their time on second-rate actors.

"Josh said he didn't take those pictures and didn't know who did, but the woman is real."

"Hmmm...who is she?"

He shook his head. "I don't know. He called her and I guess she did get a check. He swears he didn't send it. I asked him who Erin and Pedro were and he threatened me."

Bill chuckled until he caught Ryan's gaze. "He seriously threatened you?"

"Said if I bothered them, my face wouldn't be so pretty after he was done."

"Shit." Bill rubbed his chin. "It doesn't make sense. If he's that protective of them, why would he do something that would lead to them?"

"Now you're thinking logically and I don't want to do that right now. I want to wallow in my self-pity a little longer."

Ryan really wanted to lock his door and ignore everything outside it. Bill stood, grabbed the bottle and headed to the kitchen.

"We'll order pizza and watch some movies. No need to go out tonight since I'm sure Raz would like you to lay low. Tomorrow, you and I can go to Universal. I want to check out the theme park."

"You always did love roller coasters, jackass." Ryan made it to his feet and walked toward the hallway. He needed a shower in the worst way.

"What can I say? I like the speed." Bill glanced around the kitchen door. "Go get cleaned up and I'll order."

"Thanks."

"Least I can do since I did sort of goad you into the whole thing."

Bill was to blame to a certain extent, but Ryan didn't have to go through with it. Even Josh had given him an out when they were in the alley. No, the blame was his because he trusted Josh not to screw him over. *Yet Josh might not have done it*, a voice spoke up in his head. True, Josh could have been telling the truth and if he was, where did that leave Ryan? He had to hope the whole thing blew over quickly.

His phone rang the next day as he and Bill stood in line for one of the rides in the park. He pulled it out of his pocket and frowned.

"Who is it?" Bill asked, stepping forward as the line moved.

"Raz." He didn't want to answer. He'd been having fun goofing around with Bill and forgetting about the pictures for a while.

"You better answer it or he'll just keep calling until you do." Bill stepped out of the line. "We can get back in line when you're done."

"Thanks." He grimaced and flipped the phone open. "Hey, Raz."

"I told you to go home and fucking let me handle it," Raz shouted.

"I know." He should have done what his agent told him, but he had wanted to look Josh in the face and ask him about the pictures.

"Then why am I looking at pictures of you punching that fag in the face?"

"What?"

No way. Who had taken pictures of that? It made him think that maybe Josh's suggestion of someone following him might be true.

Raz barked out a laugh. "I hope you leveled the bastard, but you shouldn't have done it. Now all of the Internet gossip sites have it and I'm sure *The Hollywood Enterprise* has them as well."

He shot Bill a startled look. "I barely made the guy stumble."

"Why the hell did you go there, Kellar? It doesn't look good for you to be there if I'm trying to deny any of it took place."

Pressing a fist to his chest, he said, "I needed to ask him myself about the pictures and the money. He said he didn't do it."

"Of course he's going to say that. He probably set up the whole fight in the club as well. He had to have known you were angry and suspected you'd show up at some point. The photographer was waiting for you to show and get just the right shot." Raz sighed. "Where are you now?"

"Bill and I are at Universal." He wasn't going to cut this outing short, no matter what Raz wanted. He needed a day to relax and do silly things.

Raz mumbled something to someone. Ryan didn't ask who was with the agent. One of his many assistants more than likely.

"Good. Don't do anything stupid and don't let that redneck friend of yours talk you into anything. I'm going to start trying to put out this fire. You haven't been helping, you know that?"

He shrugged, realizing afterward that Raz couldn't see him. "I know, but you'll take care of it for me. That's what I pay you for."

"That's right. That fag bartender doesn't know who he's dealing with."

Ryan bit his tongue, stopping the objection to that word from pouring out. He didn't want to get into an argument with Raz. The agent was already worked up over everything else.

"I'll call you tomorrow to let you know what's going on." Raz hung up.

After turning his phone off, he stuck it in his pocket and gestured for Bill to join the line again.

"Do we have to leave?"

"No, we're staying here and having fun, even if it kills me."

And it just might because more than anything he wanted to go and talk to Josh again. Sit with the man and discuss this whole thing without the anger, hurt and alcohol clouding his mind. As much as he believed there were people in the world willing to ruin someone else's career for their own personal gain, he couldn't bring himself to believe Josh was one of them.

Chapter Thirteen

Josh arrived home from his second job. Tossing his keys on the small table by the door, he checked his answering machine. The blinking light informed him he had ten messages. Ten? He normally went days without even having one message left for him. He pushed the button and took the Styrofoam box containing his dinner into the kitchen.

"Josh, it's Rachel. Give me a call when you get home. I did a little digging and talked to some of my friends. I want to tell you what I've found."

He rested his forehead against the cool plastic of the refrigerator. No, he didn't want to know what Rachel had found. His weekend was free and he planned on heading up North to visit Erin and Pedro. Dealing with Pedro took all his energy, so he didn't want to bring a lot of tension with him.

"Mr. Bauer, my name is Simone Richardson. I'm a reporter for *The Hollywood Enterprise*. I was wondering if you would consent to do an interview with me about your relationship with Ryan Kellar."

Fuck, they'd found him. He thought back to how busy his section at the small Italian eatery was. Working the evening shift usually was a busy time, but there seemed to be more than the usual amount of people there. How many of them were reporters trying to get his attention and ask for an interview?

The next eight messages were all from reporters as well. He deleted them all and called Rachel.

"Hey," he said when Rachel answered.

"Josh." She sounded relieved. "Are you home now?"

"Just got in. I got your message plus nine more from reporters wanting to know all about my relationship with Ryan Kellar."

"I'm not surprised. I didn't say anything, but more pictures have surfaced."

"Fuck." He punched the wall next to the window he stood at. "More kissing?"

God, Josh hoped they weren't pictures of the other thing they'd done in the alley. That would be way over the line, even for the tabloid. Rachel's laugh filled him with relief.

"No, this is one of him punching you. He tagged you one, didn't he?"

He slumped onto his couch and sighed, touching his jaw. "Yeah, my jaw is still sore from it. Good thing I'm used to taking hits. Who knew all that boxing I've done would come in handy someday?"

Rachel laughed again. "Can I come over? I have some news and I wanted to see you before you head North."

"Sure. I have some lasagna from Mia Leone's. I'm willing to share."

"Yum. I'll bring a bottle of wine. I can be there in ten minutes."

"Good. I'm going to take a shower, so let yourself in."

He'd given Rachel a key to his apartment several years ago when he'd first moved in. She kept an eye on things when he went away.

Josh dried off after stepping from the shower fifteen

minutes later. Pulling on the sweatpants he'd taken into the bathroom with him, he thought about what he was going to do. So far no one had bothered Erin, but Josh didn't doubt some intrepid reporter would find out about her and go to talk to her.

How could any good gossip reporter miss the chance to announce to the world that the guy Ryan Kellar was seen kissing is keeping a woman and a child up North? His heart skipped a beat as he thought about how all the hoopla would affect Pedro.

Josh braced his hands on the counter and stared in the mirror. He couldn't allow that to happen. He'd promised Erin that he would keep them safe, but he didn't seem to be doing a great job of it.

A gentle knock on the door drew him from his depressing thoughts.

"Josh, are you ready for dinner?"

Rachel's voice drifted in through the door and Josh relaxed. He wasn't alone in this, plus it wasn't only his life being turned upside down. Ryan was dealing with the same issues, though he had an agent to field the harassment and Josh didn't have anyone like that.

He opened the door and smiled at his friend. "Yes."

Rachel hugged him. "Don't worry. We'll figure something out that doesn't involve risking your sister and nephew."

Burying his head in her blonde curls, he let the tension ease from him. "God, there are times when I wished I liked girls, Rachel. You're going to make some man very lucky."

"Yeah well, I'll worry about finding that guy later. Let's get some food in you and talk about my news."

She'd set his kitchen table and heated up the lasagna, dishing it out and pouring the wine as well.

After taking a few bites, Josh set his fork down and looked at Rachel. "What kind of news did you find?"

Rachel took a sip of her wine before she looked at him. "I looked at both sets of photos that have been in *The Enterprise*. Even though the ones of you two kissing are blurry, I think those were altered to look like that. You would think the others of Ryan punching you would be taken by someone's phone, since not many people come to the club with a camera."

"They weren't?"

"No. Those are quality images taken by a good camera."

He frowned. "Are you saying that they were taken by a professional?"

"I believe so."

"But why would there be a professional at the Lucky Seven? It's not like our clientele is the crème de la crème of Hollywood." He pushed his food around his plate.

Rachel leaned on her elbows and met his gaze. "I think Ryan's being followed. I just don't know whether it's just an opportunistic photographer or if all of this is a deliberate publicity ploy on his part."

Josh jumped to his feet, pacing around the kitchen and clenching his hands. He didn't care how good an actor Ryan was. The hurt and anger he'd seen in the man's eyes the other day wasn't faked.

"I can't see Ryan doing this. He doesn't seem like the type."

She shot him an incredulous look. "And you know this from all the time you spent talking to him, right?"

He blushed, but stuck to his gut feelings. "I don't think he's the type of guy who would use someone like that for personal gain. Especially not when it could backfire and force him out of the closet."

"What's the old saying, 'There's no such thing as bad publicity'? Remember that, Josh. I don't know for sure that he's the one behind it, but what if someone close to him is?"

Rachel stood and left the kitchen. When she came back, she carried several papers.

"Look at these. This is Tuesday's edition of *The Hollywood Enterprise*. The infamous kiss. On Thursday, came this one."

Josh took the one she handed him. It showed Ryan in the process of slugging him in the jaw. The headline said, "Lover's Spat?"

"Great," he muttered, tossing the paper on the table.

"This was today's cover."

"Fuck." He stared at a picture of Ryan and the guy he'd been with at the bar. Bob? Bart? No, Bill. They seemed to be standing in line at some amusement park. This headline said, "Cheating already?"

"Jesus, do these people get off on being as rude and crude as possible?" He crumpled the paper in his hand.

"Probably, but that isn't the point. The point is that these were not pictures of opportunity. If more pictures show up, I'll be led to believe someone is following him."

"Wonderful. Ryan has his own stalker now. He's made it to the big leagues, I guess."

Josh started cleaning off the table. As he scraped the uneaten portions into the garbage, he struggled with his inclinations.

"Do you think I should call Ryan and warn him?" He stopped and looked at Rachel. "There really might be things and people he doesn't want the public knowing about."

Rachel shrugged. "Is there someone you trust who could either follow Ryan themselves or could give you a name of a private investigator?"

He thought while they cleaned up the kitchen in silence. When they went into the living room, his gaze landed on a picture of him with two other men. Morgan and Vance.

"I used to bartend at this club downtown. I became friends with three of the bouncers. They quit and opened their own personal security business. Bodyguards and drivers. You know the kind of protection the big-name stars need."

"You think they'll help you?" Rachel cradled her coffee in her hands and smiled at him.

"They'll at least know who I could get a hold of to follow Ryan for a while." He set his cup down and dug out his cell phone. "I have Morgan's number in my phone."

Scrolling down the numbers, he found Morgan's and pushed the call button.

"Josh, you old dog. I see your face in the tabloids. I thought you didn't want anyone to recognize you." Morgan's voice boomed over the phone, almost drowned out by the loud music in the background.

"Hey, Morgan, did I catch you at a bad time?"

"Nah, just having a little party. It's Brody's birthday and him and his partner came to visit. Vance and I thought we'd help him celebrate."

"Tell Brody I said hi and happy birthday. I was wondering if you and Vance would have time to meet me sometime this weekend."

"Just a second. Have to move somewhere quieter." The music disappeared and Morgan laughed. "Much better. Sure, we can meet you whenever, but I thought this was the weekend you went up North."

It was and he really didn't want to screw up Pedro's routine by not showing up, but Josh couldn't see any other way out of the predicament except to take care of it right away before it spread.

"I have to cancel it. Would noon tomorrow at the coffee shop on the corner of my block be okay?"

"Sure. Make it closer to one and I'll make sure Vance is awake for it." Morgan snorted.

Josh smiled. Vance wasn't a morning person and for him to get out of bed before two was a miracle.

"Thanks and just so you're prepared, it has to do with those tabloid photos."

"Are you in trouble?"

"No, but I want to figure out how they were taken and who took them. It needs to be dealt with before my family gets involved."

"Don't worry. We'll help you with anything you need." Someone must have opened a door because the music grew loud for a second. "I have to go. I'll catch you tomorrow at one."

"Thanks, Morgan."

He hung up and set the phone down. Dropping on the couch next to Rachel, he hung his head and rubbed his neck. Rachel pushed his hand out of the way and started massaging his back.

"I hate to tell you this, but you should probably call Ryan and tell him what's going on."

Josh jerked away and stared at her. "You're kidding, right? First of all, he's not going to want to hear from me. Second of all, I don't have his phone number. I can't call him."

"I pulled some strings and I got his home phone for you." She held out a piece of paper for him to take.

"You found a number for him. Now he's going to think I'm a

stalker."

"No, he won't. Just leave him a message to meet you at the coffee shop. It'll be up to him whether he wants to come or not. If he doesn't, then you don't have to tell him anything. If he does, then you can get his input."

"He's not going to believe me." He dropped his head back down and Rachel started rubbing again.

"Tell him you've found a solution to your mutual problem. Hopefully that'll peak his interest enough to make him come see you."

Rachel was right and he hated that. Ryan needed to know what was happening and even though Josh didn't think the man would come, he still had to tell him.

Reaching for the phone, he took a deep breath and dialed.

Chapter Fourteen

The phone rang as Ryan collapsed on his couch. Growling silently, he considered not answering it. Didn't having an unlisted number mean people couldn't find it and harass him? Bill wandered in as the answering machine clicked on.

"Hello, you've reached Ryan Kellar's phone. He isn't here right now. So please leave your information and he'll get back to you. If you're a reporter, call his agent."

Bill shot him a grin. "Already talking about yourself in third person?"

He flipped his friend the finger, but the voice coming through the answering machine had him sitting up and paying attention.

"Ryan, this is Josh Bauer. I know you probably never want to hear from me again, but I wanted to let you know what I've been doing in trying to solve our mutual problem."

Ryan flung himself across the couch and snatched up the handset. "What mutual problem, fucker? I'm the one whose career is teetering on the brink here."

"Very melodramatic," Josh drawled. "Screening your calls?"

"Hell yes, I'm screening my calls. My phone has been ringing almost non-stop since those first pictures came out. The fucking reporters won't leave me alone."

"Join the crowd. You're not the only one who's caught in the middle of this shit storm, but I'm going to stop it before it spreads and drowns people I care about." Josh's voice filled with anger.

Ryan glared at the phone for a second. "This isn't my fault."

"And it's not mine either." Josh sighed. "Listen, I'm meeting some friends of mine for lunch at one tomorrow. I'm getting some advice from them about how to handle all this. Plus I think someone's following you specifically. The pictures appearing in *The Enterprise* are too good to be taken by amateurs with cheap phones."

He rolled over on his back and stared up at the ceiling. "You seriously believe that?"

"Yes."

A voice he heard in the background made him frown. "Who's there with you?"

"Not that it's any of your business, but Rachel is here and she's the one who suggested that the pictures might be more than moments of opportunity." Josh sounded tired.

Ryan bit his lip, not wanting to feel guilt or sympathy, but his conscience punched him. Josh hadn't signed on for all the media hype. Ryan at least knew that the possibility of it becoming a media frenzy existed. Being a star had its good and bad sides. Unfortunately, it did mean that there were innocent people hurt in the process.

"I'm sorry," he said softly.

Bill stood and left the room. He appreciated his friend's discretion.

"So am I. You're the best fuck I've had in a long time and any chance of it happening again has been ruined."

He blushed at Josh's crude words and he shifted on the

couch, his cock stiffening in his jeans. His head and good sense told him he shouldn't reply to that comment. There couldn't be anything between them. It was too risky to his career if he was seen with Josh again.

His body seemed to be ruling his tongue though. "There is a chance of it happening again."

Ryan hit his forehead with the hand not holding the phone. Fuck. He seriously needed to watch what he said.

"Really?"

"Yes." He sat up and rested his elbows on his knees, staring at the floor between his feet. "Listen, I'll be there. Give me the directions and I'll come. I think I need to talk to you without alcohol or sex getting in the way."

Josh's chuckle was low and hit Ryan low in his gut. Heat rolled over him, landing in his groin and causing his prick to press against his jeans like it wanted to burst out.

"Ryan, I think sex will always get in the way for us."

"Not tomorrow. I plan on being good. Never know who's watching," he joked.

"Damn. You're right. Here are the directions and I'll see you there at one."

He dug out a pen and some paper, jotting down the name of the coffee shop and Josh's cell phone number.

"That's in case you change your mind."

"I don't plan on it." He tossed the pen on the coffee table in front of him.

"Good. I'll see you tomorrow, honey."

Josh hung up and Ryan pushed the off button on his handset, staring at it while contemplating whether he had enough energy to throw it across the room. With one husky "honey", Josh had returned all the memories from their one night together to Ryan's head and he wasn't sure he was thrilled with that.

"Did I hear you right? You're going to meet the man who tricked and used you for money." Bill dropped into the chair across from the couch and grinned at Ryan.

Instead of throwing the phone at the wall, Ryan tossed it at his friend. "Yes, I am, and be glad I'm not going to make you come."

"Why not? I'd love to get another look at that bartender." Bill licked his lips.

"Stop it, asshole. If you were any straighter, you'd have a ruler shoved up your ass." He flopped back on the couch and folded his arms behind his head.

"Sure, I'm straight, but I'm secure enough in my masculinity to say when I find another man attractive." Bill snickered as Ryan flipped him the finger. "Are you really meeting him tomorrow?"

"Yes. He has an idea how to solve this problem and I should hear him out, right?" Ryan peered at Bill. "I don't believe he did it, no matter what Raz says."

Ryan's cell rang and Bill grimaced.

"Speak of the devil," he muttered before standing and leaving again.

Bill had never tried to hide his contempt for Raz and maybe his friend was right about Raz being a slime ball. He'd reserve comment until after this whole tabloid crisis was over.

"Kellar, I have a news conference scheduled for you at one tomorrow at the Roosevelt Hotel," Raz ordered.

"I'm sorry. I already have a previous engagement. I can't make it."

"What? Of course, you can make it and who are you

meeting?" Raz sounded shocked that Ryan would dare to tell him no.

He shouldn't say anything, but again his tongue took control. "I'm meeting Josh at one to talk about the whole picture thing."

"Josh? That fag bartender? You've got to be kidding me. I told you after the picture of you punching him came out. Stay as far away from him as you can. He'll only drag you down in the gutter with him and make a lot of money doing it." Raz was practically screaming by then.

Ryan held the phone away from his ear and waited until Raz took a breath.

"I don't think he had anything to do with it and I want to talk to him about it."

"You're thinking with your God damn dick, Kellar. You better think long and hard about this. I'm doing my bloody best to clear this mess up and you're bound and determined to screw it up."

Ryan didn't want to listen to Raz's rant anymore. "I'm going, and there isn't anything you can do about it. Reschedule the news conference and get back to me."

He snapped his phone shut and this one he did fling across the room, smiling at the satisfying crunch it made as it hit the wall.

"Destroying your phone can't change the fact that your agent is an ass," Bill commented from the hallway.

"I know, but it'll make me feel better for a while."

He glared at the dent in his wall for a moment before jumping to his feet. "Let's go to Olivera Street and get some good Hispanic food. I refuse to hide out here like some criminal."

Bill laughed and slapped him on the shoulder as he headed to his room. "Good for you, buddy. The best way to beat them at their own game is to refuse to play it."

Yeah, Ryan was done being ashamed of what happened. He was sure that at the news conference, Raz expected him to read a prepared statement denying the pictures were real. He still had to decide if he'd do that or not, but until then, he'd have fun with his best friend and not dwell on it.

Chapter Fifteen

"Bauer, old man. You're looking good."

Standing, Josh smiled as Morgan and Vance strolled up to him. The three men hugged before the others went to order their drinks. Josh had been at the coffee shop for about ten minutes and already had his black coffee in hand. He watched his two friends standing in line, laughing and talking quietly together.

Morgan touched Vance on the small of his back. Hmmm...friendship seemed to have moved into something more serious.

"Josh."

He turned and saw Ryan standing a few feet away from him. Smiling, he gestured for the actor to join him.

"Thanks for coming, Ryan. I know you have no reason to trust me, but I'll keep saying it until you believe me; I had nothing to do with those pictures."

Ryan reached out, stopping inches from Josh's arm. "I know. After the shock, hurt and alcohol wore off, I came to realize that you seem to have something to lose as well."

Josh started to speak, but Ryan interrupted.

"I don't know what and I don't need to know. That's why I'm here to bury the figurative hatchet and see how we go about getting us both off the front page."

He relaxed and took Ryan's hand, giving it a squeeze. Morgan and Vance joined them.

"Guys, this is Ryan Kellar. Ryan, these are two of my closest friends, Morgan LaFontaine and Vance Colvin. They own a private security company."

"Personal security in like bodyguards?" Ryan shook their hands before they sat.

"Do you want something to drink, Mr. Kellar?" Vance asked.

Ryan grinned. "I'd like an espresso, Vance, but please call me Ryan. I'm not anywhere near famous enough to rate that kind of respect."

Nodding, Vance headed back to the counter to order Ryan's drink. Morgan watched the tall blond walk away for a moment before meeting Josh's gaze.

"Do you think Ryan needs a bodyguard?"

Josh shook his head. "I don't think we need to go that far, but I'd like to see if you have any recommendations about someone we can hire to follow Ryan."

"Follow me? Why?" Ryan took the espresso Vance handed him with a nod.

"Because like I told you last night, Rachel thinks someone is following you specifically and I agree with her."

"Rachel, your new boss?" Vance sat and put his arm over the back of Morgan's chair.

"Yes." Josh sipped his coffee and organized his thoughts. "She's looked at all the pictures in the tabloid. She says the first blurry one of us kissing has been altered to look grainy. The others of you punching me and hanging out with your friend are crystal clear. No one took those with a camera phone or anything amateur."

Morgan frowned. "You think someone is following Ryan, waiting to see if he does something scandalous for good pictures."

"Yes. After we find out whom, we have to find out if someone paid him, or her, to do it or if they decided he might be a likely candidate for tabloid fodder."

Ryan glanced around the room, obviously trying to see if he could spot the culprit. Josh laid his hand on Ryan's and drew the man's attention back to him.

"I don't think he'd be standing there, holding up the camera and yelling 'it's me, it's me'."

Blushing, Ryan ducked his head slightly, but didn't move his hand away from Josh's. In fact, he flipped his hand over and threaded their fingers together. A smile broke over Josh's face and he caught Morgan eyeing him with curiosity.

Josh realized he'd never held hands with another guy in public before. It had nothing to do with being ashamed or worrying about what other people would think. It had more to do with the men he'd dated. None of them caused a reaction close to what Ryan did to him. Josh wanted to protect the younger man from all the bad things that could happen to him while in Hollywood and the film industry.

It was a strange reaction to have when they had sex one night followed by Ryan hitting him four nights later. Not a promising start to any relationship, if that's what Josh wanted it to be.

"We know the names of a couple really good private investigators. They won't talk and they get results, but they aren't cheap," Vance informed them.

"That's not important," Ryan spoke up. "I can cover the cost. I really want this whole thing cleared up before Josh gets involved any further."

Josh's phone rang. Excusing himself, he checked the caller ID. It was Erin and he knew she wouldn't be calling if it wasn't an emergency.

"Erin, sweetheart, what's wrong?"

Erin's sobs came over the phone mingling with the screams of an angry child in the background. Shit, something bad had happened. He hadn't heard Pedro act like that in over a year.

"There was a reporter here, Josh. He surprised us when we were coming back from Pedro's therapy. He kept yelling questions and snapping pictures. Pedro's on overload and I can't get him to calm down." His sister's words ran together and Josh knew her reaction to the reporter was fueling Pedro's issues.

"Fuck. God damn." He kicked a chair and everyone looked at him.

Ryan, Morgan and Vance all stood and headed toward him, herding him out of the coffee shop without any other incident.

"Take deep breaths, Erin. You know he's reacting to you and if you're not calm, he won't settle." He held on when Ryan took his hand, gripping it tight to ground himself, so his anger wouldn't upset Erin more.

"I know, but I'm scared. What if that reporter puts our pictures in the paper? What if Geraldo sees it and comes after us?" Erin's fear grew in her words. "I can't run again. Pedro won't be able to cope and he was doing so well."

Josh growled deep in his throat at the thought of his ex-brother-in-law. "I know, sweetheart, and I'll drive up to visit you. Tell Pedro I'm coming. That might help calm him down a little. It's at least ten hours if the traffic isn't bad."

"I'm sorry to do this to you, but both of us will feel better with you here."

"I'll get there as soon as I can. Keep the doors locked and the shades drawn. Don't answer the door or the phone. I've got a key, so I'll let myself in when I get there."

Erin sighed and Josh heard the relief in her voice.

"Thank you."

"I'm your big brother. This is what I do and I brought this on you. Try to get Pedro calm and I'll see you soon."

He hung up and swore, remembering he held Ryan's hand only when he tried to punch the brick wall he stood by.

"Shit."

"What's wrong?" Morgan gripped his shoulder.

"How can we help?" Vance stood beside Morgan, blue eyes filled with concern.

"I'll get my car and drive you wherever you need to go."

Ryan's offer was the only one that really sank through his anger and fear. He glanced at the actor and saw sincerity in his eyes.

"You'd do that for me?"

"Sure. This is all happening to you and Erin because of me."

"Take him up on his offer, Josh. You're in no condition to drive. Morgan and I will get on the investigator. You said your boss knows about this whole thing. We'll get a hold of her and have her bring us up to speed on it." Vance hugged Josh tight.

Morgan gave him a quick hug as well. "Text us with Erin's address and we'll send two of our guys up there to keep an eye on them. Unfortunately, you can't be with them all the time, though you might want to consider moving up there to be closer to them."

Josh nodded. "Thanks, guys. You're right, but we don't want Geraldo to find them and he tended to follow me around every so often before he went to jail."

"We'll do what we can to keep your sister and nephew safe."

He watched his friends walk away, both pulling out phones and dialing. Ryan tugged on his hand and he looked at him.

"Do you want to stop by your apartment and get anything?"

Josh shook his head. "No, I have clothes at Erin's place to save me from having to lug a duffle bag or suitcase with me each time."

"Good. My car's just around the corner and I have some clean clothes with me." Ryan smiled at Josh's silent question. "I picked up some dry cleaning on my way to our meeting."

Checking his watch, he started down the street toward where Ryan pointed. They needed to get to Erin as quickly as possible. Usually his sister was more than capable to handle Pedro's fits, but when she was scared herself, it all compounded and things could get worse.

Ryan caught up with him and led the way to where his red Cadillac CTS was parked. Josh waited until they were both seated before reaching across the console and wrapping his hand around the back of Ryan's head. Pulling the man to him, he kissed him gently without the force and passion that created their last kiss.

There was desire and need in this one, but there was mostly thankfulness and maybe a quiet plea for Ryan to be there for him. Ryan's answering movement pleased Josh and he smiled against the man's lips.

Chapter Sixteen

Ryan sank into the kiss, allowing Josh to lead him where he wanted them to go. He opened and moaned slightly as Josh swept his tongue in, stroking and learning each tooth and every nook of Ryan's mouth.

As the kiss grew deeper, he wished they weren't in the front seat of his car. He wanted to press tight to Josh's chest and feel him over every inch of his body. He drifted his hand down the other man's side to where his shirt was tucked into his jeans.

Tugging on it drew Josh's attention and he sat back, breaking the kiss. Ryan pouted, not wanting to take his hands off the man.

"We need to get going." Josh rubbed his thumb over Ryan's swollen bottom lip. "As much as I'd love to drag you back to my apartment for another round, Erin and Pedro need me."

Ryan took a deep breath and settled back in his seat, letting his heart beat calm down before he spoke.

"I know. It's just that I've been dreaming of your mouth for the last several days, pretty much ever since I left Friday morning."

Josh blinked and a smug smile crossed his face. Laughing, Ryan shook his head as he turned the car on.

"Don't be all pleased with yourself. It could just have been that I haven't been kissed in a while."

He pulled out of the parking lot and headed north. "What highway do I take?"

"Hop on I-5 north. It's pretty much a straight shot from here to Etna." Josh pulled out his phone. "I'm going to call my sister and let her know we're on our way. Also, I better let Rachel know that I won't be in tonight or tomorrow night. Luckily, I already had the days off from the restaurant."

Keeping his gaze on the road, he tried to ignore the conversations going on beside him. He smiled at the gentle tone in Josh's voice when he talked to his sister. There was a great deal of love present between the siblings. Ryan could tell that much just from Josh's side of the discussion.

"No, Erin, don't open the door. If the guy's still around, we'll take care of him when we get there." Josh's firm command would have made Ryan obey. "Put on one of Pedro's movies and try to relax a little. Help is on the way."

Erin must have asked who was coming with Josh because he said, "A close friend agreed to drive me up. I'm pretty angry right now. I don't want to become a road-rage statistic."

Josh's laughter washed over Ryan and warmed him. A close friend? At least he didn't say it was no one. Josh hung up and dialed again.

"Hey, darling, I'm heading up to Erin's. A reporter accosted her and Pedro today. She's freaked, plus he's having an episode."

Pause.

"I should have known someone would figure out where she was. I need you to do me a couple of favors."

Another pause.

"Ryan's going with me...I know... Don't worry. I didn't get

much of a chance to explain everything to Morgan and Vance, so they'll be contacting you to set up an investigator. Plus I need you to use your contacts and find out where Geraldo is. Vance promised to send a couple of his guys up to Etna to keep an eye on Erin and Pedro for me. I want to know if I need to worry about Geraldo showing up or one of his associates."

A lengthy pause and Josh chuckled.

"Now, I know you can handle Morgan and Vance. Trust me, those guys will treat you with respect. If not, just let me know and I'll take care of them... Thanks, sweetheart, I appreciate you helping me and I'll make up the time I didn't work next week... Bye."

Ryan waited for a little while, needing all his concentration to navigate L.A. traffic. When they finally got through the densest part, he shot a glance at Josh.

"Is Erin younger or older than you?"

Josh clenched his hands and Ryan could see it was a struggle for him to trust him with the information. He understood why, but he hoped they would get to the point where Josh wouldn't hesitate to tell him things.

"Younger and she's my half-sister. My mom never married Erin's dad. She wasn't the best mother in the world, so I spent a lot of time raising Erin."

Without thinking, Ryan reached over and took Josh's hand in his. Josh tensed and he thought he would pull his hand away, but after a moment, Josh relaxed and let Ryan rest their hands on his thigh.

"I'm not surprised you were her protector. You strike me as someone who would make sure everyone you considered family was okay. " Ryan grinned. "I'm glad you consider me enough of a friend to include me in your inner circle."

Josh flipped his hand over, so that his palm lay on Ryan's

leg and he flexed his fingers, digging into the muscle a little. Hissing, Ryan spread his thighs wider, hoping and praying Josh would move his hand higher.

"Are you saying I'm over-bearing?"

Josh trailed closer to Ryan's groin and his cock stiffened. Not a good idea when he was driving eighty on the highway.

"No, not over-bearing, just very dominant." He bit his lower lip, not wanting to beg for Josh to cup his prick.

He jerked as Josh's thumb grazed the seam of his jeans drawn tight over his balls. "Fuck," he breathed.

Josh squeezed his cock quickly before backing off. "Doing this in the car while you're driving isn't a good idea. As for including you in the family, it might sound silly, but I thought we connected the other night on more than a sexual level."

Wiggling in his seat, Ryan nodded. "When I saw the pictures of us kissing and I thought you had taken them, I was more hurt than angry. I mean, I was furious that anyone would invade someone's privacy like that, but when the possibility of it being you came up, I didn't want to believe you would do that to me."

"I think we both might be slightly cracked."

"Could be," he agreed.

Yawning, Josh settled back in his seat. "Would you be upset if I took a nap? I haven't slept well the last couple of nights."

"Nah, go ahead. I just stay on I-5?"

"Yes. I'll be awake before you need to worry about getting off."

Ryan fought the laughter wanting to burst from him. He managed to smother it to a soft chuckle. Josh shot him a curious look.

"Sorry. My mind hit the gutter with that comment. I'm already worrying about getting off." He leered suggestively at Josh.

"Goofball." Josh punched him in the arm.

"Ow... Hey, I can't help it if you're so fucking sexy, you put my mind permanently in the gutter." He shrugged. "Or maybe it's permanently in bed."

Josh's cheeks took on a pink tinge and Ryan laughed.

"You're not blushing, are you? Surely lots of guys have told you how fucking gorgeous you are?"

"Sure, I've heard it before, but it's different coming from you." Josh stared out the window.

Ryan frowned. "Why would it be different coming from me? I'm nothing special."

Josh shifted in his seat, obviously uncomfortable with this conversation. "I don't know. It just is."

Not wanting to make the man decide talking to him was too much of a bother, Ryan let the subject drop.

"I'll wake you up when I get past San Francisco."

"Thanks." Josh leaned back and closed his eyes.

Ryan turned on the radio, leaving the volume low. He enjoyed the feel of Josh's hand on his thigh and the sound of Josh's breathing next to him.

Chapter Seventeen

The silence woke Josh and he rolled his head to the side. Ryan was turning the car off and climbing out.

"Wait. Where are we?"

He pushed himself straighter and scrubbed a hand over his head, trying to shake the sleep from his mind.

"Just north of San Fran. I needed to stop for gas. While I fill up, why don't you type your sister's address into the GPS? That way if you fall asleep again, I won't have to wake you up until we get there."

Ryan leaned in and smiled, nodding toward the dash where the pop-up navigation screen was. It was a good idea, even though Josh didn't plan on sleeping anymore. By the time he'd gotten the address entered, Ryan had filled the tank and climbed back in the car.

"I'm going to stop at the fast food place across the street. You want anything to eat?"

Ryan pulled out of the gas station and into the restaurant, getting in the drive-thru line. Josh gave him his order and waited until they got their food and headed back out on the highway.

"I know I said this earlier, but I really do appreciate you doing this. I'm sure this wasn't how you wanted to spend your weekend." He munched on his fries.

"Driving anywhere in this kind of traffic is never how I want to spend my time." Ryan flashed him a wink. "Don't worry. The only thing I'd be doing would be trying to explain to Bill why I didn't want to go out to another club."

"Have you and Bill been friends for long?"

Why was he asking? At what point had Ryan gone from a great one-night stand to a friend or possibly more?

Ryan's laughter filled the vehicle. "God, yes. I think I hit him in the head with a shovel while we were playing in the sandbox at pre-school. It was the start of a beautiful friendship."

"What did he do?"

"Probably stole something from me. He's an instigator and loves to cause trouble. I've been in more bar fights because of him and his mouth."

"I'm not surprised. Is he gay as well?" He thought of the red head Bill was determined to pick up the other night. "Or bi?"

Ryan shook his head. "No. Bill is as straight as an arrow, but trust me, he doesn't let that get in the way of asking me all about my sex life. For a heterosexual male, he certainly is interested in what goes on between two guys."

"Sounds like he's a great friend."

Antonio did his best to be there for Josh, but there were parts of Josh's life he couldn't talk to his best friend about. Growing up in the *barrio*, he learned to keep secrets because certain things could have gotten him killed.

"I sometimes think there's something wrong with him. He's so open-minded that it floors me at times. When I finally came out to him, he laughed, slapped me on the shoulder and decided we needed to get me laid." Ryan took a sip of his soda.

"You should have heard some of the suggestions he came up with."

"I can just imagine." Josh smirked to himself. "So when did you get fucked for the first time?"

He handed Ryan napkins after the man spit his soda all over the steering wheel.

"Warn a guy next time before you say something like that." Ryan glared at him before pitching the wet napkins back at him.

"Where would the fun be in that?" Josh reached over and squeezed Ryan's knee. "You don't have to tell me if you don't want to."

"Nah...it's okay. I was just surprised is all. I waited until I went away to college. Bill and I went to Ohio University. We're from a small town in Ohio where being gay is the best way to either get your ass kicked or lose every friend you thought you had. So I chose to stay silent except for Bill. I never could keep a secret from him."

"Did you top or bottom your first time?"

He really didn't know why he was asking all these questions. The only person he ever talked this intimately with was Rachel and it wasn't usually about sex.

"I topped the first time I had sex with a guy." Ryan didn't seem bothered by the questions. "I liked it well enough, but the second time, when I bottomed, I found out what I liked best about sex with guys."

He waited until Ryan swallowed the bite of hamburger the man had taken. "What was that?"

Ryan blushed and didn't say anything for a minute. Had he insulted the man by asking? Josh opened his mouth to say something, but Ryan spoke up.

"I like being filled and if the guy's bigger than me, I like the feeling of being held." Ryan hunched his shoulders like he expected Josh to laugh at him.

He thought about it for a moment and then he caressed Ryan's arm. "I get it. I never learned how to top from the bottom, so I never enjoyed getting fucked. I think you've figured out I like to be in control."

"I never would have guessed that." Ryan shot him a wink.

"My first time was when I was sixteen. I snuck down to WeHo from my house in the *barrio*. I knew if any of my friends found out about me, I would be dead. The gang that ran my neighborhood didn't take kindly to anyone who was different, especially gays." Josh grimaced at the memory of his first time.

"Not a good experience?"

"No. I probably should have waited until I could find someone I cared about and all that bullshit, but I was horny and being with girls did nothing for me. It didn't even take the edge off."

Ryan nodded. "I've been with a few girls while I was trying to figure out exactly what I wanted, but it didn't do anything for me either. Not like a good-looking stud with a fat cock."

His leer heated Josh's face. God, he hadn't blushed in years and now he'd done it twice because of this man. Reaching over, Ryan took his hand and squeezed.

"Just say thank you and I'll try not to embarrass you anymore. Have you ever had a serious relationship?"

Regret flared in Josh for a second. "No. By the time I could admit out loud which side I played for, I had to take care of Erin and Pedro. Working three jobs really discourages serious relationships. Most guys like having time to spend with their boyfriends and I'll always have Erin to worry about."

"I understand. Family has to come first. I haven't had to worry about that yet since I'm the youngest and my sister's married to a great guy. They still live in my home town right next to my parents." Ryan checked the rearview before pulling into the other lane. "I had one boyfriend in college. He was only the third guy I slept with. Bobby was a great guy, but he wanted to travel the world and I was interested in acting. We parted as friends and he e-mails me every once in a while."

A strange jolt of jealousy raced through Josh. Why would he be jealous of a boyfriend Ryan had way before they'd even met? Maybe it was the fondness with which Ryan spoke of Bobby. Did any of Josh's one-night stands remember him with a smile?

"Why acting?" He shied away from the depressing thoughts of missed relationships.

"I guess I figured out I was good at pretending to be someone I wasn't. Acting comes easy to me. It's all the other shit that goes with it that I don't like. I hate talking about myself to reporters who don't really care what your favorite color is or who you idolized growing up."

Josh crumbled up his wrappers and stuffed them in the bag, gathering Ryan's trash as well. Checking the GPS, he realized they had another five hours to go before they arrived at Erin's house.

"Tell me about this movie, *Luther is King*. I've heard some great things about it."

Josh hit on the perfect topic to keep the conversation going as Ryan's face lit up and the actor started talking about the script. He relaxed into his seat, ready to listen for however long Ryan wanted to talk.

Chapter Eighteen

Ryan turned into the driveway leading up to a small one-story ranch. The headlights of his car swept over the flower-lined front porch and he smiled at the bright colors caught in the lights. He parked the car and turned it off. Josh stopped him before he climbed out.

"Hang out here while I go and check around. I want to make sure that reporter's gone before you get out. Don't want any more pictures."

The porch light came on as soon as the car door shut. A petite slender dark-haired woman stepped out, her hand resting on the head of the most vicious-looking dog Ryan had ever seen.

Josh hugged the woman whom Ryan assumed was Erin. He called the dog to him and the two of them strolled around the perimeter of the lawn.

Erin came down the steps and walked over to Ryan's side of the vehicle. Climbing out, he stayed where he was, sensing Erin needed to approach him. She stopped a few feet away, twisting the hem of her shirt with her fingers.

While waiting for Erin to speak, he tracked Josh's progress. They were headed toward them when Erin took a breath and smiled.

"Thank you for driving my brother up here."

"It's the least I can do since the whole thing is kind of my fault." He spoke softly and smiled.

Fragility shaded Erin's voice and face. She wore worry like an old familiar sweater, wrapped tight around her and held onto with fierce determination. He didn't want to do anything that might cause her to break.

She frowned. "Your fault?"

Josh joined them and Ryan got his first clear look at the dog. It was a mottled brown with a squat muscular build. Its square head and board chest were covered with scars.

"Let me introduce you to Zorro."

He took Josh's hand and let the man lead him to Zorro. The dog sniffed his fingers, watching him with intelligent brown eyes.

"Is he a pit bull?"

"Yes, and an ex-fighting dog. When I left my husband, Josh brought Zorro to protect Pedro and me. He's my son's best friend." Erin glanced at Josh. "Is he gone?"

"It looks like it. Let's go in and I'll introduce you two."

Josh slung an arm around his sister's shoulder and kept a hold of Ryan's hand. They went inside.

Zorro trotted down the hallway and disappeared into a back room. Ryan took off his shoes and hung back near the door, not wanting to force himself on Erin. It was her house and she had to make the decision of how far she was going to let him in.

"Come in and sit. Would you like something to drink? I have juice, water and milk. I could make coffee if you wanted some."

"Water would be fine."

"I'll get it, Erin. You need to sit and relax. How is Pedro?"

Josh gestured for Ryan to sit in the living room.

"He finally fell asleep an hour ago. It took me that long to calm him down."

Erin sat in one of the chairs and Ryan sat across from her. She studied him in the light. He let her look and confusion showed in her dark eyes.

"Erin, this is Ryan Kellar. He's the man I was kissing in the photos that started this whole thing."

Josh handed him his water. Taking a sip, he enjoyed the shocked look on her face.

"Ryan Kellar?" Disbelief colored her words.

"Yes, ma'am."

"Well, I always did say you got the good-taste-in-men genes in the family, Josh," Erin teased her big brother.

Ryan grinned as Josh's ears turned red. He chuckled.

"I thought I was the one with great taste when I let him pick me up. Little did I know some guy seems to have made it his life's goal to document my more private moments." Ryan shook his head.

Her gaze grew more assessing as he spoke. He met her eyes.

"I'm sorry for any trouble this situation has caused you, ma'am. Believe me, I had nothing to do with this."

"Neither did my brother, Mr. Kellar." Erin's conviction of her brother's innocence shone in her voice. "No matter how much money he may need, Josh would never ruin someone else's career or life like that."

He nodded. "I realized that after a bottle of whiskey, some anger and some hurt."

"And after you punched me," Josh pointed out, coming over to sit next to him.

Leaning against him, Ryan grinned. "True, but that punch didn't even faze you. I must not be as tough as I thought."

Josh encircled his waist with one arm, letting him rest more of his weight on him. Ryan's cheeks warmed as Erin took in just how comfortable they seemed to be with each other.

Why was he embarrassed? It was Josh's sister and she knew her brother was gay. As much as his mind screamed at him to move away, he didn't. He'd done some thinking on the way up while Josh slept. The public didn't need to know what he did during his personal time, but if he didn't want to lose any more of himself, he needed to be honest and do what made him happy.

"Josh works out at one of the boxing centers. He's been doing that for so many years, he must have an iron jaw by now."

"That could explain why all he did was stumble and that was probably because I surprised him instead of hurting him in some way."

They laughed and Erin seemed to lose even more of her tension. Ryan could see what kind of beauty Erin would have been if life hadn't beaten her down so early.

"You remember Morgan and Vance, my bouncer friends from the first club I worked at?" Josh asked Erin.

"Yes."

"They were with me when you called. They own a personal security business now which includes bodyguards. Morgan's going to send up two men to keep an eye out around here. No reporter's getting that close to you and Pedro again, and also, if for some reason Geraldo figures out where you are, they'll keep you safe from him as well."

Fear flashed in her eyes and Ryan watched the weight of her troubles crash down on Erin again.

"Do you think he'll figure out where we are?"

Her glance shot to the hallway Zorro had disappeared down earlier.

Josh shrugged. "I wish I could tell you no, but I told you I'd never lie to you and I won't start now. I just don't know, Erin. All we can do is prepare for the worst and hope for the best."

Standing, Josh followed her gaze with his own before going to kneel in front of her. He took her hands and smiled at her.

"Eight years ago, I promised you I would take care of you and Pedro. I'm not going to break my promise now. You're my family and my world. Geraldo is a sadistic bastard who deserves everything he got. He certainly never deserved you or his son."

Tears welled in Erin's eyes and she grabbed a hold of her brother, hugging him with all her strength. Ryan blinked tears from his own eyes and stood, moving quietly toward the kitchen. He didn't want to interrupt the emotional moment between siblings.

His family was close and he knew he'd do anything for his sister if she needed him, but whatever Josh and his sister had gone through had created bonds of steel between them that nothing would break. He hoped his problem wouldn't bring any more trouble down on Erin.

He stepped into the kitchen and stopped. A small brown-haired boy sat the table, rocking back and forth, mumbling to himself. Ryan couldn't make out the words, but he didn't think the boy was talking to him anyway. Zorro rumbled a deep warning in his chest.

Spotting a cup and a bottle of purple juice on the counter, he said, "Would you like a cup of juice?"

The boy didn't say anything, so Ryan took his silence to mean yes. He poured out half a cup and set it in front of Pedro, for that's who he supposed the boy was. Another low growl from

119

Zorro caused Ryan to back off and lean against the counter. There was something off about Pedro. He never even glanced at Ryan, just kept rocking and mumbling. The only other movements came when the boy took the cup and drank from it before reaching down to pet Zorro. Maybe that was the best place to start a conversation with him. Erin said Zorro was Pedro's best friend.

"Nice dog you've got there."

The mumbling stopped, but the rocking continued, slightly slower.

"I used to have a dog back when I lived with my parents." He kept his voice low and gentle. "Baxter was a mutt. He had big floppy ears like a Bassett hound and this odd curly coat like a poodle. The strangest-looking dog you'd ever seen. He was a scaredy-cat as well. Not tough like your pit bull there."

"American Staffordshire Terrier."

He managed not to move or act surprised when a soft voice answered him.

"Is that what Zorro is? I didn't know that. My name is Ryan and I'm a friend of your uncle Josh."

"Ryan, who are you talking to?" Josh came into the kitchen and paused. "Oh Pedro, I didn't know you were up. Did you get yourself a glass of juice?"

Pedro didn't answer and Josh shot Ryan a questioning glance.

"The juice and a cup were out when I got in here, so I poured him some. I hope that was okay." He didn't want to overstep his bounds with Josh's family.

"He didn't freak out when you gave it to him, did he?"

"No. He was telling me that Zorro is an American Staffordshire Terrier." He smiled. "I didn't know that. I thought all pit bulls were pit bulls, not a specific breed."

Josh grinned and bent to pat Zorro. "This dog is the only thing Pedro will talk about. They love each other so much."

"It shows. Hey, could you show me where I'll be sleeping? If there isn't room here, I can go back into town and get a room at the bed and breakfast we passed on our way here."

It was time for him to disappear for a while. Ryan was an intruder in this family and he didn't want them to feel uncomfortable around him. Something told him that Pedro didn't deal with strangers or changes in his routine.

"Don't be stupid. You can share the room I use when I come to visit, if you don't mind sharing a bed with me again."

Ryan's cock grew semi-hard at the thought of being wrapped in Josh's arms again, naked and warm under the blankets. He cleared his throat.

"I don't mind sharing."

A matching gleam of heat flashed in Josh's eyes before he turned, gesturing for Ryan to follow him. They went down the hallway to the very back of the house. Opening a door, Josh allowed him to enter first.

He strolled in and hesitated, turning to face Josh only after he heard the door shut. Josh cupped Ryan's ass and pulled him gently to him. Their bodies pressed tight together and he moaned silently as Josh kissed him.

Rubbing his hands up and down Josh's back, he absorbed the firm touch of his lover's lips. Ryan opened, letting Josh sweep his tongue in and relearn every tooth. He shivered as Josh sucked on his bottom lip.

They only pulled apart when both were panting for breath. Josh held his face and rubbed a thumb over his swollen lips.

"Thank you," Josh whispered.

"For what?" Ryan didn't think he deserved thanks for anything.

"For coming here with me and for trusting me, even though you don't really have any reason to." Josh rested their foreheads together.

Ryan let his shoulders lift in an abbreviated shrug. "It's my fault all this shit is happening, so it's the least I could do."

He paused for a second. Should he say what he'd been wanting to admit for a couple hours now?

"Even if this didn't have anything to do with me, I'd still want to be by your side helping you."

Josh's dark eyes burned into his and read every inch of his soul. Ryan couldn't hide, even if he wished to.

"I feel the same way."

Another soft brush of lips on lips and Josh stepped back.

"I'm going to talk to Erin for a little bit, get her calm and settled again. Our bathroom's through there." He nodded toward a door on the other side of the room. "Pedro gets his own bathroom. He can't stand anything touched or moved in his."

"No problem. Is there a toothbrush I can use?" Ryan moved away, letting Josh go back to dealing with his family.

"Yeah. Erin always keeps a few new ones in there." Josh opened the door to the hallway. "I'll be back in a few."

"Take your time. I'm not going anywhere. I'll be here for as long as you need."

Josh's bright smile caused Ryan's heart to skip a beat. Who knew he'd find the possibility of love in the shit storm that those pictures had created?

Chapter Nineteen

Josh returned to the living room, an odd happiness bubbling in him. His sister grinned at him as he sat.

"Ryan Kellar? Shit, Josh, when you decide to pick a guy up, you go all out." She shook her head.

"What can I say? I have good taste. But honest to God, Erin, I didn't know who he was until Rachel told me after the first set of pictures came out." He laughed. "You know I don't have a TV or time to go to the movies."

She moved to sit beside him and rested her head on Josh's shoulder. "I know and I'm sorry."

"Don't be. You're my family and I wouldn't have it any other way." He hugged her close. "Did you get Pedro back to bed?"

Nodding, she sighed. "Yes, I didn't even know he could get the juice out of the refrigerator. He's never done that before. I'm just glad that Ryan didn't throw him into a fit, which is odd since Pedro doesn't like strangers."

He thought about the man sleeping in his bed down the hall. "Ryan has a way about him, plus he was talking to him about Zorro. If there's anything that will get Pedro to talk, it's that dog."

"True. It was a good day when you brought him to us. I feel safer now on my own with him here." Erin yawned.

Josh stood, offered her his hand and helped her to her feet. "Why don't you go to bed? I'm here now and I'll fix it so you don't get bothered again. Rachel is checking her contacts to see where Geraldo is. We'll deal with him when or if we have to."

She kissed his cheek and headed off to bed. "My knight in shining armor always riding to my rescue. Maybe you should take a little time to yourself."

He swatted her butt when she nodded toward his bedroom. "I'll make sure he stays quiet. Don't want to keep you awake."

Erin covered her ears and made "la-la" noises before grinning at him. "TMI, big brother, TMI."

"Then you shouldn't make comments like that if you didn't want to know. Get to bed. We'll talk more tomorrow."

He watched Erin go into her bedroom before he slipped into his. Being as quiet as he could, he cleaned up and climbed under the blankets. Settling on his side, he stared through the darkness at Ryan. Should he reach out and pull the man close or should he let him sleep?

"Are Erin and Pedro okay?" Ryan's question was soft as the man rolled over to look at him.

"Yeah, they're fine."

He didn't fight the urge to stroke his thumb over Ryan's cheek. Warm skin greeted his touch and they both sighed.

Moving like they shared the same thought, their lips met. He slid his hand around Ryan's head to hold him still while he nibbled along Ryan's bottom lip.

"Oh," Ryan gasped, his hot breath bathing Josh's mouth.

He swept his tongue in, running the tip over Ryan's teeth. He teased Ryan, silently asking him to come and play. With a slight push from Josh, Ryan rolled onto his back and Josh rose above him.

Easing a few inches away, he looked at Ryan. "Are you okay with this?"

Nodding, Ryan slid his hands around Josh's hips to grip his ass. His gaze burned with desire and something that looked a little like caring.

"The damage is done," Ryan whispered. His serious expression touched a spot deep inside Josh. "There's no going back, and at this point, I'm not sure I'd want to even if there was."

That reassurance was all Josh needed to hear. He nudged Ryan's legs apart and settled between them, pressing their cocks together. Thank God, they were both naked. Their erections left wet trails over their stomachs as they rocked.

Ryan moaned and Josh leaned down to whisper in his ear, "We have to be quiet. Both Pedro and Erin are light sleepers. I don't think you're ready for them to know what we're doing in here."

He smiled as Ryan blushed before nodding. Nibbling along Ryan's chin, he ground their groins together. Ryan's breathing hitched and his hips arched up, silently begging for more contact. Josh kissed his way down Ryan's smooth chest, stopping to suck and bite at the hard nubs of flesh on each pectoral muscle.

Ryan stroked his hands over Josh's shaved head, trying to find something to hold on to. Josh chuckled when Ryan protested as he pulled away from his nipples.

"You want me to play with them a little, honey?"

Nodding, Ryan applied pressure to Josh's head, asking him to return and Josh complied. He bent to take one nipple in his teeth, using the tip of his tongue to tease it. He tugged on the nub, not doing it too hard since he wasn't sure how much pain Ryan was willing to take. The way Ryan moaned let him know the man just might want more.

He reached out with his other hand and pinched Ryan's other nipple, not wanting to neglect it. He twisted it hard, causing Ryan to curl up and stuff his fist in his mouth to keep from crying out.

"Is that all right?"

Whimpering, Ryan nodded, his body moving in a slow dance, pressing tight to Josh and retreating. Each movement enticed him to bite and pet. He sucked up a mark right above Ryan's left nipple, drawing the blood to the surface and making it dark. Leaning back, he rubbed his thumb over the bruise.

"Please."

Ryan's low cry was cut off. Josh looked up to see Ryan biting his bottom lip to keep from shouting. A little bead of blood appeared and Josh shook his head.

"Oh no. No hurting yourself to keep quiet." He climbed out of bed.

"Where are you going?" Ryan shifted restlessly on the sheets, running his hands over his chest and playing with his own nipples.

"To find something to keep you from biting your lips bloody." He dug through the dresser where he kept spare clothes for when he stayed at Erin's. He jerked a tie out of the back of one drawer. "Here is it."

Ryan's eyes widened as Josh straddled his hips and held up the piece of fabric for him to look at. Josh saw a little fear in Ryan's dark eyes, but there was also a flash of heat deep in them.

"Don't worry. I won't tie it too tight or anything. I just want to muffle your cries. You need to feel what I'm doing to you, not get caught up in thinking about not making noise." He brushed a kiss over Ryan's split lip. "Any time you start to feel afraid or so overwhelmed you don't think you can take it, let me know and I'll untie it. Will you try?"

His lover studied him for a few seconds before nodding slowly. The trust implicit in that nod made Josh's cock twitch and his heart swell. The tabloid pictures should have caused Ryan to think twice about letting Josh tie him up, but it was clear that Ryan didn't think Josh had anything to do with the photographs.

He eased the silk fabric between Ryan's lips and tied the ends behind his head. Ryan worked his mouth, testing the feel of the tie against the corners of his lips.

"It's not too tight, is it?"

Ryan shook his head and suddenly arched his hips, letting Josh know without saying a word that he was ready to start up where they left off.

"Oh wait, forgot something else."

He rolled off the bed, laughing at Ryan's groan of frustration. Josh padded into the bathroom and opened up the bottom drawer in the cabinet. The two condoms and the bottle of lube he'd left the last time he visited were still there. Grabbing them, he showed them to Ryan as he shut the drawer.

"I had them in my overnight bag last time I was here and tossed them in the drawer before Pedro could find them. He has a tendency to go through people's stuff." He shrugged.

Ryan's raised eyebrow showed skepticism and Josh smiled. "I don't bring guys here. You're the first aside from my best friend, Antonio, to ever meet Erin and Pedro. I don't share my family with just anyone."

The softening of Ryan's expression told Josh the man understood what Josh was saying. What was it about Ryan Kellar that made Josh feel safe about introducing him to his family? He protected Erin and Pedro as fiercely as Zorro did and no guy had ever gotten this close to them before.

He joined Ryan on the bed again, easing between his spread legs and setting the lube and condoms next to Ryan's hips. Trailing a finger along Ryan's hip, he grinned as Ryan wiggled, trying to get away from his touch.

"Hmmm...a little ticklish there? I'll have to remember that."

Leaning down, Josh sucked up another dark mark right above the nest of curls around the base of Ryan's cock. Ryan fisted his hands in the sheets under him and he shifted, so his cock bumped Josh's cheek.

"Do you want something?"

He glanced up to meet Ryan's narrowed gaze and laughed. "Open a condom for me while I take a little detour."

Ryan scrambled, searching for the condom while Josh licked his way around Ryan's erection to where his balls hung below his shaft. A struggled cry drifted through the room as Josh sucked one of Ryan's balls into his mouth.

Smiling to himself, Josh applied harder suction, bathing the lightly furred skin with his tongue. He'd make Ryan come before fucking him hard and fast.

Chapter Twenty

Seeing Josh lying between his legs and sucking on his balls made Ryan's prick ache. God, he wanted his cock buried deep in Josh's moist mouth. He struggled to get the foil packet open without being able to use his teeth. In frustration, he thumped Josh on the shoulder.

Josh pulled off him with a pop and frowned. "What?"

He waved the condom at his lover, growling low in his throat. Josh shot him a sheepish grin.

"Sorry. Forgot how hard it is to open those stupid things." Josh took the packet from him and tore it open before handing it back to him. "After you get this on, I'll suck you."

His hands trembled as he managed to get the rubber down over his throbbing dick. Josh watched him with intense focus and Ryan stroked his cock once, giving his best come hither look. Or the best he could with the tie in his mouth.

"You are a tease."

Ryan whimpered when Josh leaned forward and licked the vein pulsing along the underside of his prick. God, he wanted to feel Josh's tongue on his naked flesh. Maybe he'd suggest that for next time. Then Josh swallowed him down and his mind went blank. He moved with Josh's movements until Josh pinned his hips down and wouldn't allow him to participate.

Josh let his cock slide out of his mouth. "Stay still. If you can't, I might have to get some more ties out and bind you to the bed."

A full-body shudder wracked Ryan and his skin heated. Fuck, when had he turned into such a slut? The thought of being tied and entirely at Josh's mercy made his prick swell even more, to the point where one touch from Josh and he'd come.

He fisted his hands in the sheets and begged Josh with his eyes.

"I think someone likes that idea, but we'll wait until we get to my apartment for anything else."

Josh didn't wait for him to nod or acknowledge the statement in any way. He settled between Ryan's legs and swallowed him down again.

Fuck. His eyes fluttering closed, Ryan moaned and tried not to shove more of his prick into Josh's mouth. His lover hummed his approval and he twitched. Even through the latex, he could feel the moist heat of Josh's tongue as he licked and teased his shaft.

The low pop of the lube bottle opening got his attention and he looked to see Josh still working his cock like a pro, but also getting his fingers slick. Ryan reached down and hooked his hands behind his knees, pulling up and out to give Josh better access. His groan stuck in his throat as Josh pressed two fingers inside his channel without warning.

He arched his back, welcoming the burn and relaxing as it turned to lust. Pushing back, he signaled to Josh that he was ready for more. Josh matched the movement of his fingers with that of his head and Ryan became swamped with being pleasured front and back.

Two fingers became three and Josh pushed farther in,

hitting Ryan's gland and shooting electricity through his body. His balls drew tight and his cock ached. He needed to come and it was going to be soon.

A low keening sound filled the room and Ryan flushed when he realized it was coming from him. The head of his prick hit the back of Josh's throat and his lover swallowed around him, massaging his shaft with his muscles. Ryan's climax exploded around him and he screamed, thankful for the gag or else he'd be waking everyone up.

Josh licked and sucked until Ryan collapsed, melted into the bed. He couldn't get one of his muscles to work and his eyelids were disobeying commands as well. He heard the rip of another foil packet and the pop of the lube again.

His legs were lifted and set on Josh's shoulders.

"Open your eyes," Josh ordered.

Ryan forced his eyes open and met Josh's lust-filled gaze. They kept eye contact as Josh breached Ryan's ass and buried his cock deep inside. Fighting the urge to close his eyes again, Ryan reached out and gripped Josh's shoulders.

Josh nodded. "You can touch all you want now. It's going to be fast. You're so fucking hot when you come."

He glanced away for a second, embarrassed by how wanton he must look, gagged and spread with Josh balls deep in his ass. Leaning down, Josh licked a line from his chest to his mouth and took his lips in a quick kiss.

His lover rocked above him, bending him almost in two with each thrust. Josh's prick throbbed and swelled in Ryan's inner passage, driving him to squeeze and milk Josh with each stroke.

"That's it. You're a natural. God, your ass is so tight and hot. I jerked off to the memory of this, but it's not the same as the real thing," Josh babbled, reaming his ass harder and faster with each shove in.

Ryan reached back and braced his hands against the headboard, pushing back to encourage Josh closer and closer to his own climax. His own grunts were muffled by the gag and he growled low in his throat. He wanted to be able to tell Josh how much he loved getting fucked by him. He wanted to use his voice to push the man over the edge.

Josh slammed deep, nailing Ryan's gland and making him see stars.

"Shit," Josh whispered, his hips jerking and rolling as he filled the condom.

Ryan smoothed his hands over Josh's chest and shoulders as his lover's arms gave out and he collapsed on him. He held him tight until they both caught their breath and could move again.

Josh rolled off, eliciting a sigh from both as his soft cock slid from Ryan's ass. He untied the gag and Ryan worked his jaw back and forth to ease the ache in it.

"Are you okay?" Josh rubbed his thumb over Ryan's chin.

"Yeah," he croaked, his mouth dry.

"I'll get you some water." Josh took care of their condoms before heading to the bathroom for a glass of water and a washcloth.

Ryan lay there, staring up at the ceiling and wondering how he managed to get to this point. If he'd listened to Raz, he would have sued Josh for some stupid reason and do his best to look "straight" to his fans. Yet Ryan never believed Josh was the person behind those pictures and as crazy as it seemed, there had been a connection between them from that first night.

He knew he would be considered inexperienced in the sex department. His ambitions made it difficult to find someone who would stick through the madness that the film industry was. Knowing that Josh trusted him enough to show him this very personal side of his life made Ryan think Josh felt the same way about him.

A warm damp cloth swiped over his groin and he jumped. Bringing his gaze down from the ceiling, he saw Josh holding a glass in one hand and cleaning him off with the washcloth in the other. He pushed up to sit and took the water his lover offered him. They finished at the same time. Josh took both items back to the bathroom before climbing into bed and pulling the blankets over them.

None of his other lovers ever took such care of him. Usually they would come and leave. He'd be left to clean up and go to sleep in an empty bed. He relaxed as Josh wrapped his arms around his waist, pulling him back against his chest.

"You're thinking too hard. Nothing's so important it can't wait until tomorrow."

Nodding, he closed his eyes. Josh was right. He couldn't do anything at the moment about any of the problems bothering him. He'd enjoy being held tight by this man and worry about everything tomorrow.

"Night, Bear," he whispered.

"Night, honey."

Josh brushed his lips over the nape of Ryan's neck and Ryan shivered, knowing he'd be dreaming about their love making and looking forward to it.

Chapter Twenty-One

Josh woke, frowning as tingles shot through his arm. Something heavy rested on it. Opening his eyes, he saw the dark brown curls at the nape of Ryan's neck. He smiled and snuggled closer, enjoying Ryan's warm skin and male scent.

Ryan mumbled something, but Josh wasn't sure if the man was awake or not. He slid his hand down over firm abs to circle around Ryan's semi-hard cock and pumped.

"Bear," Ryan murmured, pushing into his hand before pressing his ass back against Josh.

He chuckled, wondering when Ryan started calling him Bear. "Morning, honey." He brushed a kiss over Ryan's shoulder.

"I was having a good dream." Ryan reached back to stroke his hand over Josh's hip.

"What were you dreaming about?" He moved Ryan's pliant body so his cock nestled between Ryan's ass cheeks and the flared head of Josh's prick bumped Ryan's hole, making his lover whimper.

"You and I were on a beach and we were making love." Ryan rocked between Josh's hand and his cock.

"Easy. I don't have any more rubbers."

Josh nibbled on Ryan's earlobe before sucking up a dark

mark on his shoulder. He made sure it was somewhere Ryan could hide it.

"But I want..."

"I know what you want and if you remember to be quiet, I'll give it to you," he growled into Ryan's ear as he took control of their movements.

He tightened his grip on Ryan's shaft, making each pump burn and rocket Ryan closer to the edge. They rocked together and Josh loved the muffled moans his lover made with each thrust.

"Soon," Ryan gasped.

On the next upstroke, Josh teased his thumb along the head of Ryan's cock, easing it just slightly into the slit. Ryan buried his face into his pillow and stifled his shout as liquid heat covered Josh's hand. He thrust twice and coated Ryan's back with his own come. He bit his lip to keep from yelling Ryan's name.

When he stopped trembling, he climbed out of bed and went to the bathroom. After cleaning himself off, Josh grabbed a washcloth, got it wet and headed back to wipe Ryan down. He took the damp cloth back to the other room and finished getting ready.

Slapping Ryan's naked ass, he waited until the other man glanced at him. "I brought your clean clothes in. They're hanging on the back of the bathroom door."

Ryan sat up and shoved his hand through his hair. "Thanks. Would it be all right to take a shower?"

"Sure. There are clean towels in the bathroom along with shampoo and stuff. I'm going to see if Erin and Pedro are up yet."

Without thinking, he leaned over and gave Ryan a quick

peck on the cheek. His cell phone rang as he left the bedroom.

"Hello?"

"Hey Josh, it's Vance."

"Vance, how's it going?"

He wandered into the kitchen and found Pedro already at the table, rocking and talking softly to Zorro. Josh's sister stood at the stove, frying bacon and eggs. He gave her a one-armed hug.

"Okay, man. Two of our guys should be reaching your sister's place in the next hour or so. They have your number and will call when they get there. That way you don't have any surprises."

Josh poured a glass of orange juice. "Thanks. You and Morgan are the best."

"We try. Oh, and tell Ryan that we hired a private investigator for him. The guy's one of the best and he's got the background info. Now we just have to see what he finds."

"Drinks and dinner are on me when I get back." He took a drink and looked around when he heard Erin greet Ryan. "I have to go. I'll give you a call when we get ready to head back to WeHo."

"Catch you later, and tell Erin hi from us." Vance hung up.

Josh ended the call and set the phone on the counter. He watched how Ryan interacted with Erin and Pedro. Each movement was slow and deliberate like he didn't want to scare them. He spoke softly and didn't ignore Pedro, even though he seemed to know the boy wouldn't answer him. Ryan kept a respectful distance from Erin, again seeming to understand without being told of Erin's nervousness around men.

"Was that Vance?"

Ryan joined him at the counter next to the refrigerator.

Josh couldn't resist tasting Ryan's bright smile. Ryan didn't flinch or move away. The actor opened for him, yet as much as Josh would have loved to take it deeper, he settled for another quick kiss.

"Yes. He called to let me know that they sent two guys up here to keep an eye on things for you, Erin. They'll keep the reporters at bay until we figure out what's going on."

He took another glass out and handed it to Ryan. "They also hired a P.I. to look into those pictures for you, Ryan."

"Those men your friends are sending? They won't be disrupting things, will they?"

Erin set breakfast on the table and they all helped themselves, except for Pedro who played with his Cheerios.

"They're professional bodyguards, sweetheart. They know how to blend in without being obtrusive."

Ryan smiled. "Your brother's friends have a good reputation among Hollywood, at least, of being very professional and discreet."

"I'm sure Morgan has warned them about Pedro's challenges." Reaching out, Josh took his sister's hand. "I just want you to be safe, not only from reporters, but from Geraldo as well. I haven't heard from Rachel about him yet."

Erin's gaze went to Pedro and Josh cursed silently. Hearing his father's name could set off a myriad of reactions from the boy; anything from silence to an all-out screaming melt-down. Today, it seemed silence would be Pedro's reaction.

"Pedro, if you're done with your breakfast, would you put your bowl in the sink for me? Remember that Zorro's water dish needs to be filled."

Every time Erin asked Pedro to do anything, it was a crap shoot as to whether he would do it or not. Again today looked like a good day because Pedro picked up his dish and put it in the sink. Afterward, he went into the mud room and filled Zorro's dish.

"Thank you. You can go watch TV until I'm ready to leave."

Josh and Erin exchanged sad smiles as Pedro wandered off toward the living room. There were dark circles under Erin's eyes and guilt started to swell in Josh.

"None of that." Erin squeezed his hand.

"None of what?"

Ryan sat, watching them and trying to be invisible. Josh knew the man had to be curious, but was too polite to ask.

"No feeling guilty. First of all, Pedro is my son and my responsibility. I won't turn my back on him like his father did. Second of all, you can't live your life worrying about me. You need to think about yourself more often." Erin's sad eyes met his and her grip on his hand tightened even more. "You've been taking care of me since you were fourteen. It's time to take care of yourself."

Her gaze shifted to Ryan for a second before meeting his with a knowing gleam. His cheeks heated and he wiggled in his chair. He shouldn't be embarrassed. He was an adult and could have as many lovers as he wanted, but Ryan was the first guy Josh had ever allowed to meet his family. That fact alone made the man far more special than the others.

Ryan cleared his throat. "This might be rude to ask and you don't have to answer if you don't want to. What is Pedro's diagnosis?"

"Thank you for not using 'problem'. Though that word can be used to describe Pedro's issues, I don't like using it because as far as I'm concerned, there's nothing wrong with my son."

Ryan stared at Erin and she laughed.

"I'm not deluding myself into thinking Pedro's a normal boy, Ryan. It's just that his brain is wired differently than yours and mine. Pedro's autistic, but he's not stupid or handicapped."

Josh stood and gathered their plates. He'd let Erin explain Pedro. He still didn't totally understand the doctor's explanation. All he knew was that his nephew was an intelligent boy who had a hard time expressing himself.

"He's challenged, but not because he's slow or dumb. It's simply because he thinks differently from us, so at times it makes it hard for him to deal with us. He's sensitive to so many things that I've worried we'd never get him to some sense of 'normalcy', but his classes and Zorro have helped a lot."

Josh's phone rang and he picked it up off the counter as he headed toward the front of the house.

"Yes?"

"Mr. Bauer, I'm Winston Austin. My partner and I were sent by Morgan LaFontaine. We're in your driveway."

"Okay. I'll be right out."

Josh hung up and tucked the phone in his back pocket. Stopping in the doorway of the living room, he snapped his fingers, calling Zorro to him.

"Pedro, I have to borrow Zorro for a few minutes."

He wasn't sure, but Pedro might have given him the slightest of nods. Anything doing with the dog got a response from his nephew.

Josh took Zorro out with him to meet Winston and the other bodyguard.

Chapter Twenty-Two

Ryan stayed in the background during the delicate process of introducing Pedro to Winston and Chad, the two bodyguards. Both men approached the boy with a matter-of-fact manner. They talked to him like they would a normal boy, even though Pedro never answered them.

He smiled to himself at the attraction that flared between Chad and Erin. If Erin allowed it, something could develop there.

His phone rang and he stepped down the hall into the kitchen. Checking the caller ID, he grinned.

"Bill, how's it going?"

"Great, but where the hell are you? When you didn't come home last night, I figured you must have gotten lucky again. Did you let that bartender fuck you again?"

Ryan's cheeks heated and he shook his head. How Bill still managed to embarrass him was a mystery.

"Well, yes."

"Fucking A, man. That's awesome."

He leaned against the counter and stared out into the backyard. "I'm sorry I didn't call to let you know where I was. I'm not used to having anyone but Raz worried about me out here."

Bill's tone held impatience. "Fine. It's all right. Now go back to getting fucked."

He chuckled and said, "No details, asshole. I met Josh yesterday to talk about how we were going to find out who took those pictures. He got a call from a friend who needed some help and I offered to drive him up north."

"Up north? How far up north?"

"About ten hours away." He wouldn't give Bill any more than that. Ryan trusted Bill with his own secrets, but this one wasn't his to share.

"Holy shit. I hope you got fucked for your generous offer."

"You're such a jackass," he pointed out.

"What? I'm just saying..."

Bill's laughter joined his.

"I know what you're saying and I'm not feeding your twisted fantasies."

Footsteps behind him caused him to turn and he watched Josh enter the kitchen. The other man winked at him as he gestured to the phone.

"I have to go. I should be home sometime tonight. I'm sorry to be abandoning you while you're visiting."

"Don't trouble yourself. I'm a big boy and I can entertain myself. Be careful and tell that stud I said hi."

He hung up and stuck his phone in his pocket. Josh stepped closer, slipping his arms around Ryan's waist and laying his head on Ryan's shoulder. Encircling Josh's waist, Ryan held him tight and rested his cheek against Josh's stubble-covered head.

"You need to shave your head," he commented, rubbing his face over the roughness.

"I planned on doing it this weekend." Josh sighed. "Erin's

141

getting Pedro ready to go to school. Chad's going with them. I'll fill Winston in about Geraldo, then we can take off."

"I'm not in any hurry, Bear. Bill can keep himself busy, though that could mean I'll need to bail him out of jail when we get back."

"Why do you call me Bear?"

He tensed for a second before deciding it couldn't matter. "It's silly, but I think of you as a big teddy bear. You're hairy, but not like Bigfoot hairy. More than that though, it's because when you hold me tight or let me hold you, I feel safe and at ease like I used to when I was little and holding my favorite teddy bear."

Josh laughed softly and pulled away a few inches. They stared at each other for a few seconds and Ryan saw an emotion in Josh's eyes that made his chest tighten. Not wanting to think about it at the moment, he leaned forward, pressing their lips together. The kiss was another short one, but it held a promise the others hadn't.

"Josh, we're leaving." Erin walked into the kitchen.

Ryan let Josh go reluctantly. He watched them hug before Erin turned to him and offered her hand.

"It was nice meeting you, Ryan. I have a feeling we'll be seeing more of each other."

He shook her hand and gave her a smile. "I hope so, and I'm sorry I caused all this trouble for you."

"Don't worry. We've handled worse and made it through."

Ryan managed to get coffee brewing while Josh walked Erin and Pedro out to their car. Winston joined him in the kitchen.

"Mr. Kellar." Winston nodded.

There was no surprise on the man's face, so Morgan or Vance had told him about Ryan and Josh.

"Call me Ryan, please." He gestured to the coffee. "Would you like some?"

"Thanks. I take it black."

After pouring and handing the bodyguard his coffee, Ryan prepared his own and sat at the table. Neither man spoke, but the silence wasn't uncomfortable. Josh returned a few minutes later. Sitting with them, he looked at Winston.

"I know you can handle the paparazzi that might come around, but there's another factor you need to be aware of. Erin's ex-husband, Geraldo Mendoza."

Winston's eyebrows shot up and Ryan wondered who Geraldo was by the bodyguard's reaction.

"Why isn't she in witness protection?" Winston's knuckles went white as he tightened his grip on his coffee mug.

"Erin never testified against him. As soon as the DEA nabbed him, Erin filed for a divorce and we got her out of there." Josh rubbed his chin and shrugged. "For a couple of months after he got served the papers, he had me followed which is why I live in WeHo and Erin lives up here."

Ryan frowned. DEA? What had Josh's ex-brother-in-law been involved in?

"Where is he?" The bodyguard tugged out a small PDA and typed something in.

"The last thing we heard he was in San Quentin, serving twenty-five to life for shooting a police officer."

"If he's in jail, why are you worried about him?" Ryan had to ask.

"Even if he's still there, he's the head of one of the most dangerous gangs in Los Angeles. The members will do anything to stay on his good side and one way is to find his wife."

"And his son, right?"

He stood and grabbed the pot for more coffee, offering Winston a refill.

"No. Once Pedro was diagnosed, Geraldo denied he was his son. A macho man like him would never have a less than perfect son."

"That's crazy. Pedro's perfect the way he is. What kind of man would deny his own child?"

He never understood why anyone would deny their own flesh and blood, no matter whether the child had a handicap or was gay.

"Geraldo Mendoza is a sadistic bastard, not a man," Josh remarked as he met Winston's gaze. "I have a friend checking out to see if he's still in prison and also if there's any news about Erin on the streets."

Winston typed a few more things in his PDA and nodded. "Thanks for letting me know. Chad and I will definitely keep our eyes open for anyone who might endanger your family. Trust us."

"I have to. As much as I wish I could stay here and protect them myself, I need to work. There just aren't as many jobs up here as there are down south."

Ryan hesitated for a second before laying his hand on Josh's arm. Josh covered his hand and smiled at him.

"I have to work in the morning, so we should get going." Josh stood and shook Winston's hand. "Thank you for coming and I'll either call you or have Morgan call you when we find out anything about Geraldo."

"I have my own contacts I'll check with as well. We'll pool our resources and hopefully find out that there's nothing to worry about with Mendoza."

Ryan grabbed his shirt and tossed Josh the car keys. "You

can drive home."

Josh's eyes lit up and Ryan could see that getting to drive Ryan's CTS brightened his lover's day. He climbed in the passenger seat and buckled up, trusting Josh to get him home safely.

Ten hours later, Ryan slid into the driver's seat and Josh crouched down next to the door.

"I'd invite you up, but I have to be up by six to head out for my construction job."

"I understand." Ryan cupped Josh's cheek and rubbed his thumb over Josh's bottom lip.

"Can I call you sometime tomorrow? Maybe you could stop by the club." Josh seemed a little hesitant to ask.

"Sure. I'll be hanging out with Bill. I have the next week off before I start my next movie. The nice thing about that one is we're doing the sound stage stuff first before we head out on location."

"Great." Josh kissed the pad of Ryan's thumb and stood. "I'll talk to you tomorrow."

Ryan waved good-bye and headed back to his apartment. After parking his car, he headed up to his place. Bill was sprawled on the couch as he walked in.

"You're home." Bill sat up and grinned.

"Thank God, I hate riding in a car for that long." He tossed his keys on the dining room table and flopped into the chair catty-corner to the couch.

"I stopped answering the phone."

Bill's statement made him frown.

"Why?"

"Were you out of cell phone range?"

"No. I turned my phone off after I talked to you. I didn't want to talk to anyone else." He got his phone out and turned it back on. Fifteen messages were waiting for him. "Who wanted to talk to me?"

"Your crazy-ass agent started calling shortly after I talked to you and then proceeded to call every ten minutes until I took the phone off the hook." Bill shook his head. "That man is fucking annoying as hell. How do you stand him?"

Ryan shrugged and tossed his phone on the coffee table. He wasn't going to call Raz until tomorrow.

"He got me my first job."

"That's wonderful, but now that you're getting great reviews for your movie, maybe you should consider finding a different agent. You're his biggest client and he shouldn't be as demanding on your time as he is. You're the boss."

Rubbing his forehead, he nodded. "I know, but I don't want to talk about it tonight. It's been a long day. How about I go change and we can head out to hit some clubs tonight?"

"Cool idea, man. And remember, you still have to tell me about your time with stud man."

"That's not going to happen at any point, no matter how drunk you plan to get me. Unlike you, I don't kiss and tell." Ryan stood and started to make his way to his bedroom.

"Now that's harsh. Where's the love since I hooked the two of you up? You should be willing to throw me a bone or something."

He flipped Bill the finger and went to change his clothes. Ryan wanted to have some fun and hang out with his best friend. He'd deal with his agent tomorrow.

Chapter Twenty-Three

"Hey, Josh, did you get up north this weekend?"

He looked up from the wood he was cutting to see Antonio standing there. Turning off the saw, he straightened and gestured for his friend to come closer.

"Yeah. I almost didn't go, but Erin got upset, so I ran up there with a friend to check on her and Pedro." Josh stretched his arms over his shoulders. "I'm getting too old to make those quick trips up there and back."

Antonio slapped his back. "You got time to hit the gym after work today?"

Josh almost said no, but he hadn't talked to Ryan yet and anyway, he needed to work some of his restlessness off before he headed to the Lucky Seven.

"Sure. I don't have to work at the restaurant tonight, so I have time between the site and the club."

"Great, I'll see you at the truck later."

Now that he'd stopped, Josh figured he'd give Ryan a call. Digging through his pockets, he found his phone and wandered off to the edge of the construction site. Punching in Ryan's number, he waited for the actor to answer.

"Hello?"

"It's Josh." He leaned against the chain link fence and

stared down at the dirt under his feet.

"Hi. How's your day going?" Ryan's voice held anger and he sounded tense.

"Good. It's work, you know, nothing very exciting. I was taking a break and thought I'd see how you were doing." He wanted to ask what was wrong, but wasn't sure if Ryan would want to tell him. What the hell? The worse that could happen was Ryan wouldn't tell him.

"Is everything okay?"

"It will be if I can see you tonight." Ryan's voice lowered like he was with someone he didn't want to hear his words.

"I'll be at the Lucky Seven around eight."

"Good. I really can't talk right now, but I'll see you then. Bye, Bear." Ryan hung up.

He shut his phone off and tossed it in his lunchbox. No point in worrying about Ryan. There wasn't anything Josh could do to help him at the moment. He went back to work, looking forward to seeing Ryan later on that night.

"Well, well...if it isn't Mr. Tabloid Star. I wondered when you would lower yourself to be seen with the rest of us."

Josh clenched his hands and turned slowly, meeting the sneering visage of Avery, one of the gym members who didn't like Josh.

"If I realized how much you'd miss me, I would have let you know I wouldn't be around."

"Forget about him, Josh." Antonio hooked an arm around Josh's shoulder and started to lead him away.

"So was Kellar's ass tight? He looks like he'd be a good fuck. Of course you'd have to be a fag and looking for a piece of ass."

Avery's insult wouldn't have bothered him if Ryan's name hadn't been mentioned. Swinging around, he stepped into Avery's personal space, glaring down at the shorter man.

"You've been gunning for me since you joined the gym. You want to go a round or two? I'll give you what you're looking for."

"Come on, man, he isn't worth it."

Antonio tried to defuse the situation, but Josh wasn't interested in walking away from the asshole. Whenever he'd been at the gym at the same time as Avery, the man always picked at him. He wasn't in the mood today to back down from anyone.

"Get some tape for my hands and my bag. I'll talk to the trainer to get the ring ready."

He started to walk over to where the manager of the gym stood. Avery grinned and strutted off to where his friends stood.

"What's going on?" The manager looked over to where Avery stood, accepting the congratulations from his buddies.

"Avery wants to spar with me. I was wondering if the ring is set up."

"Seriously?" The guy shook his head. "Avery's dumber than he looks. No one's told him about you, have they?"

He shrugged. "Probably a bunch of guys talked about me to him. He's one of those jerks who doesn't believe a fag can be tough."

The manager grinned and punched Josh's arm. "It's his funeral then. I'll turn the lights on and you can go in whenever you're ready. I'll hang out and keep an eye out for any problems."

"Thanks. I think once I hit him a couple of times, he'll get the idea that compared to me, he's an amateur."

Antonio met him at the side of the ring. Josh put his headgear on and let his friend tape up his hands before putting on his gloves. He'd stretched earlier when they got there and warmed up enough not to worry about pulling any muscles.

Stepping into the ring, he did a little shadow boxing while he waited for Avery to join him. The shorter, younger man climbed into the ring and grinned at Josh. There was arrogance in the man's eyes and bearing, but Josh didn't let it bother him. He'd dealt with lots of young men who thought they were studs and were challenging the old bull for top spot.

The manager reminded them of the rules and told them they could start. Josh circled Avery, studying every movement of the man's body and eyes. He'd watched the other man box a few times and knew he wasn't good enough to threaten or hurt Josh.

Avery set his feet and swung a wide left at Josh's face. Josh dodged it easily before driving a punch into Avery's gut.

"Ompf..." The air rushed from Avery's lungs.

"Good right, Josh," Antonio yelled.

"Lucky punch," Avery gasped.

Josh raised an eyebrow, but didn't talk. He never trash talked while he was fighting. Never saw the point in wasting his breath; he liked to let his fists talk for him.

Avery swung wildly and Josh had no problem avoiding them, but with each punch the other man threw, Josh swung back and connected with each of his. One of his punches split Avery's lip and Josh stepped back, unwilling to do any more damage or get the man's blood on him.

Spitting on the mat, Avery glared at him. Josh stood, relaxed and keeping his fists up.

"You wanted to take me on and I proved to you that you're

not good enough to even spar with me. Get your head out of your ass and realize that a fag is better than you at something."

Avery growled and lunged for him. He threw a one-two punch and Avery hit the mat.

Standing over him, Josh said, "You didn't believe what they told you about me. I mean, how can a fag be the top-ranked amateur boxer in the world? I haven't been for a while now, but don't ever think I can't take care of myself. I'll beat your ass into the ground if you want me to."

Antonio called to him from outside the ring. "No need, Josh. I think he got the message."

Josh went to his friend and let him remove his gloves. After taking off his headgear and spitting out his mouthpiece, he turned to Avery.

"You have some talent, but don't think you can defeat everyone you come up against because there will always be someone bigger and faster than you."

He checked the clock on the gym wall.

"I have to get going, Antonio. I need to take a shower and clean up before I head to the Lucky Seven."

"I'll be by to pick you up at six-thirty tomorrow morning. Take care."

He cleaned up and headed out to the club. Arriving just before eight at the Lucky Seven, he waved to Tammy and Pete as he walked by to Rachel's office.

Knocking on the door, he waited for Rachel to acknowledge him before he walked in.

"Hey, sweet lady, how are you tonight?"

Rachel looked up and smiled. "You seem to be in a good mood."

"Yes, I am. I got to beat up on some homophobe who

decided that fags couldn't be good boxers. Aside from that, I might get to see the hottest man in Hollywood tonight."

Her smile faded. "You're still seeing Ryan?"

"Well, maybe. We spent the weekend together up at my sister's and he knows I didn't set him up."

"Be careful."

He set his backpack down and sat on the edge of her desk, looking at her. "Careful of what?"

"I just don't want to see your heart broken when Ryan decides to go back in the closet." Rachel laid her hand on his thigh.

"It's my heart, and I don't think he'll do that."

"What happens when he realizes that he might lose his career and all those prized roles if he comes out? What will happen when he comes to the conclusion that it's you or his future?"

Josh pursed his lips and thought for a moment. He didn't want to just disregard her concerns. "I know you're worried about me, but I'll deal with it. I'm an adult and am responsible for my own actions."

A knock sounded on the door and Pete's voice came through the wood.

"Josh, Ryan's here to see you."

"Tell him I'll be right there." He leaned down and kissed Rachel on the cheek. "Don't worry. I'll watch my heart, but I have to risk it sometime."

"I'll be here to help you if you need a shoulder to cry on."

He winked before leaving the office and going back out to the club floor.

Chapter Twenty-Four

Music throbbed, filling Ryan's body and driving his pulse. He waved to the female bartender.

"What can I do for you?" She sashayed down to his end of the bar.

"I'm waiting for Josh, but I'd like a whiskey straight."

"Does he know you're here for him?" She grinned and poured him a drink.

He nodded. "Yeah, the other guy said he'd go tell him for me."

"Cool. Wave if you need anything else." She worked her way down the bar, filling drinks and collecting money.

Ryan rested his back against the bar, watching the crowd dance. It was slow for a Monday night, but there were still people enjoying the music and hooking up. He grinned as he remembered all those nights he blew off studying to go out dancing.

"Would you like to dance?"

As he glanced over to his left, he spotted the slender blond guy smiling at him. Ryan started to turn him down when Josh showed up. The bartender slipped his arm around Ryan's waist and kissed him, claiming him in front of everyone. Not minding one bit, Ryan cupped the back of Josh's head and nibbled at his lips.

The blond sighed. "Sorry, didn't know you were taken."

Josh broke away and grinned at the other man. "Hey, Tommy, how's it going?"

"Pretty good, Josh, though I should have known you'd get the best-looking guy in the place." Tommy pouted, but ruined it by giggling.

"It just shows how good my taste is because I think you're the cutest thing here." Josh leaned down and kissed Tommy's cheek.

Ryan waited for jealousy to rush through him at the flirting Josh was doing, but he was entertained by it, not threatened at all. Tommy blushed and ducked his head. God, Josh was right. The little blond was the cutest thing in the club.

"Tommy was asking me to dance when you showed up," Ryan told his lover.

"Oh great. I have to get to work and Tommy can keep you entertained until my break." Josh winked at Ryan. "I'll try not to be jealous and imagine that Tommy's trying to steal you away."

"Like that would ever happen." Tommy snickered.

Ryan gave Josh his glass and held out his hand to Tommy. "May I have this dance?"

Tommy pressed one hand to his chest and pretended to swoon. "Such a gentleman."

They all laughed as Ryan led Tommy out on the dance floor and Josh went behind the bar. The man in his arms was a good dancer and Ryan relaxed, knowing he didn't look like an idiot or a chicken with its head cut off.

Every time he looked over at the bar, Josh was watching him with a heated gaze. It was the lust in Josh's eyes and want on his face that made Ryan's hips swing in a sultry rhythm. He tugged Tommy closer, molding their bodies tight together. Tommy wrapped his arms around Ryan's shoulders, arching into him.

"Does Josh like watching you with other guys?" Tommy's question was loud enough for Ryan to hear over the music.

Ryan didn't stop dancing while he thought about it. Shaking his head, he leaned down to set his lips against Tommy's ear. "I think he likes seeing me dance with you, but he's not into anything other than that."

Tommy nodded. "He strikes me as a possessive guy, in a good way. You won't have to worry about him fucking around behind your back as long as you don't do it to him."

Ryan buried his face in Tommy's sweat-curled hair and breathed. Josh didn't have to worry about Ryan messing around behind his back either. Yes, his cock swelled and tried to break his zipper because of Tommy's wiry body rubbing against him, but he didn't really want to fuck the man. He kept thinking of Josh's hands gripping his hips and his fat prick driving into him, deep and hard.

They danced for a while, not listening to the words, just letting the beat dictate their movements. When a slow song came on, Ryan looked over at Josh who gestured for him to return to the bar.

"Josh wants me," he told Tommy.

The man pushed up on his tip-toes and kissed Ryan. "Go see him. I'm sure it's his break time and he's been looking over here pretty hard all night. I'll be around if you want to dance later."

He patted Tommy on the ass as he walked away. Making his way through the crowd to the bar, he kept his gaze locked with Josh's. Need burned in those dark eyes and his ass clenched as he thought about Josh taking him again.

As he reached the bar, Josh slid from behind it.

"Pete, I'm taking my break."

The other bartender waved them away with a grin. It was déjà vu all over again as Ryan was dragged through the club toward the back. Only this time instead of going into the alley, they went into Rachel's office.

"Won't your boss get upset about you bringing your boyfriend back here?"

Josh shut the door and leaned against it, arms folded over his chest. "Are you?"

"Am I what?"

Lust confused his brain and he had no clue what Josh was talking about. All Ryan wanted was to drop to his knees, unzip Josh's tight jeans and suck the man's cock like a lollipop.

Reaching out, Josh lifted his chin so their eyes met.

"Are you my boyfriend?"

He blinked. Had he said that word? He must have, but did he mean it seriously or had he been teasing? Forcing his brain to function without the haze of need, he thought about how the connotation of "boyfriend" made him feel.

"Yes, I meant it, but only if you want me to. I mean, I could have just been teasing if you don't want me to be your boyfriend. I know we've never really talked about what our relationship was or where we were headed with it."

Fuck, he was babbling now and Josh had an amused gleam in his eyes. To hear him talk, no one would believe he was a professional actor. Ryan bit his lip to stop the words from tumbling out.

Josh tapped his chin with a finger. "Get those pants off and bend over the desk."

Was he seriously going to get fucked in the boss's office?

"Do it, honey. No thinking right now."

Whirling around, he struggled with his belt and zipper while he rushed over to the desk. He got them opened and pushed down to his ankles before bending over and taking hold of the desk.

God, he was a complete slut, but at the moment, he couldn't work up the mental energy to be embarrassed. All his brain and body demanded he think about was the fact he was going to get nailed by Josh again.

"So sexy."

Josh's rough fingers trailed over the small of Ryan's back as his T-shirt rode up and exposed his skin. Whimpering, Ryan arched and rocked his ass back toward his lover.

"Pushy." Josh's affectionate tone made Ryan's heart skip a beat.

Ryan dropped his forehead onto the desk and shivered. The crinkling of foil caught his attention and he glanced over his shoulder to see Josh rip open a condom packet. His lover sheathed his prick with the rubber before reaching over to press his fingers to Ryan's lips.

"Get them good and wet. This is all the lube you're getting," Josh warned.

Moaning softly, he sucked Josh's fingers in, tasting salt, lime and the slight tang of soap. He licked and swirled his saliva all around those digits, getting them as wet as he could.

"That's good."

Josh removed his fingers from Ryan's mouth and using one hand, he spread Ryan's ass cheeks to expose his hole. Rubbing his wet fingers over the puckered opening, he drew a sob from Ryan.

"Please. Just do it."

Ryan no longer cared how he sounded or looked like. All he wanted was Josh reaming his ass. There was no hesitation as Josh breached Ryan's hole and invaded his inner channel until Ryan couldn't take him anymore.

Screwing his eyes shut, Ryan breathed through the burn and pain. He convinced his muscles to relax and accept the fullness Josh caused with his two fingers. Pushing back, he signaled to his lover that he was ready for more.

"So needy and tight," Josh murmured, stroking his fingers in and out, nailing Ryan's gland with every other thrust.

Ryan bit his lip to keep from begging for more, for Josh to move faster and harder. He needed more than his fingers.

The fullness disappeared and Ryan protested.

"No. I need you. I need more." Ryan undulated on the desk, trying to entice Josh back.

Josh's hand landed on the small of his back, pinning him there, and he felt the brush of Josh's latex-covered cock over his opening. Without thinking, he pushed back and an inch of Josh's prick slid into him.

"Fuck," he cried, the burn almost overwhelming him and he fought the urge to pull away.

"Take it. I'm not stopping until I'm buried balls deep in your hot little ass."

Josh shoved and Ryan pushed back, relaxing the best he could as his lover's fat cock filled him until he couldn't feel or think of anything else.

Finally, the cool metal of Josh's zipper brushed Ryan's cheeks and the rough fabric of his jeans rubbed against the back of Ryan's thighs. Josh slid a hand up Ryan's T-shirt to twist one of his nipples and Ryan jerked.

"I can give you a second if you need one to adjust, but no more than that," Josh rasped, and bending over Ryan, he sucked the sensitive spot behind Ryan's ear.

Ryan shuddered and trembled, but didn't ask for any time. He couldn't ask because any connection between his mouth and brain had been shot the moment Josh entered him. All he could do was grip the desk and shove back, letting Josh know without words that he wanted the man to start moving.

"I got that order." Josh laughed and gripping Ryan's hips tight, pulled almost all the way out.

He clenched his muscles, trying to keep Josh inside. He didn't want to lose their connection. Ryan shouted as Josh slammed back in and the flared head of his cock hit Ryan's gland, causing explosions throughout Ryan's nerve endings.

They settled into a driving rhythm, each thrust driving him into the wood under him and drawing cries from him. His balls drew tight to his body and Ryan realized he was going to come without touching himself. There was no way he could risk letting go of the desk because of the demanding pace Josh set.

"I'm gonna come soon," Josh grunted.

Ryan nodded the best he could without banging his head on the desk and massaged Josh's shaft with his ass, milking his lover's climax from him. One more thrust and Josh froze. The swelling and sudden heat in his ass drove Ryan over the edge as well.

"Josh," he called out, spilling his come all over the front of Rachel's desk.

They rocked together and the tremors lingered. Ryan collapsed on top of the desk, allowing Josh's weight to press him harder into the unyielding wood. He moaned softly as Josh pulled out and stepped away. Cool air washed over his naked flesh and goose bumps rose on his skin.

When he managed to stand and get his jeans pulled up to his hips, he turned. Josh stood behind him, holding out some paper towels.

"Here. Clean yourself and Rachel's desk off. My break's over and I have to run to the bathroom to wash up." Josh cradled the back of Ryan's head and gave him a rough kiss. "Thank you, and we'll talk about the boyfriend thing later tonight."

Ryan's thought process was fried and he simply smiled as Josh left him. After cleaning everything up, he threw the dirty towels away in the bathroom and went back out to the bar. Josh set a whiskey in front of him when he sat and winked.

He blushed as the ache in his ass reminded him of what they had been doing only a few minutes earlier and of how much he wanted to do it again soon.

Chapter Twenty-Five

"We're done here, Josh." Pete tossed a wet towel at him. "Get the hell out of here and take your fucking hot boyfriend with you."

Josh caught it, finished wiping down the bar and threw it back at Pete. "I'll catch you tomorrow night."

"Only if I don't get swept off my feet by some embarrassingly rich man and flown to the South of France." Pete shrugged at Josh's skeptical grin. "Hey, a guy can dream, right?"

Laughing, Josh walked over to where Ryan sat. "Ready to head out?"

Ryan nodded and stood, settling into Josh's side like he'd always been there. Josh savored the warmth and scent of his gorgeous lover while they made their way over to the door. He stopped and looked at Ryan, who frowned at him.

"I would love to have you come home with me and share my bed, but I would completely understand if you say no. We haven't figured out who's been taking the pictures and even though there haven't been any new ones lately, doesn't mean the stalker isn't lying in wait for you to do something like going home with me."

Maybe he was worrying too much, but he wanted Ryan to know he would let the actor set the pace. If Ryan didn't want anyone to know about them, Josh would deal with it. Of course, coming to the Lucky Seven and staying all night wasn't the best way to hide.

Ryan's smile was sweet as he studied Josh before saying, "It's too late, no matter what we do. I've been here all night. The guy could have taken a ton of photos when you dragged me off to the office or even before that when I was dancing with Tommy."

Ryan cupped his cheek and Josh nuzzled the man's palm. Ryan's brown eyes flared with heat. Josh wanted to do something about that passion, but decided the club wasn't the right place for it. At least, not at this point in the night.

"It might throw my agent into a hysterical fit, but I'm not going to act like there's nothing going on between us. There haven't been any more photos and the hoopla has died down. I haven't been ambushed by paparazzi or anything like that. I don't think people care anymore whether their stars are gay or not as long as I don't act ashamed of it."

Josh accepted Ryan's decision because ultimately it was Ryan's career and his choice. Holding out his hand, he grinned as Ryan took it.

"Do you need to let your friend know you won't be home tonight?" he asked as he opened the door to step outside.

"No. I told him not to wait up for me when I left tonight. We drove up to San Francisco and spent all day wandering around. He wants to go up to the Napa Valley and check out some vineries." Ryan shrugged.

"Don't you?"

Ryan's cheeks pinked in the streetlights and Josh thought how cute the actor looked when he blushed.

"It's not that I don't want to go. I just don't like the idea of not being able to see you for a couple days."

162

Josh dropped Ryan's hand and slung his arm around the man's shoulder, bringing their bodies tight together. He enjoyed the way their hips bumped together and how Ryan let him take the lead. Of course, Ryan might not remember how to get to Josh's apartment building.

"It's just the first flush of a new relationship," Josh pointed out. "If we'd been together for months or years, you wouldn't have any kind of trouble going away for a few days without me."

"Maybe." Ryan walked quietly for a few steps, obviously thinking about something. "Josh, what's going on between us? Are you my boyfriend?"

He chuckled and Ryan shook his head.

"God, I sound like I'm in high school again. Should I send you a note asking you to be my boyfriend?"

Reaching down, he pinched Ryan's ass. "You're being silly. Can you wait until we get to my place before we get deeper into this? I want to be able to see your face when we talk."

Ryan shot him a quick glance and nodded. "That doesn't sound good."

"Don't worry. It'll be fine. I don't like to air out personal stuff in the middle of the sidewalk." He gestured to the people walking around them.

"Good point. You never know who's watching or listening."

They continued on, enjoying the rather warm California night and watching the people around them. Josh was a little nervous about the upcoming talk, but from everything Ryan had babbled, he wasn't going to get rejected if he suggested they make their relationship exclusive.

After getting them home into his apartment, he dropped his backpack and dragged Ryan over to his couch. Sitting, he tugged Ryan onto his lap and pulled him close.

"Now that we're alone, we can talk about your cute babbling over me being your boyfriend." He nuzzled Ryan's chin, breathing in Ryan's musky scent.

"Hell, I swear I'm not a teenage girl in disguise. I can handle it if you've decided all you want is amazingly hot sex. I mean, I'm an adult. I understand that sex doesn't equal a relationship. But, fuck me, sex with you is like nuclear, man. I completely give it up when you just look at me with lust in your eyes."

He covered Ryan's mouth with his hand and laughed. "Breathe. You must want to spread your legs every time I look at you because I always want to fuck you. You've got a body that doesn't quit and an ass that fires my brain the minute I stick my prick in it."

Ryan drew in a breath and Josh knew his lover wanted to say something.

He shook his head. "Let me talk now, Ryan. You'll get another chance to ramble. Sex with you is great and I won't be saying no to more of it later, but more than that, I'm finding out that I enjoy spending time with you. I like talking to you, even when you chatter like a monkey. I find myself thinking about you during the day when we're not together."

Josh removed his hand from Ryan's mouth and the actor leaned forward, kissing him with gentle insistence. He let his head fall back and allowed Ryan to control the kiss, understanding that at that moment, Ryan needed to dictate what happened.

After a few minutes spent kissing and touching, relearning each bump and ridge in Josh's mouth, Ryan eased away. His gaze was serious as he met Josh's.

"I could fall in love with you, Bear, and I'm a little afraid of that. All the years I worked to make it in the movies and I'm getting to the point where I would throw it all away as long as I got to keep you." Ryan closed his eyes for a moment and took another deep breath.

"What scares you the most?" Josh ran his fingers through Ryan's curls, soothing his lover with his touch.

"That you don't feel the same. That this isn't about love for you. That you see us as two friends who like each other and have great sex, but there's nothing deeper to it."

He saw the fear deep in Ryan's eyes and knew he had to do something to reassure the man. Cradling Ryan's face in his hands, he locked eyes with him and smiled.

"I don't know what love is supposed to feel like, Ryan. Not the forever commitment kind of love anyway. I only know about the love I feel for Erin, Pedro and my friends. That's sort of like what I feel for you, only ours is deeper and stronger. It's mixed up with the sex and the attraction, but those things don't make it weaker, just bigger."

Relief flooded Ryan's face and he threw himself into Josh's arms. Josh stood, holding his lover in his arms and making his way to his bedroom.

It was time for some soft slow loving, shoring up what he admitted to Ryan. There would be more questions and compromises to work out, but for now, he'd hold his lover close and love him until any doubts Ryan had were gone.

Chapter Twenty-Six

Buzzing woke Ryan the next morning. He rolled over, reaching his arm out to hit the snooze on his clock.

"Shit, honey. Watch where you're throwing body parts."

He jerked up and looked to his right. Josh lay on his back, rubbing his nose and grinning up at him.

"Sorry, forgot where I was. I'll kiss and make it better."

Leaning down, he pressed his lips to Josh's mouth, licking along the crease and asking for entrance. Sighing, he slid his tongue in when Josh opened for him. He sank into Josh's embrace and feasted on the man's mouth, sucking on his tongue and nibbling along his bottom lip. Their bodies fit together as Ryan settled between Josh's legs and rocked their groins together.

More buzzing and Josh groaned.

"Stupid clock," he growled.

Ryan moved to lie on his side, propping his head on his hand. He watched Josh climb out of bed and start to dig through the pile of clean clothes on a chair in the corner of the room.

"I have to take a shower, get dressed and make lunch in fifteen minutes. Antonio's coming to pick me up for work."

"Don't worry. You go get ready and I'll make you lunch."

Getting out of bed, he found his boxers and jeans. He put them on while Josh headed for the bathroom. After making his way to the kitchen, he assembled two sandwiches for Josh's lunch along with three apples and a bag of chips. He wasn't sure what the other man drank, so he didn't pull anything out.

Josh's lunch box was sitting on the counter and Ryan packed everything in it by the time Josh stepped into the kitchen. Ryan's phone rang as Josh hugged him.

Jerking it out of his pocket, he answered without checking the ID.

"What?"

"Thank fucking God, I finally got a hold of you. I've been calling for the past two days and no answer, plus your stupid friend wouldn't tell me anything. Where the hell have you been? Oh wait, I know, you've been with that bartender again."

Raz's voice shot out of Ryan's phone like the high-pitched screech of a parrot. Blinking in shock, Ryan held the phone away from his ear and stared at it.

"I told you to stay the fuck away from that fag, but you just can't seem to help yourself. More pictures of you appeared in the tabloids yesterday. Is he blackmailing you? If he is, I'll get the police to haul his ass into jail."

Josh stood close to him and by the look on his face, he heard everything Raz had to say.

Ryan interrupted his agent. "I don't want to talk about it right now, Raz. I just got up and I'm not awake enough to deal with you."

Shaking his head, Josh kissed Ryan and headed out of the apartment.

"I want you in my office at ten o'clock sharp and you better be able to deal then."

Raz slammed the phone down in Ryan's ear. Swearing silently, Ryan ran and caught Josh as he started down the stairs.

"Can I call you later?" he asked, grabbing Josh's arm and bringing him to a stop.

"Sure, though if I'm working, I won't be able to answer. You can stay at my place as long as you want. Just remember to lock up when you leave."

Josh glanced out toward the parking lot where a large black truck sat.

"I have to go and your agent doesn't sound very happy. Go, put out that fire and bring your friend to Mia Leone's for dinner. I'm working the evening shift there."

"Cool. Have a good day, Bear."

He stepped back, not wanting to make Josh uncomfortable with a public display of affection. Although he was the one who should have issues with that since it seemed he was being stalked by some obsessed camera fiend.

Ryan watched Josh get in the truck and leave before he went back to Josh's apartment. He straightened up a little, tugged on his shirt and left to get his car.

As he drove back to his apartment, his phone rang again. He took the time to check the ID before answering. He didn't need another repeat of Raz's call.

"No, Bill, I'm still not telling you the gory details."

"Well fuck, if you won't share, I'm not going to tell you my news." Bill's teasing words rang in his ears.

"You know I never want to hear about the girls you screw." He stopped at a red light.

Bill's laughter danced over the phone. "True. Are you on

your way home?"

"About ten minutes away. Why?"

"Does your building have a back entrance?"

What was Bill up to?

"Yes. What's going on?"

"I'm at the window overlooking the front of your building. There are photographers all over. I swear some are hiding in the bushes."

Shit. Somehow he'd managed to convince himself that aside from the invisible cameraman following him around, he'd avoided any major fallout from the original photos. It sounded like he was wrong.

"Good news is there doesn't seem to be any TV reporters out there." His friend sighed. "Can you sneak in?"

He parked a block away, locked the car and headed toward his building.

"Yeah, I parked a block away and I'll be there in a few."

"Great. See you when you get here."

He hung up and manly resisted the urge to throw his phone. He'd already destroyed one because of this whole shitty situation.

Keeping his head down, he made it inside and up to his apartment without being spotted. Bill was sitting on the couch when he walked in.

Falling onto the couch next to his friend, Ryan groaned. "I didn't sign on for this. Raz said another set of photos appeared yesterday."

Bill shook his head. "Either you need to stop seeing the stud or you need to just come out. Either way you'll stop giving them fuel for the rumors."

"I'm sure Raz has my statement for me." He threw an arm over his eyes as he leaned back against the cushions.

"Are you going to do what he wants? I'll bet you any money, he wants you to say it was all a mistake and that you love fucking girls."

Closing his eyes, he shrugged. "I'm not sure yet. I really like Josh, and if I let him go, I'm not sure I'll get another chance at a relationship like this."

"Another option is say you're straight, find a good-looking woman to play your girlfriend and keep Josh on the side. It's a time-honored Hollywood tradition."

He gave a weary chuckle. "It wouldn't be fair to either of them. If I wouldn't want to be someone's secret or second choice, why would anyone else? I guarantee Josh isn't willing to be my secret lover."

Bill hummed "Secret Lovers" and Ryan slugged him in the arm. As they laughed, Ryan thanked God for a friend like Bill. A friend who understood him so well, he was able to make him laugh even when he was frustrated and angry.

Relaxing back, Bill grinned at him. "You know, I don't think Josh would have a problem being discreet, but what he would have a problem with is never being acknowledged by you as anyone more than a friend and no one wants to come in second to their lover's career or public opinion."

"You're probably right." Ryan glanced at his watch. "I better take a shower and change my clothes. I have to report to Raz by ten for my verbal spanking."

"Something tells me that won't be any fun at all," Bill joked.

Standing, Ryan looked at Bill and grimaced. "Nothing ever is with Raz."

"I'll be here when you get done."

"Oh right, Josh invited us down to Mia Leone's, the restaurant where he works. He'll be there tonight. I thought it might be cool for you two to meet again and get to know each other."

Bill's eyebrows shot up. "Sounds like you've already made up your mind about what's going to happen."

"Maybe."

He went to clean up and dress. It was time to face Raz.

Before he walked into Raz's office, Ryan's phone rang. He glanced down and frowned when he saw Josh's number on the screen. Moving away from the door toward the windows, he answered the phone.

"Josh, what are you doing calling me now? I thought you'd be busy."

"Hey, honey."

Something was wrong because Josh didn't sound very happy.

"What's wrong?"

"I wanted to catch you before you went in to talk to Raz."

"Why? Is there something I should know about my agent?" He rested his shoulders against the wall and stared out the window.

"We're on our way over to you. We won't let you face him without proof."

"Proof?" Ryan didn't like the sound of that.

"Yeah. The private investigator came through for you. We'll be there in five minutes."

"I'll be waiting for you."

Whether he liked the news or not, he knew it was important for him to at least hear it and make his own decisions on it.

Chapter Twenty-Seven

Morgan and Vance strolled into Ryan's agent's outer office without looking around, acting like they belonged there. No one questioned them. They looked at Josh a little strange, but he didn't care. So what if he was wearing dust-covered jeans and a sweat-stained shirt while the other two wore designer suits? He wasn't there for anyone but Ryan.

His lover stood by the elevators, staring at the floor and ignoring the crowd moving around him. Going up to him, Josh clapped a hand to his shoulder and squeezed.

Ryan's head jerked up and his dark eyes met Josh's. He saw the worry and the low simmering anger burning in them.

"Hi, honey. How are you?"

He kept his voice low. He didn't want anyone overhearing the endearment. This whole situation was fucked up.

"I'm not sure. Will I want to kill Raz when I find out what he's done?"

He shrugged. "I don't know. I guess it depends on how you feel about it."

"I think you're being evasive."

"You're right." He turned as Morgan and Vance joined them. "Are you guys ready?"

"Sure. Do you want to tell him or should I?" Morgan

glanced at Ryan.

"I'll do it." Josh moved them all off to the side where no one else stood.

"Just tell me," Ryan spit out, frustration evident in his voice.

Josh looked at the other men for encouragement. Morgan nodded and Vance gave him a quick smile.

"Okay, so remember we hired a private investigator to find out who took those pictures of us and why."

"Yeah, I remember that. I'm not an idiot."

Sarcasm dripped from Ryan's words. Josh held out his hand for the folder Morgan carried.

"The guy knows his stuff, Ryan, and he found not only who took the pictures, but who hired him to do it."

Ryan took the folder from him and tore it open, grimacing at the pictures of him and Josh kissing in the alley. Josh knew there were more graphic photographs in there that he thanked God no one saw except the photographer and the investigator. Ryan's eyes widened and his cheeks flushed when he got to those photos.

"Don't worry. The investigator told me the photographer never showed those to the tabloid. The only people who have seen those are you, me, the investigator and the photographer."

Relief washed over Ryan's face and he flipped through the rest of the pictures. Looking up, he said, "Are we sure the guy who took these doesn't have the digital versions? I mean getting all his hard copies is one thing but he could still have them on his hard drive."

Morgan pulled a memory card out of his pocket. "Our investigator bought the card from the guy and wiped them off the man's computer himself."

Ryan looked at the card, but didn't take a move to take it. Josh gave Morgan a quick smile and took the card, putting it in his pocket.

"So you found the camera guy and got the pictures. What does that have to do with Raz?"

"He paid the guy to follow you and see if he could get pictures of you doing something embarrassing."

"Are you sure?" Ryan flipped the folder shut and slapped it against his thigh. "Raz had no idea that I would go out and do something stupid like I did. He couldn't have guessed I was gay. I never did or said anything to make him think that."

"Yes, we're sure," Vance spoke up. "We wouldn't have told you any of this if we weren't a hundred percent positive. The photographer gave us Raz's name and the investigator went to the bank where the money order was purchased. He showed a picture of Raz to all of the tellers. One remembered him coming in and getting it."

Ryan swung away, staring out of the window. Josh wanted to touch him or offer some kind of support, but he wasn't sure if Ryan would accept it from him and they were in public. He wasn't about to do something that would "out" Ryan if the man didn't want that.

"Why would he do this?"

Josh shrugged, even though Ryan wasn't looking at him.

"I don't know. That's something you'll have to ask him. Taking this kind of risk with your career is crazy." Morgan frowned. "It could easily backfire on you."

"I had to sneak out of my apartment this morning to get here. The paparazzi have it staked out, probably waiting to see Josh stroll out of my building like he lived there."

"I can't afford your place," he joked.

His friends laughed and Ryan did crack a smile, but it was obvious his lover was thinking about other things. Checking his watch, Ryan sighed.

"I better get up to see Raz. He'll be furious as it is since I'm a half hour late." Ryan looked down at the folder in his hand. "I'll keep these if it's all right with you."

"They're all yours, Ryan." Morgan grabbed Vance's hand and strolled toward the doors. "Call us later, Josh."

"Thanks, guys. I appreciate all you've done."

"We're not completely finished yet. We still need to figure out what's going on with your sister, but that'll be taken care of soon enough, I'm sure." Vance waved good-bye as they left.

Josh reached out, touching the back of Ryan's hand with the tips of his fingers. "Are you okay? Do you want me to come with you?"

Surprise shot through him as Ryan turned his hand and threaded their fingers together. The other man tugged him close, resting his head on Josh's shoulder. Without regard to the people wandering in and out of the area, Josh wrapped his other arm around Ryan's waist, hugging him tight and resting his cheek on the top of Ryan's head.

"I'm sorry," he whispered.

Ryan laughed wearily. "You have nothing to be sorry for. I'm an adult and I'll accept responsibility for my part in all this."

Josh let Ryan step back when the man moved. Ryan took Josh's face in his hands and stared up at him with serious chocolate brown eyes. God, he could look into those eyes for hours and never get tired of them.

"As much as all of this makes me furious, I don't think I'd change one thing as long as it ensured I'd get to meet you." Ryan paused. "Okay, so I'd change the fact that this has disrupted Erin and Pedro's lives. That's something I don't think I'll ever forgive Raz for. I'll go face him alone. There's no need for you to deal with the ugliness he can spew out."

"Okay. Letting you handle it is probably best anyway because I'm furious that he would do something like this to you. It's your career, my jobs and it could be Erin's life if Geraldo finds her. And all for what?"

"I don't know but I plan on finding out." Ryan gave him a quick kiss before easing further away. "I'll call you after the meeting. Bill and I are still planning on coming to Mia Leone's tonight."

Josh nodded. "Great. I'll make sure there's a table reserved in my section. Take care and I'll talk to you in a little bit. I have to get back to work. My boss was pretty understanding about me having to leave, but I don't want to strain his good will."

"Oh, have you heard from Erin today?" Ryan asked, turning back to look at him.

"Yeah. Having Chad and Winston there has really lifted a burden off her shoulders. I'm thinking there might be something going on between her and Chad. All I heard about this morning was how great Chad was with Pedro."

Ryan chuckled. "I noticed some attraction between them when they met. I hope things work out. Your sister deserves a good man and I think Chad might be the right one for her."

"We'll see." He waved Ryan away. "Get going before Raz calls out the National Guard to come looking for you. I'll be waiting for your call."

He watched Ryan stride to the elevator and disappear inside. Damn, why did he feel like he was sending Daniel into the lion's den? He shook that feeling off. Ryan was a big boy and could deal with Raz. No matter the outcome, he was glad they managed to get rid of the photographer. At least, now Ryan wouldn't have to worry about someone snapping pictures of him at inopportune times.

Josh went outside to find Morgan and Vance waiting for him.

"We thought we'd drive you back to the work site. He's going to confront Raz on his own, huh?" Morgan gestured to where Vance had their car pulled to the curb.

"Yes. I guess since it's his career that's the most affected, he has the right to do it alone. He knows I'm here for him if he needs me."

He climbed in and after Morgan got in, Vance pulled away.

"Ryan seems like a good guy. Too bad he has to make this decision so soon into his career. If he'd had a few more years and a couple more movies, coming out might not bother his roles."

Shrugging, he looked out the window as they drove away. "Ryan hasn't made the decision to come out publicly yet, so who knows? This might not affect him as badly as we think."

And if Ryan didn't come out, where did that leave Josh? Guess he couldn't worry about what he couldn't control. He would just go back to work and wait for Ryan's call.

Chapter Twenty-Eight

"It's about damn time you dragged your ass in here."

Raz jumped to his feet when Ryan walked into the office. He didn't reply to his agent, simply tossed the folder on the man's desk and stared at him.

"What's this?"

"Take a look and tell me what the hell you thought you were doing." Ryan folded his arms over his chest and glared at Raz.

His agent frowned, but Ryan saw a flicker of fear in his eyes. The man opened the folder and a sneer of disgust crossed his face. He shut it without looking through the rest of the pictures.

"How did you get these?"

"I had an investigator check into things for me. Imagine my surprise when I was told that my agent was the bastard who hired him to take pictures of me. Little did my agent realize just what kind of photographs his little camera guy was going to get."

"You hired a private investigator? Why would you do that? I told you I had things handled."

Raz sat, but Ryan remained standing, not interested in getting comfortable.

"Sure you were handling things. You were making sure that more photos appeared in *The Hollywood Enterprise* every other day. You didn't want the buzz to die down yet. Did you figure that no matter what they were talking about, at least they were talking?"

Raz shook his head. "I really didn't think you would get caught kissing some fag, Kellar. I never pegged you as queer. I was hoping to get photos of you drunk and being an ass or with some girl. That's why I wanted you to go to the A-List clubs where all the big stars hang out. Little did I know your redneck friend would drag you to some piss ant club in WeHo."

"If you weren't expecting to catch me with a guy, why did you send those pictures to the tabloid then? Did you seriously want everyone to know I was gay?"

"Fuck no. I don't want anyone to know a client of mine is gay. You're going to burn in hell for sucking dick and I don't want that taint on me. I'd never get any more clients."

His agent shoved the folder back at him.

"You know what I was doing? I was planning on building up a buzz and get your name out there even more. The talk shows and the photo shoots are great, but no one really pays attention to them. They pay attention to the tabloid news and magazines. It's working. I'm getting a ton of requests for interviews and even some casting directors calling me to get you."

Stunned, Ryan didn't move or say anything. He just stared at Raz.

"When the photographer brought me those pictures on Friday, I had my assistants do some digging. I found out who that queer was and about his sister up in Etna. I mailed the money order to her. I wanted you to think he did it. That way you'd have a falling out and never want to see him again. I should have known better. You fags stick together."

"It's not just my privacy you invaded. You could cause Josh to get fired because of all this and you endangered someone else's life." Ryan clenched his hands at his sides.

"What do I care about some bartender? I could care less if he loses his job. It has nothing to do with me or your career. I've set up a press conference for you at one today. You'll be reading this statement."

Raz held out a piece of paper, but Ryan didn't take it from him. No way was he doing anything his agent wanted him to do.

"Cancel the press conference. I'm not going to be there and don't worry about your reputation anymore. You're fired and my lawyer will be contacting you about all the pertinent issues in our contract." He leaned over and braced his hands on the desk. Staring straight into Raz's eyes, he growled, "I better not see any more pictures of me show up in the tabloids or I'll see what sort of damages I can collect from you for defaming my character."

He made his voice as mean and fierce as he could, channeling a little bit of Josh as well. Easing back, Raz paled and Ryan could see that his threat got through to his now ex-agent.

Straightening, he grabbed the folder and headed toward the door. He stopped and turned at the entrance.

"When and if I choose to come out, it'll be at a time and place of my choosing. I won't be forced into lying by anyone."

Leaving, he strolled to the elevators and pushed the call button. Raz stormed out after him.

"You're nothing but a no-talent fag. I'll make sure you're black-balled for breaking our contract. You won't get one new role, so you might as well to go back to Ohio," the agent screamed at him. "I can ruin that bartender with one phone call. He's the one who has turned you against me. All I was doing was helping your career out. Any kind of scandal is good for a new actor."

He swung around and grabbed a hold of Raz's shirt, fisting his hands in the fabric. He slammed the smaller man against the wall beside the elevator.

"You make that phone call and you'll regret it the rest of your life. I'll ruin your career without a thought." He shook Raz. "And don't say you were doing this only for me. You did this all for yourself. The bigger I get, the more money you make, so there's no way you can convince me all of this shit was for my career."

Pushing Raz away from him, he got in the elevator and left.

He had forgotten all about calling Josh or the herd of paparazzi outside his apartment building. When he strolled up the sidewalk to the front door, several photographers jumped in front of him, blocking his way and snapping pictures of him.

Stopping, he held out his hands and grinned. "Take all the pictures you want, guys."

"Hey, Kellar, where's your lover? Has he moved in with you yet," one of them yelled.

Keeping silent, he let them get bored taking his picture. Bill pushed open the front door and looked out.

"Ry, do you need help?"

The sharks circled, sensing an interesting photo-op. Ryan shook his head.

"No help, man, though you do realize that your photo's going to be splashed all over the tabloids tomorrow. I'm sure these guys will think you're my new lover." He made his way to Bill's side.

"Oh hell no," his friend groused. "They truly don't believe I have that bad of taste, do they?"

All of the camera guys laughed and Ryan ducked inside. He and Bill went up to his apartment.

"Thanks for coming to my rescue." He slapped Bill on the shoulder.

"No problem. That's what I'm here for. How did it go with your agent?"

He grabbed two beers from the refrigerator and, handing one to Bill, joined his friend on the couch. He twisted off the top and took a drink before answering.

"Raz hired the photographer to follow me and take pictures. Even though he didn't plan on me actually being gay, for some reason, he decided to send the pictures to the tabloid anyway. I'm not sure what he expected me to do. Probably say it was the alcohol or that Josh seduced me. That I'm as straight as you are, I suppose." Dropping his head back, he stared up at the ceiling fan and sighed. "Why are people so worried about who I sleep with?"

"I just ask to irritate you. I don't know what I'd do if you really ever told me about your sex life." Bill grimaced. "Probably need to clean my ears out with bleach and see a pig slaughtered to get the image out of my head."

He rolled his head to the side to look at Bill. "Does the thought of two men having sex scar you that much?"

"The thought of you having sex with a guy does. I really don't care what two, or three, people do in their homes. You haven't had sex or a boyfriend for so long, I think I've gotten to the point where I see you as asexual."

"Umm...thanks a lot." He yawned. "You know what? I'm going to take a nap. When I get up, we'll head out to Mia Leone's. Josh said he'd reserve us a table in his section."

183

After saying that, he remembered he was supposed to have called Josh after his meeting with Raz. He found his phone and speed dialed Josh's number.

He got Josh's voicemail.

"This is Josh. I can't come to the phone, but leave a message and I'll get back to you as soon as I can."

Beep.

"Hey, Josh, it's Ryan. I wanted to let you know I fired Raz. He didn't deny that he did it. Seemed to believe he was helping me out. I told him not to bother you or Erin again. Hopefully he'll listen to me. Bill and I will be at the restaurant around eight. See you then."

Flipping the phone shut, he stood and nodded to Bill. "My keys are on the table if you want to go for a drive. I'll be up in an hour or so."

"I'll hang out here and watch a movie. You still owe me a trip to Napa Valley."

"We'll head up there tomorrow."

Ryan went to his room and stripped, climbing in bed and pulling the covers over his head. He made a mental note to call his lawyer when he got up. He needed to double check his contract with Raz.

Chapter Twenty-Nine

"Josh, your guests are here," Russell yelled through the kitchen.

Looking out through the kitchen door, he saw Cybil seat Bill and Ryan in his section. He grinned and grabbed the pitcher of water off the staging station.

"How are you this evening, gentlemen?"

He nodded at Bill and barely brushed his hand over Ryan's shoulder. It was obvious by the way Ryan looked tired and sad that the choice to break his contract with his agent weighed on his mind. Josh wished he could talk to Ryan, but it wasn't time for his break.

"What can I get you to drink?"

Bill pursed his lips in thought. "I'll take a Jack 'n coke. I don't know what he'll have."

"Ryan, what do you want to drink?" Josh kept his voice low.

"I'll just have lemonade right now." Ryan reached out and took Josh's hand, squeezing it tight before letting it go. "How's your day going so far?"

"Good, but it would have been better if I could have spent it with you." He risked brushing his thumb over Ryan's cheek.

His lover sighed and nuzzled into his hand, kissing his

palm softly. Bill snorted and looked away.

"Come on, you two keep this up and I'll go into a sugar coma."

"Ass." Ryan stuck his tongue out at Bill, but pulled away from Josh.

"I'll go get your drinks and when I come back, I'll get your dinner order. When your food is done, I'll take my break and sit with you."

He got everything ordered and made sure he didn't neglect his other customers while stopping by Ryan's table and chatting with Bill. Ryan stayed pretty quiet, but he joined in the teasing and joking.

Setting their food in front of them, he took his apron off and sat next to Ryan. His lover flashed him a smile before digging in.

"Bill, have you convinced Ryan to take you to the Napa Valley?" Josh leaned back in his chair, easing his foot over to rub against Ryan's ankle.

Bill eyed them before nodding.

"Yeah, we're leaving early tomorrow morning and going to spend the night up there. I'm not a big wine guy, but everyone told me I had to go and check out the wineries up there while I was in California."

"They're some of the best in the world. I can get you a list of places to stop and visit. Just don't go crazy with the taste-testing unless you're planning on taking a designated driver with you."

"Thanks, Josh. I've been here a year, but I still don't know where to take people outside of the theme parks." Ryan shifted closer to Josh, pressing his thigh against Josh's.

"You're here for the rest of the week, right, Bill?" Josh

smiled.

He slid his hand from his side to lie on Ryan's knee and trailed his fingers over the seam of Ryan's pants up toward his groin.

"I fly out next Monday." Bill shot him an amused smile, proving that he had some idea what was happening between Ryan and Josh.

Josh grinned. "Great. I usually don't work the construction sites on the weekends, so I can give you both a tour of L.A. I've lived here all my life."

Ryan spread his legs and Josh grazed his zipper with his finger. Josh couldn't help but chuckle when Ryan bit his lip to stop from moaning.

"You guys are terrible." Bill laughed.

Glancing around and seeing that no one was paying attention to them, Josh turned back and kissed Ryan hard on the mouth before standing.

"My break's over. You guys want to see the dessert menu?"

Ryan blinked, the change in the subject a little fast for his mind to absorb. Bill shook his head.

"No thanks. We should call it an early night. Tomorrow morning's going to come fast."

Josh tamped down his disappointment. Bill had been Ryan's friend far longer than he'd been Ryan's boyfriend. Of course, Bill would expect Ryan to spend more time with him since he was only here for another week.

"I get off in thirty minutes or so. Why don't you have some dessert and hang out until I'm done? Then we can head over to my apartment and I'll get that list of wineries for you."

"We can do that," Ryan spoke up before Bill said anything.

"Great. I'll bring out the dessert plate."

He wandered back into the kitchen and swept up the tray holding their desserts. When he got back out into the main room, he noticed there was a crowd around Ryan and Bill. Frowning, he pushed his way through and glanced at his lover. Ryan didn't seem overly worried about the people.

"Are you okay, Mr. Kellar?" Josh asked.

Ryan nodded. "Just some fans who wanted a few autographs."

"I'm sorry, everyone. Mr. Kellar wants to get his dessert. How about we give him some privacy?" Bill stood, carefully herding them away and giving Ryan and Josh a few seconds to themselves.

"Are you really okay?" Josh didn't want Ryan lying to him. "I can make sure you're not bothered again."

Ryan seemed to think about it for a few seconds before shaking his head. "No, I'm fine actually. It was nice to have them ask for my autograph and about my next movie, instead of questioning me about who my boyfriend is or am I really gay."

"That's because I truly believe a majority of the public doesn't care. They like your movies and your talent isn't affected by your sexual orientation. There were a lot of male stars in the old days who were gay, and everyone in the business knew, but they kept the secret. None of the movie goers knew and they still went to watch all those romantic movies those men were in."

Laughing, Ryan tapped him on the hip. "It doesn't matter because there wasn't a love interest in *Luther is King* or in my next role either. They just might be more accepting of me as an action hero than as a romantic lead."

"Well, you're my hero, does that count?"

He fluttered his eyelashes and they both burst out

laughing. After calming down, he set the tray on the table and rested his hand on Ryan's shoulder again.

"How are you feeling about firing Raz? I know you've been with him since you got into the business."

"I'm still angry and hurt, but it's fading a little. He thinks we were going to hell because we were gay. I don't want to work with an agent like that."

"I don't blame you and there are plenty of agents out there who don't care about your bed partners as long as it doesn't get splashed all over the front covers of the tabloids." He winked. "Pick out something for yourself and Bill. I have to check my other tables."

Ryan pointed to the two desserts he wanted and Josh put the order in before circulating through his section, making sure everyone had what they wanted. By the time Ryan and Bill were done with their coffee and food, Josh's section was empty of customers.

He rang them out and grabbed his stuff from the employee's room. The other two men were waiting for him in front of the restaurant. Surprise froze him when Ryan stepped into his space and cupped the back of his head, bringing his mouth down to his. Holding onto the strap of his pack, he encircled Ryan's waist and crushed his lover to him. Josh had no idea how much time he'd spent lost in Ryan's kiss, but he pulled away when Bill snorted.

"Okay, I know I'm annoying with all my questions about what the hell you two do together, but really, I don't want to know or see for that matter."

Ryan blushed and stepped further away, but slid his hand down to take Josh's. They made their way down the street, chatting and being normal guys. Josh tried not to worry about people taking their picture or approaching Ryan for an autograph. If his lover didn't freak out about those moments, then Josh wouldn't either.

Chapter Thirty

Wiggling his key, Josh managed to get the door to his apartment open. Ryan chuckled when his lover looked back at him and grinned.

"Great. Now, can you help me drag Bill's ass inside before the man passes out in the hall?"

He sighed as Josh took all of Bill's weight. Letting Bill drink that much at the Cuban restaurant they went to wasn't a good idea. Shutting the door behind him, he watched Josh drop Bill onto the couch.

"Did he get this bad when you went to the wineries?" Josh flopped into the chair next to the couch, grabbing Ryan's hand and tugging him into his lap.

Shaking his head, Ryan curled into Josh and ran his hand over the man's chest. "No. We were good, except he bought a ton of wine and shipped it back to his place in Ohio. I'm not sure why unless it's to impress the girls he brings home."

Josh slid his hand under Ryan's shirt and ran his fingers up and down his spine. Ryan sighed and rested his head on Josh's shoulder.

"It's been an exhausting week. I should have stayed home after firing Raz. The trip up to the Napa Valley, hitting those wineries and then taking Highway One back down to San Francisco. We wandered around San Fran and I should have known Bill would want to see everything." He leaned back a little to look at Josh. "We should take a trip up there and hit some of the clubs. Maybe go to Castro Street and check out the shops there."

"Going to San Jose and hitting The Winchester House isn't romantic or fun for you?" Josh's grin told Ryan he was teasing.

"I can't believe you took us there."

"I figured Bill would enjoy the genuine creepiness of the place." Josh hugged him close. "Plus it gave me a chance to spend time with you."

Ryan couldn't believe how much he had missed Josh in the four days they'd been gone. Talking to him on the phone wasn't the same as being able to sit in his arms and soak in his warmth. He shook his head mentally. When had he become so touchy-feely about Josh? Of course, he'd been that way with his first boyfriend, needing to be with him or talk to him every day.

That boyfriend didn't stick around long since he wasn't looking for anything more than sex, but something told him Josh might be looking for more than sex.

He brushed a kiss over Josh's chin and smiled. "I'm glad since I think next week when I start filming my next film, we won't get a lot of time together."

"I'd love to take you to my room and fuck you senseless, but I'm not sure about leaving Bill by himself out here."

They laughed as Bill's snores filled the room. A knock sounded on the door and Josh grunted.

"I wasn't expecting anyone."

Ryan climbed to his feet and let Josh go answer the door. He settled back in the chair, watching Josh greet Rachel.

"Hey, what brings you here? I still have time before work."

Rachel hugged Josh and came in, smiling at Ryan when

she saw him. "I have some news that might be good or not, depending on how you look at it."

"Okay." Josh stared at Bill for a moment. "I guess we should move into the kitchen because I don't think Bill will be moving any time soon."

Following them into the other room, Ryan went to the refrigerator. "Do you want something to drink?"

"I'd love some wine if Josh has any." Rachel hung her purse on the back of one of the chairs and sat, flipping her hair over one shoulder.

He pulled a bottle of white wine out of the refrigerator. Josh handed him a corkscrew and took down three glasses from the cupboard while he opened it. Pouring the wine, he let Rachel and Josh talk.

"So what's the news?"

Josh sat across the table from Rachel and Ryan leaned against the counter, sipping his drink and listening.

"I got in touch with my friends in the corrections department, to see what they could tell me about Geraldo. It seems that Geraldo isn't the head of the gang anymore. There was a coup, or whatever you call it, a couple of months ago and someone else is in charge now. I'm not saying that he isn't still looking for your sister, but the rest of the gang won't come in search of her."

Rachel pulled out a folder and tossed it across the table at Josh. Opening it, he started reading. Ryan held up the bottle to Rachel and she nodded.

"Is Geraldo still in jail though?" He refilled her glass.

"Yes. As far as I can tell, he has at least thirty more years on his sentence without any possibility of parole. He killed a police officer for God's sake. People don't let cop killers get away or go free."

"I guess I'll call Morgan and Vance to let them know that they can pull the bodyguards from Erin and Pedro. Geraldo has to know that he'll never get them back and even if he did find them, what would going after them prove to anyone? He's weak enough to have lost his position in the gang."

"Would getting Erin back shore up his strength in the members' eyes?" Ryan sat next to Josh, resting his hand on Josh's thigh.

"I'm not sure, but I don't think so. I think he's lost any standing in the gang that he once had. It's hard to run a gang while you're in prison for so long, especially if you have jealous members who have coveted your position for a long time."

Josh stood and snatched up the phone on the counter. "Can you call Morgan and let him know that they can call the guys off?"

"Sure."

Ryan started to pull out his phone, but Rachel stopped him. "I'm meeting Morgan and Vance for dinner tonight. I'll let them know. It won't hurt to keep their men up there for another day or so. We have to make sure the reporters don't bother her anymore."

"I think as long as the photos stop appearing, some other story will appear to make the front page. I mean, really, does it matter who my boyfriend is or even that I have a boyfriend? We don't plan on having sex in the alley again or running naked on a beach somewhere." He laughed as Josh pouted. "I'll try not to embarrass myself in public and most people will forget who I love."

Josh encircled Ryan's shoulders and Ryan rested his head against Josh's side. He listened to his lover's heartbeat. Rachel eyed them for a moment before she smiled.

"It's a nice thought and for the most part, you might be right, but there will be paparazzi following you around, especially the bigger your career gets. Just keep a low profile outside the movies and you should be able to live relatively normal."

She finished her wine and stood. "I better get going. I have to get ready for dinner. I'll catch you later at the club, Josh. Will you be stopping by later on, Ryan?"

He shrugged. "I don't know. It depends on Bill and if he feels up to go out to another club."

"What's up with him anyway?" Rachel nodded toward the sleeping Bill as they walked by.

"He had way too much to drink at dinner tonight." Ryan chuckled. "Bill's been really enjoying his vacation."

"I'll say," Josh murmured, letting Rachel out after giving her a hug and a kiss.

After Rachel left, Josh grabbed the phone. "I'm going to call my sister and let her know about Geraldo."

"Great. I'm going to see if I can get Bill moving. We need to get back to my place and you need to get ready for work."

He managed to wake Bill up and get him standing. Josh finished his phone call and came to help him get Bill down to the car. They poured his friend into the Cadillac, with Bill hindering more than he helped.

"I'll call you later tonight when I go on break," Josh promised, wrapping his arms around Ryan's waist and tucking his hands in his back pockets.

Ryan gripped Josh's shoulders and leaned on his hard body, trusting him to take his weight. "Do that. I'll be up for a while. Maybe we can get together for brunch tomorrow, if you're not working or anything."

"I have the evening shift at Mia Leone's along with a shift at the club tomorrow night, so brunch would be great."

Sliding his hands up to cradle the back of Josh's head, he brought their lips together. He swept his tongue inside Josh's mouth, tasting wine and the spices from their dinner. Their lips rubbed and teeth nibbled. Each kiss brought a promise of tomorrow and a hint of passion.

Ryan shivered as Josh slipped a hand up under his shirt and scratched his nails lightly down his back. Gasping, he pressed his growing erection against Josh's. His lover moaned and took a step back, bringing his hands around to hold Ryan's hips.

"We had better stop while we still can. Any more of that and I'll be dragging you back into the apartment for a good reaming before I go to work."

Licking his lips, he nodded. "You're right and it wouldn't be fair to leave Bill sitting in the car."

Josh glanced over Ryan's shoulder at Bill listing to one side in the seat. "You could always leave the window rolled down a little, so he could get some fresh air."

"Just like the family dog, huh," Ryan joked.

"Yes, but at least with the family dog, you wouldn't have to worry about it wandering off on you." Josh kissed him quick. "I'll call you later."

"Have a good night at work, Bear." He went around to the driver's side.

"Bye, honey."

Driving away, he was already counting the hours until he talked to Josh again.

Chapter Thirty-One

Josh leaned back, his arms folded under his head and called for Ryan.

"Ryan, come here for a second."

Ryan was nervous about the Golden Globe ceremony later that night and had been pacing the past couple of hours, trying to decide if he should risk writing a speech or not. The nomination had come as a surprise since *Luther is King* was Ryan's first role and he was going up against some pretty established actors. The last several months had gone well for Ryan's career. No more tabloid pictures and no real prying questions about his relationship with Josh.

Also, their relationship had progressed well. Josh had moved into Ryan's apartment and they'd been sharing the bills ever since. He had quit his job at Mia Leone's, and keeping the other two allowed him to continue sending money up to Erin. So far the press had laid off them and he planned on keeping a low enough profile, so that Ryan never had to explain him to anyone.

Ryan's conversation with his parents about being gay had been rough on him, but Josh had held him and dried his tears before carrying Ryan into the bedroom to nail him to the mattress.

Today, as excited as Josh was for Ryan, all the mumbling

and pacing was driving him crazy, so he came up with the perfect plan to get his lover to relax and enjoy the evening.

"What do you want, Bear?" Ryan walked into the bedroom, his mouth dropping open when he spotted Josh spread naked on the bed. "Oh my."

He stretched, flexing his muscles and letting his abs ripple a little. "You never did lick all of my tattoos. I thought maybe if you weren't doing anything important, you could do that."

In seconds, a naked Ryan joined him on the bed. "I'm not doing anything that can't wait until I'm done tasting every inch of you."

Reaching out, he ran his thumb over Ryan's plump bottom lip. "I'm all yours and I have a special treat for you when you're ready."

Ryan's eyes lit up. "A treat, really? Can I have it now?"

"You're like a kid who wants to open his presents on Christmas Eve. No, you can't have it. You have to earn it. Now, get that talented tongue to work."

Grinning, Ryan swirled his tongue around Josh's thumb, drawing it into his mouth and sucking. Josh jerked, fighting the urge to yank his thumb out of Ryan's mouth and shove his cock in there instead. *No, this is all about Ryan and what he wants. If he wants to suck your cock, he will. You have to let him control the love making.* This was going to be harder than he thought.

He pulled his hand away from his lover and spread his arms out wide. "I'm all yours. Show me what you can do."

Ryan rocked back on his heels, eyeing Josh's body and obviously trying to decide where to start. Of course, Josh had his own plans on how this whole thing would work and he wasn't above manipulating Ryan into what he wanted. He flexed a bicep, drawing Ryan's devouring gaze to his left arm.

"Mmm..."

Licking his lips, Ryan focused on Josh's arm and Josh sighed. He should have had Ryan tie him up because he wasn't going to be able to resist trailing his hand over Ryan's naked body and teasing the man's cock when he could reach it.

His lover squeaked when he encircled his cock and squeezed. Ryan batted his hand away.

"Do you want me to tie you up? I don't think I can do this if you keep touching me like that." Ryan glared at him.

He laughed and shook his head. "No, I'll be good."

"You better be."

The warm, moist touch of Ryan's tongue running over his skin caused shivers to rock Josh's body. He fisted his hand into the sheets on both sides of him to keep from grabbing Ryan and fucking him. Wiggling, he laughed as Ryan licked his underarms.

"I don't have tattoos there," he protested.

"I know, but I think I want to taste you everywhere, not just your tats."

He was so fucked. "Whatever you want."

Closing his eyes, he breathed deep, trying to keep control. His cock swelled and rose proudly from his groin. The blunt head wept like it was begging for attention from its favorite person. Ryan ignored it, inching down Josh's shoulder and chest to one of his nipples.

Josh managed to keep from whimpering when Ryan swiped his tongue over the little nub of flesh before pinching it between his teeth and tugging. The quick flash of pain shot through Josh to land in his groin, making his cock harden even more.

Ryan moved to the neglected nipple at the point when Josh was about to beg him to suck his prick. Teeth and mouth on one nub and fingers continuing to torture the other one until both pieces of flesh were red and throbbing.

Leaving those, his lover moved down Josh's body to circle his belly button and drew chuckles from Josh as Ryan blew a puff of air over the wet lines. Josh tilted his hips, bumping the head of his cock into Ryan's chin.

"No, I don't think I'm ready for that and besides you don't have any tattoos there."

He growled and Ryan flashed him a wicked grin.

"Just remember, pay backs are hell."

"Those types of warnings aren't incentives to get me to do what you want," Ryan reminded him.

He held onto his control with the tightest grip he could. How many times had he teased Ryan until he begged Josh to come, so he couldn't complain too much about the situation. He grinned to himself, remembering the other night when he tied and gagged Ryan before using a feather to tickle him everywhere. It had been so much fun and he had made Ryan come by just breathing on his cock.

He was so caught up in the memory, he jumped when Ryan slapped his hip.

"Turn over. I want to lick that dragon on your back."

Josh rolled onto his stomach, trapping his painfully stiff prick under him. It hurt just enough to ease him away from climaxing.

"Hmmm..." Ryan hummed. "I love your body."

"That's a good thing because it's all yours."

Ryan scraped his nails down Josh's back and over his ass. Shouting, Josh arched, absorbing the pain and transforming it into pleasure. Bite marks peppered his back as his lover feasted on him. He was going to have to keep his shirt on at work for the next couple of days.

He flexed and shifted, encouraging Ryan to investigate every inch of skin. Ryan's hands landed on Josh's ass and he froze, waiting for his lover's reaction as Ryan spread his cheeks apart.

"What's this?"

Ryan's finger pushed gently on the plug in Josh's ass and he moaned as it hit his gland.

"It's your treat, honey."

"If it's mine, why are you wearing it?" Amusement sounded in Ryan's voice.

Rising on his elbows, Josh glanced over his shoulder at Ryan. "I want you to fuck me, Ryan."

"But..." Surprise and shock filled Ryan's face. "You've never bottomed before."

Josh turned over so he could take Ryan's hands in his.

"I bottomed the first time I ever had sex with a guy. I didn't like it because he didn't take the time to make it good for me. I've never wanted a guy to fuck me like that again until I met you." He grinned. "Don't get me wrong. I'm not going to suddenly want to be fucked all the time."

"Thank God," Ryan breathed.

Chuckling, Josh brushed his fingers over Ryan's cheekbones. "I love how tight your ass is around my cock, but this is my gift to you. To prove once and for all that I trust and love you. It's your reward for being nominated for a Golden Globe as well."

He gestured to where a piece of paper sat on the night stand. "Plus I got my results this morning and I'm clean."

Ryan's eyes lit up like a Christmas tree. "You mean?"

"Yes."

Josh leaned back, set his hands behind his knees and spread his legs, offering everything to Ryan.

"Get the lube."

Ryan couldn't seem to take his eyes off Josh's ass.

"Ryan, if you don't get the lube, I'm going to take a shower because we do have to get ready at some point today for the ceremonies."

Yanking his gaze back to meet Josh's, Ryan shook his head. "No, I'm not missing this for the world."

His lover launched himself across the bed to the night stand and jerked open the drawer, digging around for the lube they kept in there. With a crow of triumph, Ryan held the bottle aloft, grinning ear-to-ear.

"Slick up and get rid of this plug. You don't have to worry about stretching me. I want to come on your cock, and feel you fill me with your come."

Ryan whimpered, his hands trembling so badly, he struggled with the top of the slick. Josh took pity on the man and grabbed the lube, popping the top and squirting some out into Ryan's palm.

While Ryan slicked his shaft up, Josh removed the plug with a hiss. He'd put it in earlier in the day because he didn't want to waste time having Ryan stretch him. His ass ached from the unfamiliar object.

"Are you all right?" Ryan rubbed one slick finger over Josh's hole, pressing in a little with each pass.

"I'm fine, just been a very long time."

He took Ryan's cock in his hand and positioned the head at his opening. They both watched as Ryan pushed in, breaching Josh's virgin opening slowly, but without hesitation.

Josh dropped his head back, biting his lip and breathing

through the burn. Having the plug in had helped but Ryan's cock was slightly bigger than the plug. Ryan circled his hand over Josh's stomach, trying to soothe him.

"Breathe, Bear, and relax. Push out and it'll get better."

He closed his eyes and listened to his lover. Soon, he relaxed enough for Ryan to bury his shaft all the way in Josh's ass. Josh wrapped his legs around Ryan's waist, locking his ankles together. Ryan bent over him and rested his head on Josh's shoulder. Their chests heaved and their sweat mingled.

Josh tried to think of the things Ryan did to drive him crazy. Clenching his muscles tight, he rocked up and brought his hips to a different angle, hitting his gland with Ryan's cock.

"Fuck me," he cried.

"All right," Ryan said and started to move, his thrusts slow and gentle like he didn't want to break Josh.

"No." Josh clasped Ryan's ass with his hands and showed him how he wanted to be fucked.

"Are you sure," Ryan gasped, his body shaking with the need to ream Josh's ass.

"Yes, I want to feel you every time I move."

Ryan's next stroke slammed into Josh, forcing shouts from both of them. Grunts and moans filled the room along with the smell of sex and sweat. This wasn't love making, it was sex, pure and simple, and Josh loved it.

Tingling started at the small of his back and he knew his climax was about to explode through him. Clamping down hard around Ryan's prick, he came, shooting his come all over his stomach and chest.

Two more strokes and Ryan froze, flooding Josh's inner channel with hot liquid. Ryan collapsed on top of him and he ran his hands over Ryan's back as tremors shook his lover.

"Fucking amazing," he murmured, letting his legs fall to each side of Ryan's hips.

Ryan mumbled something and Josh got the feeling the other man was about to fall asleep. He pushed at his shoulder.

"Move to the side and I'll get us cleaned up."

They groaned as Ryan's limp cock slid from Josh's ass and Josh stood, secretly enjoying the feeling of Ryan's come trickling down his thighs. After washing up, he brought a damp cloth back to the bedroom and cleaned Ryan off.

He tossed the cloth toward the door and climbed back into bed, spooning with his lover and threading their fingers together to rest their hands on Ryan's chest.

"Do we have time for a nap?"

Josh smiled into Ryan's hazy eyes and nodded. "We have plenty of time. I set the alarm."

"Thank you, Bear." Ryan's voice trailed off.

"Anytime, love. Anytime at all." Josh kissed the back of Ryan's neck and closed his eyes, tired and satisfied that he managed to get rid of Ryan's nervousness.

Chapter Thirty-Two

Shit. The Golden Globes. Ryan never imagined he would be there among Hollywood's best and brightest. Not only sitting among them, but nominated as well. A firm squeeze on his hand had him glancing at Josh, who sat next to him at the table.

He stared at his lover. With his shaved head and rough good looks, Josh shouldn't fit in with the polished crowd surrounding them, but wearing a tuxedo like he'd been born to it, Josh was the best-looking guy in the room.

Ryan had seen how all the people's gazes had followed them as they made their way up the red carpet into the Beverly Hilton Hotel and he wasn't positive it was him they were all staring at. By bringing Josh with him, he made a silent declaration of his orientation. Hopefully, the reporters wouldn't be compelled to search him and ask him about it.

"I had a feeling I'd be running into you again."

Ryan looked up to see Garrett Johnson standing beside him. Garrett's partner stood next to the actor, tugging on the cuffs of his shirt.

"CJ, stop fidgeting. You've done this shit before; you should be used to them." Garrett chided the dark-haired man.

"Doesn't mean I like them. It looks like we're sitting with you gentlemen." CJ grinned. "I guess this is the gay table. I'm

CJ Lamont, Garrett's partner."

They all laughed and Ryan introduced Josh.

"Josh, this is Garrett Johnson and CJ Lamont. Mr. Johnson, Mr. Lamont, this is my boyfriend, Josh Bauer."

It was weird saying that out loud, but he discovered it got easier every time he did.

Josh shook their hands. "It's nice to meet you both. I'm afraid I've never seen any of your movies, Mr. Johnson. Working three jobs didn't leave much time for extracurricular activities."

"Now you've crushed him, Josh. He believes everyone to know who he is." CJ winked at Ryan.

"Jackass," Garrett said with fondness. "Please, call me Garrett, and he's CJ. We aren't very formal."

Sitting, they ordered drinks and Ryan studied the two men. Even when they weren't touching, anyone looking at them would know they were a couple. Private smiles and shared touches said more than if either man spoke of their commitment.

"I heard you fired your agent, Ryan." Garrett met his gaze over the rim of his glass.

"Yes. I told the public it was a mutual decision, but I'll be honest, I broke our contract because he was the one who hired the photographer and leaked those photos of Josh and me to the tabloids." Anger still swelled in him at the mess his ex-agent created.

"Why would he do that?" CJ frowned.

"I guess Raz believed any publicity is good for a career. He figured the possibility of being truly 'outed' would scare me into going along with his plan." Ryan shrugged. "He didn't count on two things. I might not advertise my orientation, but I never lied about it and I wasn't willing to further my career by destroying someone else's life."

Both Garrett and CJ nodded in approval. Josh gripped his knee for a second.

"You're a strong man." CJ toasted him with his whiskey.

Blushing, he laughed. "I don't know about that. My father always told me that integrity and honesty started within. If I was honest with myself, I could be honest with others and never regret it."

"Smart man."

He silently agreed with Garrett's statement, remembering his father's reaction when he called his parents a few days ago to formally come out to them. They had been stunned at first, but after a few minutes, Ryan's father had told him that if Ryan truly thought he was gay and was prepared for all the prejudice he would have to deal with, then his parents would support him.

After he hung up, Josh had held him while he cried. Knowing how blessed he was to have parents who accepted him no matter what had overwhelmed him.

"You know, CJ, I have seen your show on one of those learning channels. All the things you can do to cars amazes me." Josh broke the silence.

"Thanks. It's been fun doing the show. At least, I can keep playing with cars, even if I can't race them anymore."

"When have you seen the show?"

"It's one of Pedro's favorite shows. I watch it with him when I visit them." Josh turned to Garrett and CJ. "My nephew's autistic, so it's hard to get him to interact at times. If we find things he likes, we encourage him to either do them or watch them."

Pride welled in Ryan at Josh's willingness to talk about

Pedro's autism. A lot of families acted like autism and those who suffered from it should be hidden away or acted like there was nothing wrong with the one who suffered from it. Pedro was a remarkable boy and he didn't deserve to be shuffled aside because he didn't fit into society's image of what a child should be like.

"Garrett, would you be interested in donating something to a charity auction I'm arranging? All the proceeds will go to different autism foundations."

The actor's bright smile made Ryan's pulse stutter for a second and he could see why Garrett had been voted one of the most beautiful people in the world.

"I'd love to. And I can get my brother to donate some stuff as well. Kasey plays pro basketball. He could probably get some of his teammates to send things too."

"Great. Can I call you next week and talk to you a little more about it?"

"Sure." Garrett wrote down his number. "That's for my personal cell phone. That way you can get a hold of me no matter where I am."

"Cool."

He stuck the card in his pocket. After that, the ceremony started and he settled back to enjoy himself.

Halfway through the night, Garrett leaned over toward him and asked quietly, "Have you found a new agent yet?"

Ryan shook his head. "I haven't had time. I want to do some research, make sure I find one that isn't totally homophobic. I'm sure a majority of the agents could care less who I sleep with, but I also understand that it might not matter how talented I am, being gay will be a huge black strike against me with some studios and directors. I'd just prefer an agent who didn't believe I was going to burn in hell for who I love."

"Fortunately, there are more of those in Hollywood these days. Here." Garrett handed him another card. "Sam Browning is my agent. He's a real hard-ass, but he won't harp on you about being gay. If he doesn't want to take you on, he'll be able to give you names of some agents that fit your criteria."

"Thanks a lot."

"You're welcome. Like I said last time we met, it will get easier. Hollywood isn't quite the queer utopia a lot of people believe it is, but it's close. Still you'll lose roles for no other reason than you're gay and you'll get offered roles you'd never consider doing for the same reason. Being 'out' in society is a hard choice to make and you have to be tough to deal with things."

Ryan reached out and took Josh's hand, flashing his lover a smile when Josh looked at him. Ryan had dealt with the tabloids exposing his sexuality and came through it determined to live his life on his terms, not dictated to by public opinion, even if it meant his career stalled.

"The best advice I can give you is keep your personal life private, but on those occasions when you can't, conduct yourself with class. Don't punch out photographers, no matter how much you might want to. If you treat them with respect, most of them will treat you well."

"I appreciate the help, Garrett."

"If I might offer a piece of advice as well," CJ spoke up.

He nodded and noticed Josh doing the same.

CJ took Garrett's hand in his and smiled at the actor. The love shining in his eyes drew a gasp from Ryan. Josh tightened his grip on Ryan's hand, letting him know he was just as affected.

"Hold the ones you love close, especially the man who holds your heart. It's easy to lose each other in this business, but if you keep your grip tight and your love strong, you'll both survive."

Watching Garrett kiss CJ, Ryan marveled at their ability to ignore the people around them and sink into each other. He turned toward Josh.

"I want that," he whispered, tilting his head to indicate the other couple.

Josh's smile was gentle and full of love. "We'll get there, honey. We've got all the time in the world to build a solid foundation. I love you, Ryan, and you being willing to bring me as your date to this award thing is enough for me right now."

Ryan leaned against Josh, absorbing heat and strength from his lover's presence.

"I love you," he murmured.

Josh was right. Speaking their love out loud to each other was enough for now and he had taken the first steps to being "out" by having Josh escort him to the ceremony. From here on, they would deal with everything that happened together and be the stronger for it.

With This Ring

Dedication

To all my readers who fell in love with Josh and Ryan.

Chapter One

Snow drifted across the bright blue sky, transforming the Vermont hills into a picture perfect winter wonderland postcard. Skiers dotted the slopes, racing down or riding up. Even with all the movement, there seemed a hushed expectancy to the air, like everyone was waiting for something special to happen.

Ryan Kellar snorted silently. The only one waiting was him as the hours crawled closer to midnight and one of the biggest moments in his life. New Year's Eve and his wedding.

"Ry, are you all right?"

He turned away from the windows in the dining room to find his parents eyeing him with mild concern. He smiled and nodded. "I'm fine, Mom."

"Not having second thoughts, are you?"

"If I didn't have second thoughts while planning the wedding, Dad, what makes you think I'd have them now?"

His dad shrugged. "Well, your marriage won't be legal in most of the country and the tabloids will go crazy once word gets out about this."

He and Josh had talked about the whole tabloid angle. After everything that had happened to them when they first met, avoiding any publicity should have been foremost in their minds. Yet neither Ryan nor Josh were willing to hide in a closet or act ashamed of loving each other.

"We're hoping no one will spill the beans about what's happening tonight. We only invited friends and family, plus Morgan is providing security. No one without an invitation gets in."

"Good thing we remembered to bring ours."

Ryan laughed as his mom's mouth dropped open. He recognized the voice. Garrett Johnson and CJ Lamont strolled into the room, hand-in-hand. Ryan tapped his mother's shoulder.

"It's not polite to stare." He nudged his dad. "Do you have a napkin for Mom to wipe the drool off her chin?"

She blushed and Garrett winked at her before kissing her cheek.

"Mrs. Kellar, I see where Ryan gets his good looks from."

The pleasure in his mother's eyes made Ryan swallow his snicker. CJ's fond expression told him that the man was used to Garrett's subtle flirting.

"All you actors can't stay away from the beautiful ones, can you?" Ryan's dad joked.

"No, sir. We can't." Garrett focused his gaze on CJ.

CJ blushed as well and Ryan's gut tensed. God, he hoped Josh would look at him forever like Garrett looked at CJ with such longing, love and desire in his eyes.

"Mom, Dad, this is Garrett Johnson and his partner, CJ Lamont." Ryan remembered his manners long enough to introduce his parents to his friends.

"Soon-to-be husband, actually." CJ held up his left hand, showing off a brushed yellow gold band.

"Awesome news!"

214

Ryan whooped when the pair nodded and Garrett revealed his matching band. He hugged them both tight and waved down a waiter.

"We need a bottle of champagne."

The waiter nodded before heading toward the bar.

"Celebrating already?"

Whirling, he spied Josh leaning in the doorway between the lobby and the dining room. He kept his gaze on his fiancé as Josh strolled through the room toward him. Josh slipped his arm around Ryan's waist and Ryan relaxed against him.

"Garrett. CJ. Glad you could make it," Josh greeted the men.

"Congratulations. We wouldn't have missed it for the world." CJ slapped Josh's back. "Maybe we'll pick up a few pointers for our wedding."

"Seriously?" Josh grinned. "That's great news. So you're going the wedding route as well, huh?"

Garrett laughed. "Yes, we are. Kasey and Gram are having a commitment ceremony, but we decided we wanted the whole shebang."

"Your brother and his partner are engaged too? It's an epidemic." Josh took the bottle from the waiter while Ryan passed out the glasses.

Josh extracted the cork with a soft pop and managed not to spill a drop of the bubbly liquid. Ryan admired the confident way his lover poured the champagne.

As the others laughed and toasted, Ryan thought back to the night he asked Josh to marry him.

Chapter Two

Six Months Earlier

The ice in Ryan's glass clashed together like castanets and people around him looked worried. Maybe they thought he was suffering from some kind of anxiety attack because of his shaking and the beads of sweat trickling down his face.

He set his drink down before he dropped it. Christ. His nerves were worse than when he had to speak at the Golden Globes. The way he acted, one would think he'd never done interviews or acted before.

Yeah, but none of those events were as important as what he was about to do. Nausea roiled his stomach. Whose idiot idea was this?

Oh right. It had been Bill's. He'd called his best friend a few weeks ago, in a panic over what to get Josh for his birthday and his ever-helpful friend suggested a ring, like Josh was a girl or something. Unfortunately, he couldn't get the idea out of his mind, especially after seeing a news segment on TV about states that allowed same sex marriage.

Ryan wiped his palms on his thighs, bumping the square lump in the pocket of his jeans. Josh's laughter rang out over the noise of the crowd at the club. It was now or never.

He pushed his way through the crowd toward the area

where Josh held court with their friends. They'd come to the Lucky Seven to dance and hang out, celebrating Josh's birthday.

Josh Bauer, Ryan's boyfriend, stood, talking to Rachel, Josh's boss, as Ryan slipped up behind him and wrapped his arms around Josh's waist.

"Hey, Rachel, can I borrow Josh for a few minutes?" Ryan rested his chin on Josh's shoulder and flashed a shaky smile in Rachel's direction.

Her shrewd gaze studied him and he hoped his nervousness didn't show too badly. Ryan grimaced when Rachel winked at him. How could he get rave reviews for his acting if he couldn't even convince Rachel he was fine?

"You certainly may. Happy birthday, Josh." She kissed Josh's cheek and patted Ryan's hand before leaving.

"Ready to dance?" Josh turned in his arms and embraced him, large hands cupping Ryan's ass.

"Mmm..." He brought Josh's mouth down to his and kissed him.

He loved kissing Josh. Once his lover took over, Ryan held on, allowing Josh to plunder his mouth. He sucked on Josh's tongue and nibbled on his bottom lip. Josh lifted him up on his toes and he entwined his leg around Josh's thigh.

"Shit." Moaning, he dropped his head back to give Josh better access to his skin.

"I missed you," Josh murmured, scraping his teeth over Ryan's jugular. "I'm glad you got back in time for my birthday. It's the best present I ever got."

Birthday? Present? There was a reason he'd come over to get Josh, but his body overruled any other thought in his head.

"I want you. Please."

Pleading with Josh to fuck him was something Ryan had grown accustomed to doing.

"I love it when you beg."

Josh stepped back, grabbed his hand and dragged him across the club floor, ignoring the catcalls as their friends teased them.

They pushed through the door of Rachel's office, and he slammed back against it as Josh plastered his body tight to Ryan's.

"Rachel's going to get tired of us doing it in her office." He panted, arching his hips into Josh.

"She understands," Josh mumbled.

Ryan wasn't sure about that, but he pushed it out of his mind. Josh unbuttoned his shirt and shoved it out of the way, baring his chest to Josh's gaze. Ryan's head banged on the door as Josh pinched one of his nipples between his teeth while twisting the other nipple with his fingers.

"Damn."

"Get those pants off right now."

It didn't seem to matter that Ryan couldn't get his mind focused enough to move his hands. Josh took control, drawing a groan from Ryan. Soon naked flesh rubbed naked flesh. Sweat mingled with sweat and Ryan shivered as Josh's chest hair scratched over his sensitive skin.

His jeans fell to his ankles with a thud and Josh flipped him around. Ryan rested his cheek against the familiar wooden door. How many times in the last six months had he found himself in this position?

"What are you laughing at?" Josh whispered in his ear.

Stifling his chuckles, he shook his head. "Not important."

"I don't have any lube." Frustration ran in Josh's voice.

"Just do it, love." He canted his hips, offering his ass to Josh.

Ryan heard a slurp an instant before Josh pressed wet fingers inside his channel.

"Oh."

Relaxing, he pushed back, taking them in as far as he could. He loved that feeling, but in seconds, he wanted more.

"Josh, please. I'm ready." He rocked back and forth, fucking himself on Josh's fingers.

"Okay. Wait a second."

"No," he protested when Josh moved away.

Clothes rustled and a buckle jingled. They sighed as their bodies came together. The crown of Josh's cock breached the stretched ring of Ryan's ass.

Josh slipped one arm around Ryan's chest and grasped Ryan's cock with his other hand. Within seconds, they danced to a rhythm they loved. Give and take. Push and pull of sex. Each thrust in drove a soft cry from Ryan, and Josh's grunts filled the air.

After months of making love, Ryan learned all the signs of Josh's impending climax. The loss of grace as he reamed Ryan. How his fingers tightened around Ryan's cock, demanding Ryan's come as payment.

It was a price he willingly paid. He shouted as his pleasure burst and nerve endings fired. His come spilled over Josh's hand, onto the door supporting them and the floor beneath them.

Josh slammed into him twice more before freezing. Ryan milked as much of the wet heat flooding his inner passage as he could from Josh. They slumped forward, their hearts racing in time with their breathing. Ryan didn't know how many minutes they stood there before Josh straightened and eased out of him.

"Wow."

"It's been a while, honey." Josh patted Ryan's bare ass and pulled him away from the door. "Stay here. I'll be right back."

"Like I have any muscles to move," he muttered as he snatched up his jeans enough to get out of the way of the door opening.

If they were going to continue fucking in Rachel's office, they had to make sure to pack lube and towels in Josh's backpack. Ryan's hand brushed the square shape in his jeans pocket. Josh's birthday present. He'd forgotten all about it the moment Josh kissed him.

"Here." Josh came back and cleaned Ryan up with a wet towel. "We better straighten up and head back out before Tammy or Pete come looking for us."

Ryan fastened his jeans and grabbed a hold of Josh's wrist before his lover could leave again.

"Wait. I wanted to give you your present."

Josh's grin held satisfaction and a hint of lust. "I thought you already did, but give me a little while and I'll be happy to get another one when we get home."

"That's a present you can have any day, any time." He tugged Josh over to the couch and pushed him down on it.

Ryan's hands trembled so badly, he had a hard time getting the box out of his pocket. When he finally had it in his hand, he dropped to his knees in front of Josh. Josh eyed him in confusion.

He cleared his throat and took a deep breath. "This is the hardest thing I've ever done. I had a pretty speech memorized, but nothing's in my head anymore. I mean, you're not a girl, so I don't think you want to hear poetry or confessions of undying love." He rubbed his forehead. "I'm supposed to be a suave leading man, yet I can't tell you how I feel."

Josh frowned. "What's going on, Ryan? What's so important that you're all tied up in knots?"

"Josh Bauer, will you marry me? Tie the knot with me?" Ryan opened the box, holding it up for Josh to see.

The one dim lamp on Rachel's desk reflected off a pair of etched platinum rings.

Josh's mouth dropped open and shock claimed a spot in his eyes. "Ryan, are you serious?"

"I know it's only been seven months since we met, but I know I love you and I want to spend the rest of my crazy life with you." He held his breath.

He didn't expect a lot of emotion from Josh. His big bad construction worker had grown up believing emotions were best tucked away, unacknowledged for the most part.

"Yes!"

Josh launched off the couch, knocking Ryan onto his back. The kiss they shared was filled with joy, promise and love. He set the ring box on the floor and framed Josh's face with his hands. Their tears blended together and it was one of the happiest moments in Ryan's life.

Chapter Three

Sipping from his champagne glass, Josh glanced over at Ryan standing at the edge of the crowd with a silly grin on his face. He wandered over and bumped their hips together.

"Where'd you go?"

Ryan blinked like he was waking up from a dream and graced him with a quick peck on the cheek. "Just thinking about your birthday."

The night Ryan proposed to him. Josh doubted he'd ever forget it. Once Josh accepted he was gay, he'd also come to grips with the fact that he'd never get married. He thought he was fine with that. He'd never even seen what was so special about marriage anyway.

It took falling in love with Ryan for him to understand why some of his straight friends spoke of it in such glowing terms. He'd said yes to Ryan without thinking about what came next.

"It was the perfect birthday," he murmured.

CJ filled their glasses again and Garrett raised his to Josh and Ryan.

"A lot of words will be spoken tonight as you say your vows," Garrett said in a serious tone. "The most important ones are the three words you say to each other every day as often as you can. I love you."

"You must never forget to say them, no matter how angry you may get with each other or if one hurts the other," CJ said, encircling Garrett's waist with one arm while holding up his glass as well. "Love is a solid foundation upon which to build your new life together."

"Love," they all said together before draining their glasses.

"Now, CJ and I are going to our room to unpack. Then maybe we'll go out and try the slopes." Garrett set his glass down, hugged them both and headed out of the dining room.

"We'll see you tonight." CJ waved as he followed his lover out.

"Your father wants to take a nap and I want to check with the girls to see if they need any help." Ryan's mother kissed them. "We'll catch up with you boys later."

Ryan's dad rolled his eyes a little at the mention of a nap, but he left without protesting.

Josh set their glasses on a table in the dining room and flagged down their waiter. After charging the champagne to their room, he took Ryan by the hand and led him out to the great room where a huge stone fireplace dominated the main lobby area with smaller, more private nooks spread around the edges.

He picked the one furthest away from people, more intimate and quiet. Josh drew Ryan down in the chair with him, arranging it so Ryan sat on his lap. It was a gay-friendly ski resort, but even if it wasn't, Josh wouldn't have cared. He had the right to show affection to the man he loved and no one had the right to say he couldn't.

Ryan rested his head on Josh's shoulder and they sat in silence for a few minutes, absorbing each other's warmth.

"Not having second thoughts, are you?"

Ryan chuckled. "My dad asked me the same question before you showed up."

"And your answer is?"

"The same as I told my dad. If I didn't have second thoughts in the six months leading up to this, I'm not going to change my mind today." Ryan nuzzled Josh's chin. "Though I will admit there were times when I wished we could elope to Vegas."

"Someday it might be possible for gay couples to do that." He pinched Ryan's ass. "What did you have to worry about with the planning? Erin and Rachel did it all for us."

"You're right. And I appreciate them involving my mom in the process."

"I think most women love weddings and everything that goes with them," Josh stated.

"All I can say is thank God for Rachel and Erin. We'd be getting married by a justice of the peace in Iowa if I was in charge of the nuptials."

Josh smiled. His lover would have asked Bill's advice and Ryan's best friend would have suggested something like that.

"Has Bill arrived yet?" Josh eased Ryan closer, breathing in the man's woodsy cologne. It was a scent that had come to represent home to Josh.

As crazy and annoying as Bill could be at times, Josh loved the way the man supported Ryan in everything. The love between Ryan and Bill was that of brothers and since the rest of Ryan's extended family declined to attend, Bill's presence was doubly important.

"He got in this morning, dumped his stuff and headed out to the slopes. Probably trying to pick up snow bunnies." Ryan placed his hand on Josh's chest where his heart was.

"I should have known. Let's hope he doesn't injure himself trying to impress the ladies."

Ryan didn't reply, but Josh had a feeling he was thinking about something. Leaning his head back on the top of the chair, he closed his eyes, allowing the peace and quiet ease him. The craziness of their party later on would drive any relaxation out of him.

"What do you think the papers will say when this gets out?"

Ryan's question was soft, but Josh heard the touch of worry in it. He re-adjusted their positions, getting Ryan to straddle his lap and face him. He cradled Ryan's face in his hands.

"Same as they always do when a celebrity gets married. Some will make a big deal of it. Some will make fun and others will ignore it. We've been in the tabloids before and somehow we fell in love despite their intrusion." He brushed his thumb over Ryan's bottom lip. "Now that Sam's your agent, he'll help you figure out which ones to ignore and which ones to respond to."

"And you're not giving any interviews," Ryan reminded him.

Not that he needed that pointed out to him. When Ryan and Josh first decided to try a serious relationship, Josh explained to the movie star that he would support Ryan's career a hundred percent. He'd attend award shows and other events with him, but he wanted to stay out of the spotlight as much as possible.

Ryan accepted Josh's request and tried to honor it as much as he could.

"We both know it's better if I just keep my mouth shut."

Their laughter mixed as Ryan leaned forward and brought their lips together. Josh opened to Ryan's questing tongue. He shivered as Ryan sucked on his tongue. His cock started to stiffen and Ryan rocked against him once before backing away.

What did he do to deserve Ryan? There wasn't anything special about him and Josh knew that. He worked as a bartender now that Ryan had convinced him to quit his other jobs. He still sent money every month to Erin and Pedro, but that didn't make him a saint or anything.

Yet he held in his arms, and heart, one of the most gorgeous and talented men in the world. God must have been smiling down on him the night Ryan stepped foot in the Lucky Seven.

"Okay, no more of that, gentlemen."

Rachel's crisp British accent cut through their peaceful contemplation. Ryan scrambled off Josh's lap and hugged her.

"No more of what?" Josh asked, climbing to his feet and kissing her cheek.

"All that staring into each other's eyes along with all that sugary sweet nonsense. It's enough to put people into a sugar coma." The twinkle in her bright blue eyes balanced out the sarcasm in her voice. "You can do that when you say your vows."

"Yes, ma'am," they said in unison.

She hooked their arms with hers and they escorted her to the elevator.

"Sam has been looking for you, Ryan. He needs to go over the final version of the press release before he sends it out."

Ryan looked skyward and exhaled heavily as they entered the elevator.

"Oh, I know. The trials and tribulations of being a movie star." She patted him on the cheek. "Also, your mother said that your Great Aunt Edna is here. Seems none of you thought she'd show at an event like this, but the old lady surprised you all. She wants you to go and visit with her for a little while before the party."

"And you said you wouldn't have any other family here." Josh was happy that some other relative came. Ryan's other aunts and uncles refused to be a part of their wedding.

"Let's see how happy I am after I talk to her. Which floor is her room on?" Ryan frowned, uneasiness shining in his eyes.

"I had the resort put her next to your parents."

"Thanks."

Ryan kissed Josh and stepped off the elevator. Turning, Josh looked at Rachel.

"Did you meet Great Aunt Edna?"

"Yes, I did, and your man has nothing to worry about. I was talking to the resort manager about the changes you and Ryan decided on when Edna checked in. She's a feisty ninety years old and rather put out that no one thought she'd come to a gay wedding." Rachel smiled. "All the other members of her family are pea-brained bigots who wouldn't know true love if it bit them on the ass. Her words, not mine."

Relief washed the tension in Josh's shoulders away. "Now I can't wait to meet her."

"Oh, and she requested that I seat her at Garrett's table because a meal is always better with good-looking men as dinner companions."

He burst out laughing and Rachel joined him. They lurched into the hallway from the elevator. The honeymoon suite took up half of the top floor of the main building at the resort. He'd checked in yesterday morning and Ryan arrived late that night after wrapping a movie.

Swiping the key card, he waved Rachel in as he held open the door.

"Hey, Josh, wait."

Erin raced down the hallway, shaking a piece of paper in his direction. "Was that Rachel with you?"

"Yeah." He stepped back to let her in.

"Great. I need to talk to you both about seating."

He groaned and Erin took a swipe at him as she went by. He motioned to the couch as he went to the mini bar where he pulled out three bottles of water. When he returned to the living area, Rachel and Erin were already seated, heads together as they talked about arrangements for the tables.

Josh bit back a smile. It was a good thing he and Ryan were relatively neat guys or there might be a bottle of lube on the coffee table from their early morning activities.

"What do you think?"

He glanced up to see the ladies staring at him with expectant expressions.

"About what?"

"Where were you? We asked if it would be okay to put Ryan's great aunt at the table with Garrett and CJ." Erin gave an exasperated sigh.

The red marring his cheeks informed Rachel about where his thoughts might have been.

"Josh was thinking about Ryan, I'm sure." She winked at him.

He didn't acknowledge that. "Sure. She'll embarrass the hell out of CJ, but Garrett will love her."

"Okay, then as far as we're concerned, everything is taken care of. You and Ryan can enjoy yourselves without worrying about anything."

He sat between his two favorite ladies and threw his arms around their shoulders, hugging them close.

"I'm not sure what Ryan and I would have done if you two

hadn't stepped in like you did. Thank you both."

"You're my big brother, and heck, you're the closest thing to a brother Rachel has. We just wanted to make sure you had a perfect day. You've done so much for Pedro and me. I wanted to return the favor." Erin hugged him hard.

Rachel squeezed his knee before standing. "I have to go. Maybe you should take a short nap. It's going to be a late night for all of us."

Erin bounced to her feet. "Good idea. I want to check on Pedro and Zorro. Chad took them out on the kiddie slopes and I want to make sure they're okay. I'm thrilled the resort understood about Zorro."

"So am I. There wasn't any way I'd get married without you and Pedro, though I assume he's going to bed before the actual ceremony." Josh joined them and wandered with them toward the door.

"Yes. There's a young lady who works here that Pedro seems to trust. She'll look after him until Chad and I get in. But he won't miss out on the fun part since you're holding the reception first." Erin hugged him again before she left.

"That was a brilliant idea, by the way," Rachel commented. "Having the party first and then the ceremony, so you're pronounced man and husband right at midnight. The perfect New Year's Eve celebration."

"Ryan's a romantic at heart." He blew her a kiss and shut the door.

Josh went back to the couch and flopped on it, staring up at the ceiling. Again, he thanked God for Rachel and Erin. If not for them, he and Ryan would still be floundering, trying to figure out how to get anything organized.

Chapter Four

Josh picked up his phone from the center console of Ryan's Cadillac. He pressed number two on the speed dial while glancing at Rachel, who sat in the backseat.

"Josh, how far out are you?" Erin's voice burst over the line.

"About ten minutes. Just calling to give you warning." He smiled at the happiness he heard in his sister's words.

Once they found out that Erin's ex-husband was no longer a threat to them, his sister had blossomed. Of course, the attention of a certain bodyguard helped.

"Chad's here and Pedro's ready for the birthday cake already. Did you have a good time last night?"

He looked over at Ryan and smiled, resting his hand on Ryan's thigh.

"It was one of the best birthdays I've ever had."

Ryan flashed him a quick grin before looking back at the road.

"Rachel's with you, right?"

"Yes, I wouldn't leave my other favorite girl at home."

Especially with the news he had to share with them. He hoped they'd be happy for him.

"Great. I'll see you when you get here."

"Love you, sis."

"Back at you, bro."

Hanging up, he tossed the phone back in the console.

"Well, Erin's in a good mood," he commented, leaning back against the seat.

"Must be because her older brother's coming for a visit," Ryan teased.

"I'm not sure. It could be that or it could be the fact that Chad is visiting."

"Chad?" Rachel piped up from the backseat.

"He's one of the body guards Morgan and Vance sent up to keep an eye on her when we were worried about Geraldo."

"And you're okay with them dating?" Ryan pulled onto Erin's street.

"If Morgan and Vance trust him enough to ensure my sister's safety, that's good enough for me."

Chad had to be vetted before he went to work for the security company. Anything suspicious or bad in his background would have red-flagged him. Plus, Chad seemed to get along with Pedro and Josh trusted his nephew's intuition.

Ryan parked the car behind Chad's truck and Zorro stood, barking, on the front steps of the porch.

"Hush, Zorro," Josh called as he climbed out of the car.

They sat down to dinner soon after arriving. Pedro fidgeted, eyeing the frosted cake sitting on the counter. The adults didn't waste time with eating, not wanting to frustrate him anymore.

The plates were rinsed and stuck in the dishwasher. Erin placed the candles and lit them. Josh almost busted a gut laughing as the adults sang with Zorro howling as accompaniment. He managed to get the candles blown out without them melting all over. Erin cut the cake and tried to hand the first piece to Josh.

"Let Pedro have the first piece."

She wrinkled her nose and he hid his smile behind his hand as Pedro pounced on the dessert. It was a special treat for him to have that much sugar. Erin tried to keep him from eating too many bad things.

Once everyone devoured the cake, Josh asked for them to gather in the living room. Erin let Pedro go to his room and turn on the TV.

Josh tugged Ryan to his side and stood in front of the others. "We have some news to tell everyone."

Erin's eyes lit up and Josh figured his sister might have guessed what he wanted to tell them.

"Last night Ryan asked me to marry him and I said yes."

Screaming, Erin catapulted herself into Josh's arms. He caught her and whirled her around, smiling as she covered his face with kisses. He noticed Rachel hugging Ryan and Chad shaking Ryan's hand. When he set Erin aside, she raced to Ryan and enveloped him in a hug while Josh accepted congratulations from Chad and Rachel.

"Have you decided on a date yet," Erin asked after everyone settled down and were seated.

"No. Not sure where we want to go and do it at. There's only four states that allow them right now and I have to admit I never saw myself getting married in Iowa."

The rest agreed and he rested against Ryan.

"That leaves Massachusetts, Connecticut and Vermont." Rachel pursed her lips and narrowed her eyes, thinking. "Maybe you could do a destination wedding."

"Oh, how about Vermont on New Year's Eve? It would be so romantic and a great way to start your new life together." Erin almost clapped her hands in excitement.

"Not sure how to go about planning something like this." Ryan shook his head. "Heck, as guys, aren't we supposed to get the tux and make sure we get to the church on time?"

"Men." Rachel mock-punched Ryan in the arm. "Tell you what. Why don't Erin and I do the research and logistics? We'll get your input, plus you'll have to get us guest lists."

Josh met Ryan's gaze and his lover nodded.

"Sounds like a good idea to me."

"Yeah. I have to head out to some on-location shit for this movie. I'd hate to leave you to do all the work." Ryan frowned.

Josh knew he'd have to deal with Ryan being gone for months at a time, but he figured they could enjoy the time they were together.

"Great, then don't worry. We'll make sure everything is perfect, but you'll get final say over everything. We'll be like your wedding coordinators."

Rachel winked at Erin and Josh's sister's face lit up. What had they gotten themselves into?

But over the next six months, the ladies proved to be worth their weight in gold as wedding planners. They arranged everything while keeping him and Ryan in the loop. They also included Ryan's mother, which won over Ryan and his parents.

Chapter Five

Ryan entered his room with a relieved sigh. Boy, he hadn't realized how much work Great Aunt Edna would be. She could talk, and did, for hours about her time in Vaudeville. All the marvelous men who courted her and the ones who taught her how to sing and dance. He felt bad about not having spent a lot of time with her while he was growing up, but he promised her that he and Josh would come and visit her in New York when he got a break between movies.

It never occurred to him that someone from her generation would be so open about homosexuality. Maybe it stemmed from her time in the entertainment business. Or it could simply have been that she understood love couldn't be defined by narrow parameters. Love came in all shapes and sizes, whether it was two men in love or a man and a woman, love was the same.

He strolled into the living area and grinned at the picture Josh made sprawled out on the couch. Wandering over to his soon-to-be husband, he knelt and pressed his lips to Josh's.

Ryan licked a line along the seam of Josh's mouth. With a soft exhale, Josh opened to him. He stroked and teased Josh's tongue, drawing a moan from him. Josh raised his hand and thrust his fingers into Ryan's hair, taking the kiss deeper. Within seconds, he covered Josh like a human blanket.

They kissed, bit and sucked while grinding their hips together. His erection rubbed over the hard length of Josh's cock. He grunted as Josh grabbed his ass and humped against him faster.

"Please."

Josh managed to flip them until Ryan lay underneath and there was more pressure for Ryan to rub against. His soft cries were swallowed by Josh. Tingling pressure built at the base of his spine and his balls drew tight to his body.

"Josh." He bit his lip as he came in his jeans.

With a shout, Josh shoved against him and jerked as he came a few seconds after Ryan. Ryan smoothed his hands down Josh's back as Josh collapsed on him, driving him into the cushions of the couch.

"I haven't come in my jeans since I was a teenager." Ryan grimaced at the sticky mess in his underwear.

"You're going to give me a swollen head if you keep talking about how horny I make you."

Standing, Josh popped the button on his own jeans before offering a hand to Ryan.

"Ugh!" Ryan tugged at his crotch. "Good thing we need to get dressed for the party."

They made their way to the bathroom, stripping as they went. Josh turned on the shower while Ryan pulled their tuxedos out of the closet.

"Guess it wasn't a complete waste of money getting tailored tuxes for the Golden Globes. At least we didn't have to rent any for tonight."

He heard Josh's snort from the bathroom and he smiled. They had argued for days about the tuxedos. Josh didn't believe it was worth the cost to get them custom made, but Ryan had

235

persevered, wearing his lover down by explaining about all the award ceremonies they would be attending from now on.

"The water's ready," Josh called, and Ryan joined him in the shower.

As much as he wanted to play some more, they didn't have time. They washed quickly and dried off. While Josh shaved, Ryan dressed.

He was tying his bow tie when Josh came in from the bathroom. Pausing, Ryan admired Josh's body. All that olive toned skin beautifully marked with tattoos. Wings, wolves and stars adorned Josh, highlighting well-defined muscles earned from hard work and gym time.

Josh didn't move as Ryan walked toward him and reached out, holding his fingers inches away from the newest design on Josh's chest. It had been a Christmas present for him. Gothic lettering spelled out his name over Josh's heart.

"Are we ready for this?"

He didn't protest as Josh embraced him. He entwined his arms around Josh's body and soaked up his lover's strength and warmth.

"I've never been more ready for anything in my life. I love you, Ryan Kellar, and whether we have a marriage license or not, I'd still consider you my husband."

The kiss they exchanged this time was gentle and he could imagine them in their golden years, kissing and loving. He couldn't wait to grow old with Josh.

A knock on their door broke them apart. He trailed his fingers over Josh's shoulder as he headed out to answer it. "Get dressed. It's probably my parents."

Shutting the bedroom door behind him, he tugged on his cuffs to straighten them before going to get the door. He opened it to allow his parents in.

"Mom, you look so beautiful. Maybe next year if I go to the Oscars, I'll take you as my date." He hugged his mom carefully, not wanting to mess up her hair or dress.

"Josh would probably pay for my dress, just so he could get out of going." She laughed, but there were tears in her eyes.

"What's wrong?" He swiped a finger under her eye and caught a tear.

"Don't worry about her, Ry. She's been like this since we started to get ready. Must be a mother thing."

His dad looked quite handsome, and very different from his usual causal jeans and polo shirt outfit.

"You're looking quite dashing, Dad." He waved them toward the couch. "Would you like a drink before we head down? Josh is getting dressed. He'll be done in a minute or so."

"Nothing at the moment. We wanted to give you something."

He noticed the box his mother carried. She gestured for him to join them on the couch. Sitting down, he wondered what his parents could have gotten him.

"You didn't have to get us anything."

In fact, he and Josh had requested that if anyone wanted to give them something, they preferred donations to several Autism organizations that helped kids like Pedro.

"This isn't new, Ry. It actually was your grandfather's."

His mother held out the box to him. As he took it, he glanced at his dad. "Which grandfather?"

"It was my father's," his dad said.

Both sets of Ryan's grandparents had died when he was quite young, so he never got to know them. Neither of his parents ever really spoke about them to him as he was growing up.

"Why now?" He opened the box and a thin gold band winked up at him.

"This is yours. I know you and Josh have matching bands, but your grandfather always wanted you to have this. You were only three, yet he said it was important that it got passed on. Your grandmother worked three jobs to buy it for him and he never took it off until the day before he died."

He eased the fragile circle out of the satin pillow it rested on. Holding it up to the light, he saw the words engraved on the inside: Forever Be My Love.

"Thank you." Tears welled in his eyes and he felt silly for getting emotional over a piece of jewelry from a man he never knew.

"You keep it and give it to your son or daughter." His mom folded his fingers around the ring.

"Mom."

"I know you're gay and everything, but that doesn't mean you can't adopt if you want to. There are a lot of needy children out there who could use good parents. Being a gay couple doesn't mean you're evil people who are going to corrupt children." She puffed up, indignant that anyone might consider her son a terrible person.

He patted her hand. "I know that, Mom, but we're not ready to talk about children yet. I mean we're getting married tonight and it isn't accepted in most states or by most people yet. Maybe we'll try changing the world one baby step at a time."

"What are we taking baby steps for?" Josh stepped from the bedroom and Ryan almost swallowed his tongue.

Someone should make it illegal for Josh to wear a tux. The man filled the fabric out so well, he looked like a cover model. If

Ryan wasn't careful, some starlet was going to try and steal Josh away. Good thing Josh wasn't attracted to women.

"Josh, you look wonderful." Ryan's mother approached Josh with her hands held out.

Josh clasped them in his and kissed her cheeks. "I swear people are going to think you're Ryan's sister, not his mother."

"You're such a charmer." She swatted his arm. "I can see why Ry fell in love with you."

While Josh and his mom chatted, Ryan turned to his dad.

"Do you think Grandpa would have disowned me like the rest of the family if he were alive?"

His dad seemed to think for a moment before shaking his head. "I'm not sure. My dad was stubborn. It took him a year to accept your mother into the family simply because she was Protestant. Aunt Edna wore him down on that, so he probably would have come around after a while."

He thought about all his extended family and how none of them chose to come to the resort for his wedding.

"I used to think we were a pretty close family. Now I'm not so sure." His disappointment showed up in his voice.

His father laid a hand on his knee. "Ryan, I know it hurts to have them turn their backs on you, but you know what. Your mother and I still love you. Your Aunt Edna does as well. Plus, you're marrying a guy who thinks you hung the moon. Build your own family with him."

Glancing over at Josh, he caught his lover's gaze and he saw all the love Josh had for him in his face.

"You're right, Dad. Thank you for being such a great father."

They embraced and Ryan appreciated how hard his father tried to understand what was going on. He knew his parents didn't completely understand what his being gay meant, but from the moment they met Josh, they'd welcomed him with open arms.

Chapter Six

Ryan tapped his fingers on the steering wheel, and his muscles tensed each mile closer they got to his parents' house. Josh smoothed a hand down his thigh to his knee.

"Stop worrying. It'll be fine."

"How can you say that? The first time my parents hear about you is actually a picture of us kissing in an alleyway."

Nervousness caused his pulse to race. His parents had seemed very accepting when he broke the news about being gay. It was one thing to hear it over the phone, but to be confronted by your son's lover was something totally different.

"You need to calm down, honey, or you're going to make yourself sick. They know we're coming. It's not like we're showing up on their doorstep without warning them first."

Josh slid a hand around the nape of Ryan's neck and started massaging the knots out of it. Ryan dropped his head forward slightly, letting Josh soothe his sore muscles.

"I guess I'm just worried about what my dad's going to say when he meets you," he admitted. "My mom's been helping Rachel and Erin with the wedding plans and I know she's excited about it. It's the only wedding she's going to get since I don't have a sister. I'm pretty sure she never thought I'd be marrying another guy though."

"It's probably not first on the list of announcements parents expect from their sons." Josh winked. "Just try not to worry about things until you need to. I think your parents will surprise you."

He hoped so, and they were going to find out soon. He pulled their vehicle into the driveway and parked behind his mom's car. They hadn't even shut the doors yet before his mother raced down the steps and flung herself at him.

"Ryan, I'm so glad you were able to come visit." She peppered his face with kisses while he tried to dodge her.

"Mom, you'd think I've been away at war the way you're carrying on. I've only been gone seven months."

"You've never been gone that long before. Not even when you were away at college."

He got her calmed down in time to see his father approach Josh. His mouth went dry as he waited to see what would happen.

"You must be Josh." His father walked up to Josh.

"Yes, sir. Thank you for inviting me to your home, Mr. Kellar."

Josh offered his hand and Ryan relaxed when his dad shook it. If his dad had any doubts about Josh, he wouldn't have shaken Josh's hand. To Ryan's father, a man's handshake was a sign of respect.

"Introduce me to your fiancé, Ryan." His mom tucked her arm in his. "I've heard a lot about him from his sister and his friend."

"I hope it was all good, Mrs. Kellar." Josh's smile was gentle.

Ryan could see that Josh had made an effort not to look so bad-ass the first meeting with Ryan's parents. His lover wore a button-down dress shirt over a blue T-shirt and faded jeans. Instead of his usual motorcycle boots, Josh wore running shoes. As much as Ryan loved the clothes Josh wore while working at the club, he also adored Josh when he dressed like a preppy. Of course, he lusted after Josh no matter what the man wore or didn't wear.

"I'll let you know later after we've spent some time together. I do have to say that I enjoy talking to your sister very much. She's a wonderful girl and such a good mother."

"Yes, Erin is a great mother. Pedro isn't an easy kid, but she does her best to make his life better."

Ryan watched his mother steal his boyfriend. Smooth move, Mom, he thought as he went to the back of the car and popped the trunk.

"Let me help you, son."

"Thanks, Dad." He handed a suitcase to his dad before grabbing their carry on.

"Did you have a good flight?"

They headed into the house. Pausing in the hallway, he shot his father a look.

"You and Josh can use the guest room. The bed's bigger in there."

Surprise shot through him. "Um...thanks, Dad. I wasn't sure if you'd want us to share a room."

"You're adults, Ry. I can't tell you how to live your life. I trust you to respect my house, but if your fiancé was a girl, there wouldn't be any doubt where you'd sleep."

He followed his dad upstairs to where they left the bags in the guest room. His dad stopped him before they went down.

"Ryan, your mother and I are trying our best to make Josh feel welcome here. We might not get everything right, but we're trying."

He couldn't help himself. He hugged his father hard.

"I haven't said it enough, but I appreciate all you've done for me in my life. It was difficult for you to send me to college money-wise. Then when I told you I wanted to go to Hollywood and try my hand at acting, I know you thought I was crazy, but you helped pack me up and sent me out there." Tears welled in his eyes. "I hope you aren't ashamed of me."

"Ashamed? Why would we be ashamed of you?" A puzzled frown marred his father's forehead.

Ryan ducked his head. "For getting my picture in the tabloids. I'm sure it was embarrassing for Mom to go to the grocery store and stuff like that. You don't know how low class I felt seeing myself on the covers of those rags."

"You're a handsome young man and an up-and-coming actor. People are interested in you. Unfortunately, it means your private life isn't as private as you would wish it to be. You and Josh will have to be careful the bigger your career gets." His dad grinned. "It'll be hard, but I think the two of you can make it."

"Ryan, get down here and help me with dinner."

"Just like old times, huh?" His dad slapped him on the back as they went back downstairs.

Ensconced on a bar stool at the island counter, Josh munched on chips and dip while Ryan helped his mom prepare dinner. As he moved around the kitchen, he'd brush up against Josh and tiny chills would chase over his skin at the contact. Would the day ever come when he didn't get turned on by the mere presence of Josh? He hoped not.

Dinner consisted of good food and lots of laughter. Josh kept them in stitches with stories from both the club and the construction site. Ryan told anecdotes about being on set for

Luther is King and some of the other funny tales that happen while making a movie.

The dishes were washed and put away. They retired to the living room with coffee and homemade cookies. As they settled, Ryan leaned into Josh while they sat on the couch. Josh grinned at him, reassuring him silently that everything was okay.

"Now, I sent Erin the guest list for the family, Ryan. I have to admit, though, I'm not sure any one will come." His mother didn't look happy.

His heart dropped. "Really?"

"Well, it is just your father's side. There aren't any aunts or uncles on my side anymore." She touched his father's arm.

"Right, and I'm afraid my siblings aren't all that open-minded. I've already received several phone calls from them about gay marriage being wrong and all that rot." Anger flashed in his father's eyes. "I told them in no uncertain terms that you were my son and I wasn't going to turn my back on you. That marriage has nothing to do with the sex of the people getting married, but everything to do with love."

Josh took Ryan's cup and set it on the coffee table before embracing him. He laid his head on Josh's shoulder and sighed. It hurt to know that people he thought cared for him couldn't see beyond one aspect of his personality to help him celebrate a special moment in his life.

"It's all right, I guess," he mumbled.

"No, it's not." His mom stiffened. "We've supported them when their children did far worse things than fall in love. Yet they dare to preach to us and tell us that our son is going to hell. You're not a murderer or a druggie. It isn't right and I think we're better off not having them there."

He sank deeper into Josh's arms, letting his lover's

strength soothe him inside. "You and Bill will be there. That's all the family I need."

"Don't forget. Garrett and CJ have RSVP'ed and they are more your friends than mine. Mostly because you talk to them far more than I do," Josh pointed out. "And you know, my family is yours. Erin considers you another brother. Pedro loves you as much as I do."

True. The best type of family was the one he created from friends because they chose to care for him.

"Heavens yes, Bill will be there. He wouldn't miss a chance to harass you at the reception. I assume he's your best man." Ryan's dad chuckled.

"Yes. He complained about having to rent a tux and the cost of flying to Vermont, but after I explained that it was all his fault and he had only himself to blame, he changed his tune."

"His fault? How so?" Josh looked at him with interested eyes.

"A couple of weeks before your birthday, I called him in a panic because I couldn't think of anything to get you. He suggested a ring and I joked about you not being a girl and not interested in jewelry. A few days later, I was watching TV and saw a news piece on same sex marriage. The next thing I know I had the rings and plans to ask you to marry me."

"Another thing I have to thank the man for. He really is a great friend." Josh nudged him slightly.

He blushed when he realized what the other thing Josh was talking about. If it wasn't for Bill, they would never have hooked up in the first place.

"He's done a lot of stuff to answer to over the years. Good and bad. I can't wait to hear his speech at the reception." He smiled fondly at the thought of his best friend.

"About your reception."

Obviously his mother had been waiting for an opening. The rest of the night was spent discussing the reception and ceremony. His father deserted them when colors for the table arrangements entered into the conversation. Josh retreated soon after, leaving Ryan and his mother to bond over wedding plans.

It was one of the nicest times he'd ever spent with his mother.

Chapter Seven

The cocktail hour was in full swing when Josh and Ryan arrived at the ballroom they'd rented for the reception. Erin greeted them with hugs. His sister looked gorgeous in a black strapless dress and her hair up. Josh knew the glow of happiness making her skin shine came from two sources. His wedding and the good-looking man who never left her side.

When Chad came to shake his hand, he gave him a hard one-armed hug. "Thank you for taking care of my sister, Chad."

The look Chad sent in Erin's direction made Josh think there might be another wedding to plan sooner rather than later.

"She's a wonderful woman. You did a good job raising her."

"I have a feeling she did most of that on her own."

With their mother out of the picture at an early age, he and Erin had learned to rely on each other, but there were times when Josh felt he'd let his sister down. Especially concerning her marriage to Geraldo.

Chad shrugged. "Maybe, but you set an honorable example to follow and you took care of her when she needed you."

Pedro raced up and hugged Josh's leg hard. Crouching down, he studied his nephew. Excitement and happiness gleamed in Pedro's dark eyes. The crowd and noise didn't seem to be bothering him so far. Zorro bumped his elbow with his nose. Looking over at the dog, he burst out laughing. Someone, most likely his sister, put a garland of white roses around the pit bull's neck. Zorro ducked his head like he was embarrassed to be seen like that.

"Are you having a good time?" he asked Pedro while patting Zorro's broad head.

His nephew nodded his head vigorously, almost falling over with the effort.

"Good. Make sure you don't get into trouble. There will be cake later."

Pedro's eyes lit up at the mention of the dessert. Josh straightened as his nephew and dog disappeared back into the crowd. Chad laughed.

"You've created a monster now. He'll bug Erin every second, wanting to know if it's time for cake yet or not."

"As long as he's not getting upset or having a meltdown, I think we're doing okay. I was afraid the crowd would overwhelm him, but he seems to be handling it well."

"Having Zorro with him helps." Chad spotted someone across the room. "Morgan and Vance just arrived. I'm going to head over to say hi."

"Let them know I'll catch up with them later." Josh acknowledged Morgan's salute.

Ryan waved at him from the side of a petite white-haired lady draped in diamonds and a hot pink feather boa. The infamous Great Aunt Edna must have arrived. Josh hurried over, anticipation surging in his stomach. Something told him that she would be a marvelous support for Ryan, not just at the wedding, but in the rest of his life as well.

"Aunt Edna, this is my partner, Josh Bauer. Josh, this is

my great aunt." Ryan introduced them.

He took the elegant hand offered him in his and bent, kissing the paper-thin skin gently. An expensive perfume wafted over his nose and he was sure Erin or Rachel could tell him the name of it, but whatever it was fit the older lady perfectly.

"It's wonderful to finally meet you, Ms. Kellar. I must say the women in Ryan's family are some of the most beautiful I have ever seen. That's saying something considering I live in Hollywood."

"Quite the flatterer." Edna fluttered her eyelashes at him and smiled, her faded blue eyes cool like she was gauging his worthiness for Ryan.

"I call them like I see them, ma'am." He tucked her hand in the crook of his elbow. "Would you like a drink?"

"I never turn down a drink from a good-looking man." She flapped the end of her boa at Ryan. "You can go mingle with your guests, Nephew. Your beau will take care of me, I'm sure."

"Yes, ma'am."

They shared fond smiles over Edna's head and Josh escorted her to the bar. The bartender's eyebrows shot up when they arrived.

"What would you like, Ms. Kellar?"

"Call me Edna. I'd like a Jameson on the rocks, please. And, young man, I'd like more whiskey than rocks." She winked at the bartender, who laughed and nodded.

Resting an elbow on the bar, Josh ordered a beer. They got their drinks and Edna held hers up.

"To the man who won my nephew's heart. May you treat it as the precious gift it is."

He clinked his bottle to her glass and said in as serious a tone as he could, "I will cherish it every minute of my life."

"I knew you were a smart man, Josh." She turned to survey the room.

Her movements were graceful and she carried herself like a dancer. She had a kind of timeless beauty and he imagined there must have been hundreds of men who fell in love with her when she was younger.

"May I ask a personal question?"

She looked at him from the corner of her eye and nodded. "Certainly, Josh. I have no secrets from family."

"Why did you never marry? I'm sure you could have had your choice of men, but you never picked one."

Sighing, she waved the bartender over to fill up her glass. "I did pick one."

The sadness in her sigh warned Josh there wasn't a happy ending to her story. He caressed her arm.

"You don't have to tell me. I was being nosy and it's definitely none of my business."

"Let's go for a stroll." She picked up her glass and slid her arm through his when he offered it.

Josh picked up his beer and wandered with Edna around the edges of the room. Maybe it was the look on her face or the way she carried herself, but no one interrupted them. They found a private alcove and she sat, primly tucking her dress around her legs and arranging the boa around her shoulders.

"I had gone over to England before the second world war. I met Frank at one of the clubs the soldiers frequented. We started dating, as best as anyone could back then. The Nazis were taking over Europe and we all knew that Britain would be entering the war soon. He wanted me to marry him before he got shipped over to the continent."

"Why didn't you?" He sat next to her.

"Arrogance in a way. I was young and believed, even with the war looming, we had all the time in the world. I didn't want to be tied down, though I loved him with my whole heart. I told him we would talk about marriage again when he returned." Wisdom filled her soft laugh. "I should have known it wouldn't work out that way."

"What happened?" Josh had already figured out that Frank hadn't made it back.

"He died at the Battle of the Bulge and I lost my chance at love."

He tugged the handkerchief Ryan had tucked in his pocket out and handed it to Edna. She dabbed the tears from her cheeks.

"I'm sure there have been many more offers since then, Edna. Why didn't you accept any of them?"

She twisted the cotton square with her hands. "Maybe part of me didn't believe I deserved to be happy when Frank died, protecting his country. He loved me so much and I know I hurt him when I didn't say yes. The other thing is I never felt the way about any of those other men like I did Frank. I've had lovers by the dozen since then, but I couldn't give any of them my heart."

Josh let the silence reign for a few minutes while he thought about Edna's past and losing her chance at love. He angled his body to look at her.

"That's why you came tonight."

Edna waved to someone in the crowd and Josh turned to see who it was. Ryan stood next to his parents, but his gaze was on them. Josh didn't stop to think before he blew a kiss in his lover's direction. Ryan's face lit up with such love that Josh caught his breath at the beauty of it.

"Yes, that's why I came tonight. Being gay isn't looked down on quite as harshly as it was in my heyday, but you still have your battles to fight. Supporting Ryan at his wedding is my way of making up for the fact that I didn't take a chance on love when I should have." Edna met his gaze with her own, determination firming her lips. "You are grasping love and holding tight to it. No one has the right to tell you you're wrong."

Leaning down, he brushed a kiss over Edna's cheek. "You are a strong woman, Edna. I know Ryan is honored that you came. Hopefully, you can grow closer now. With all your Vaudeville experience, I know you can help him with his career."

She patted his cheek. "I'll do what I can."

Erin caught his eye and mimed eating. He stood, held out a hand to help Edna to her feet.

"It looks like dinner is ready to be served. May I escort you to your table?"

"Did that blonde lady put me at the same table as Garrett Johnson?"

"Yes, she did." He swallowed his chuckle.

"Marvelous. When Cynthia mentioned he would be here, I knew I wanted to sit with him. He's a nice piece of eye candy." Edna practically wrung her hands together in glee.

Josh couldn't keep his laughter from bursting out that time. The oddness of this dignified lady saying something like "eye candy" struck him as hilarious. "Oh, you and Garrett are going to have such fun teasing CJ."

Everyone made their way to the dining room where the tables were set and the wait staff stood ready to serve the meal. Josh nodded toward Edna when he saw Ryan looking for him. Ryan smiled and took a seat next to Bill at the head table which included Bill's date, Erin, Chad and Pedro. Ryan's parents sat with Rachel and Josh's friends from the Lucky Seven.

Both Garrett and CJ stood when Josh and Edna approached them.

"Gentlemen, I'd like to introduce you to Ms. Edna Kellar. She's Ryan's great aunt and specifically requested to be seated at your table."

"We're honored, Ms. Kellar, and again, I'm forced to say that the Kellar women are some of the most attractive ladies I've ever met." Garrett bowed over Edna's hand, earning an actual giggle from the lady.

"This time I have to agree with my partner." CJ claimed Edna's hand after Garrett let it go.

"Oh my. Two gorgeous hunks and they're all mine." Edna waved Josh away. "You go and enjoy your dinner with Ryan, Josh. I'll be fine."

Josh did just that. He knew Garrett and CJ would take good care of Edna, so he could focus his attention on Ryan and their upcoming vows.

Chapter Eight

Ryan leaned over when Josh took the chair next to him. "Did you have a good talk with Aunt Edna?"

"She's an interesting lady. We're going to have to keep in touch with her after the wedding. I think she'd be able to help you." Josh grinned.

A strange clinking sound filled the air and Ryan turned to find Bill hitting his wine glass with a fork. Narrowing his eyes, he glared at his friend.

"Come on. You've been to a wedding reception before. When the guests hit their glasses, the bride and groom have to kiss. Okay, technically you're not married yet and we have two grooms, but still the idea's the same." Bill's smile was pure evil.

"You're going to be doing this all night, aren't you?"

"You better believe it, buddy." Bill waved a hand at him and Josh. "Come on now. Pucker up."

Josh was laughing as they leaned toward each other. They took their time kissing, not caring that it held up the meal or that their friends were whistling at them. It was their night.

"All right. All right. That's enough for now. We would all like to eat before the dancing starts," Bill yelled.

Laughter erupted throughout the room and Ryan flopped back in his chair, laughing as loudly as the others. God, he never imagined that he would have this much fun at his wedding. Of course, he never thought he'd get married.

His best friend stood and gestured to the waiters. "Make sure everyone has some champagne. It's time for the toasts."

Light chatter filled the room while the waiters uncorked the bottles and distributed the champagne. Ryan looked at his friend.

"Are you going to embarrass me or Josh?"

Bill turned away from the busty brunette he'd brought as a date. When Ryan had asked who she was earlier, Bill explained that he met her out on the slopes and since she wasn't busy she agreed to come with him. Only Bill would bring a stranger to his best friend's wedding.

"Isn't that what the best man is supposed to?" Butter wouldn't melt in Bill's mouth.

"Just remember that my parents are here," he whispered urgently over the table.

"Don't worry. It'll be fine."

He rolled his eyes and Josh reached under the table to squeeze his knee.

"Relax, Ryan. Your parents know what Bill's like." Josh's warm breath washed over his ear.

"I just don't want him upsetting them or you," he admitted.

"I'm a big boy. I can handle anything your friend dishes out."

Their champagne glasses were filled and Bill stood, raising his in the air.

"Like everything else in his life, Ryan had to have a different kind of wedding. So here we are, having the reception first before he and Josh exchange vows."

Everyone chuckled.

"None of us ever imagined that Josh and Ryan would be vanguards in a way by actually getting married instead of just having a commitment ceremony, but more power to them as far as I'm concerned."

Their friends clapped.

"I've known Ryan for a long time and I consider him my best friend. Too many times I saw him walk away from relationships because of the inherent problems involved with being gay in our society. Yet from the first time I saw Ryan and Josh together, I knew that this was one relationship that Ryan had to fight for."

Bill nodded at Josh.

"Josh, you will be the rock my friend can cling to when he needs support and strength. You will anchor Ryan while he spreads his wings and learns to fly." After clearing his throat, Bill took a little sip of champagne. "Ryan, what can I say? You've been my best friend for years and no one deserves happiness more than you. I love you, man. Congratulations."

Everyone drank and Josh wiped a tear off Ryan's cheek with his napkin.

"Who would have thought Bill could be such an eloquent speaker?" Josh teased, flicking some drops of water from his glass at Bill.

"I was inspired, jackass." Bill flipped Josh off.

"Classy, dude." Ryan rolled his eyes.

"Uh-hum." Erin cleared her throat.

They all turned to where she stood on the other side of Josh, her hand lying on his shoulder.

"I was honored when Josh asked me to stand up with him. It surprised me a little since Antonio has been Josh's best friend since we were little." She pointed to Antonio sitting a table away with his wife.

Antonio acknowledged everyone's stares, but Ryan noticed the man looked a little green around the edges. It might have been caused by the kiss Ryan and Josh shared. Antonio never turned his back on Josh when he came out, yet he wasn't comfortable with public displays of affections between Josh and Ryan. It had been Marcelia, Antonio's wife, who told her husband that they were coming to Josh's wedding. Ryan owed the lady a personal thank you because he knew it meant a lot to Josh to have the man there.

"When I asked him why he was asking me, he told me it was because for so many years, our family had just been the two of us. I was the only one he could trust with his deepest darkest secrets."

Tears pooled in Erin's eyes and Chad handed her a handkerchief to dry them. She took it with a warm look in the man's direction.

"Then Pedro came along. I floundered, trying to learn how to deal with my son and how to make him comfortable in a world that doesn't always understand him. Josh struggled to keep the two of us safe from the poor decision in a husband I had made. Through it all, we leaned on each other, taking strength with the knowledge that our little family of three was stronger for the trials we went through."

Josh reached up and covered Erin's hand while grasping Ryan's hand with his free one. Ryan almost gasped at the strength in Josh's grip on his hand, but looking at the emotion in his lover's face, Ryan didn't say a word. Erin's speech hit Josh in the heart and Ryan understood the man was trying not to cry.

"But we persevered and settled into a routine. It worked for us, though we were both lonely for companionship of a different kind. Josh had his chances, but he wouldn't stop being my big brother long enough to allow those chances to grow."

Ryan felt her gaze rest on him and he met her eyes with an encouraging smile.

"One night, Josh met someone and their first kiss put into motion events that led us to this night. After all that trouble, I wouldn't have been surprised if Josh and Ryan had called their budding relationship quits, but both men are stronger than any of us give them credit for being. They held tight to each other, believing that love was more important than career or reputation."

Erin moved to stand between them, her hands on both their shoulders.

"Ryan is perfect for my big brother in so many ways. He makes Josh laugh and smile, something he hasn't done very often. He gets Josh to relax, which we all know is a major feat. He fits into our family without any sharp edges or doubts, opening his heart to Pedro and me as quickly as he did to Josh."

A drop of liquid rolled down Ryan's cheek and he swiped at it with his hand.

"Congratulations, Josh and Ryan. May your marriage make all your dreams come true and prove that love will last no matter who is in love."

Their guests took a drink of their champagne while Josh jumped to his feet, dragging Ryan with him. They wrapped Erin in a tight hug as she cried on their shoulders. After a few moments, they gained control again and stepped away from each other. Erin returned to her seat while Josh and Ryan remained standing.

Holding hands, they turned to face the rest of their guests. Ryan's mother sobbed quietly into a handkerchief while Ryan's dad encircled her shoulders with his arms. There were tears in numerous eyes and smiles on everyone's face.

"We want to thank you all for coming and making our wedding so very special. It means a lot that you gave up holiday time to come here. Of course, Vermont is a rather beautiful place to be on New Year's Eve." Josh waved his free hand toward the windows looking out of the snow-covered hills.

"In many ways, you are all our family, whether by blood or by choice. I guarantee that when both Josh and I admitted to ourselves we were gay, neither of us ever imagined getting married, but here we are, and though we haven't said the words or made it official yet, I think, in our hearts, we've felt married for months now." He raised his glass, which had been refilled by the efficient waiting staff. "Thank you and enjoy yourselves."

The glasses were emptied again and Josh signaled the manager that the food could be served. A low hum started as people chatted at the tables as the dinner plates were delivered. Josh talked to Erin, Chad and Pedro while Ryan chatted with Bill and his date.

Chapter Nine

After everyone ate their fill, Josh stood, knocking on his glass to get everyone's attention. Of course, that caused everyone to start hitting their own glasses and he ended up having to kiss Ryan. It wasn't a hardship by any means. He even slid his hand to the small of Ryan's back and dipped the man back to give a dramatic flair to the kiss.

Hooting and hollering, their guests encouraged it. By the time he let Ryan stand up, both of them were panting and Josh wished he could adjust himself. There seemed to be a decided lack of room in his pants all of a sudden.

"Now that you're done with that rather impressive display of making out, what did you want to say, Josh?" Bill smirked as Josh reached across the table to smack him upside the head.

"What I wanted to say, before I was so pleasantly interrupted, was it's time to cut the cake and after that, there will be dancing until twenty minutes before midnight. That's when the ceremony will start. Now, hopefully, everything will run as smoothly as it did last night at the rehearsal."

Pedro and Zorro led the way to where the wedding cake stood, in regal splendor. They'd chosen to go with a non-traditional cake and when their guests realized what it was, they all erupted into laughter. The two miniature grooms stood on top of a camera with a replica of *The Hollywood Enterprise* folded up next to it. A friend of Erin's at work made the cake for them.

"Oh my God, that's perfect." Rachel spoke up from where she stood between Morgan and Vance. "You two are evil."

"Hey, the tabloid brought us together in a way." Ryan picked up a cake knife before gesturing to Sam, his agent. "That's why the *Enterprise* will get exclusive pictures from the wedding and an interview from me about getting married."

Ryan had discussed the interview possibility with Josh and as long as Ryan and Sam were comfortable doing it, Josh didn't mind, though it had been understood that Josh wouldn't be participating in said interview.

He cut a small piece of cake and turned to Josh. His lover smiled and opened his mouth. With a wink, he shoved the cake into Josh's face. Josh grabbed another piece that Erin had cut and slipped a hand behind Ryan's head, holding him still to pay him back. After struggling a few seconds, Ryan froze.

"Stop it, you two. You're going to ruin your tuxes before you even get married." Erin pulled on Josh's arm.

Breaking away, Ryan laughed as Josh wiped a towel through the layer of frosting coating his face. He took the napkin Rachel handed him and cleaned the mess off himself. One of the waiters came by and took the cake away to cut up and serve.

"We still have two hours before the ceremony begins, maybe we should do some dancing." He nodded toward the band, who had set up while they were eating dinner.

Whirling around, he searched out Josh and grabbed his hand, pulling him to the dance floor. Ryan slipped his arms around Josh's shoulders, lying his head on Josh's chest as the slow song started. They strolled around the empty floor. Josh hummed in his ear, hands cupping his ass and pulling him closer.

Ryan eased back a few inches to look into Josh's eyes. "Why does this feel so much different than every other dance we shared?"

"Because even though we haven't said the actual words yet, we're married and this is our first dance as a married couple." Josh nuzzled his cheek.

Not caring who was watching, he brought Josh's face to his and kissed him. Their mouths moved leisurely together, tasting and testing. Relearning each touch that made the other shiver or moan. Each taking in the breath of the other, sharing the very thing that helped them live. Ryan allowed Josh to take the kiss deeper. Giving up control was easy for him and Josh liked to be in charge.

He slipped one hand up under Josh's jacket, stroking it up and down Josh's back, caressing each bump on his lover's spine. "I love it when you hold me like this."

"I'll hold you like this forever, Ryan."

The music died away and they came to a halt. Someone started clapping and they looked around. All of their guests were gathered around the dance floor, watching them dance. All the ladies had tears in their eyes. Some of the men looked uncomfortable, but most were smiling.

"Everyone grab a partner and join the happy couple on the floor," the lead singer said.

Garrett and CJ were the first pair to walk out. Soon the floor was crowded with people dancing and laughing. Ryan patted Josh on the ass before moving off to mingle with everyone.

Morgan and Vance were dancing next to Rachel and Pete. He kissed them all before moving on. He wanted to say hi to everyone who took time out of their holidays to support them.

He was leaning on the bar when Morgan and Vance joined him.

"What are you gentlemen drinking?" He waved the bartender over.

"I'll have a scotch and water," Morgan ordered.

"I'll have a beer." Vance laughed as Ryan grimaced.

Morgan shook his head. "The only taste Vance has is in men."

"I say the same thing about Josh. But hey, as long as he stays with me, then he can drink beer all he wants." Ryan sipped his whiskey while he watched Josh foxtrot Aunt Edna around the floor. "I didn't know Josh could foxtrot."

"What did he tell us?" Morgan glanced over at Vance.

"He learned to dance for Erin, so he could teach her. That way when she went to dances in high school, she wouldn't be embarrassed because she didn't know how to dance." Vance nodded toward Erin and Chad as they danced past. "Until you, everything he did was for her and Pedro. It's nice to see him doing things for himself."

"I never got to thank you for helping out with security for tonight."

Ryan gestured toward the discreet men in black suits wandering around the edges of the room, keeping an eye out to make sure no one got in who wasn't invited.

"Least we could do. You're a big star now, Ryan. Any thing you do makes the news and for some strange reason, people think your personal life is fair game." Morgan ran his finger through the circle of water left by his glass.

Ryan grunted his agreement. Aunt Edna waltzed over to him and grabbed his hand, dragging him out on the floor as she winked at the other men. Grinning, he twirled her around. She was pretty spry for being ninety. Soon, she'd moved on to another partner while he caught his breath.

Josh came up behind him, encircled his waist, and tugged him close. Lying his hands over Josh's on his stomach, Ryan let Josh support his weight while they rested and watched their friends party.

The preacher approached them and Ryan checked the clock on the wall. It was twenty-five minutes to midnight.

"Are you ready?"

Ryan turned in Josh's arms to face him. "You ready to get married, Josh?"

"I was ready the day you asked me."

Chapter Ten

Josh got the bandleader's attention and the man stopped the music. Everyone turned to look at him and Ryan.

"We need to get this wedding started. Can everyone gather around?" He held out a hand to Erin.

Bill strolled up with his date on his arm. "Are we going to do this thing?"

"Yes, we are."

Ryan and Josh stood arm-in-arm before the preacher with Erin on Josh's side and Bill on Ryan's. Rev. Harold Rutherford greeted everyone with a bright grin.

"I have to admit that weddings are my second favorite ceremony to perform. My first is, of course, baptisms. There is such joy and hope at weddings where a couple is willing to join their lives together." Rev. Harold held open his arms to include everyone in the room. "I know that you who will be witnesses to this wedding will help them continue on the path of love and happiness by supporting them and reminding them why they love each other."

Ryan trembled and Josh slipped his arm around Ryan's waist, supporting him. He didn't know if it was nerves or just excitement that affected the man, but he had no doubt that Ryan would go through with it.

"Dearly beloved, we are gathered here today to witness the union of these two men." The reverend stopped and laughed. "It's odd to be saying that, but so refreshing at the same time."

Josh silently agreed with the man. How strange it felt to be standing, surrounded by friends and family, about to exchange vows with another man. It was something Josh never thought to see in his own lifetime, aside from never thinking he'd experience it for himself.

Ryan's laugh had just a touch of hysteria to it. Josh couldn't believe that the man who could be so calm and collected in front of a camera had sweaty palms about one little ceremony.

"Joshua Kenneth Bauer, do you take this man, Ryan Jonathan Kellar, for your lawful wedded husband, to live in the estate of holy matrimony? Will you love, honor, comfort and cherish him from this day forward, forsaking all others, keeping only unto him for as long as you both shall live?"

"I do."

Rev. Harold turned to Ryan and asked him the same question.

"I do."

"Turn and face each other, gentlemen. Josh, repeat after me."

Josh gripped Ryan's hands tight in his and smiled softly at his lover.

"I, Joshua Kenneth Bauer, take thee, Ryan Jonathan Kellar, to be my lawful wedded husband, my constant friend, my faithful partner, and my love for this day forward. In the presence of God, our family and friends, I offer you my solemn vow to be your faithful partner in sickness and in health, in good times and bad, and in joy as well as sorrow. I promise to love you unconditionally, to support you in your goals, to honor

267

and respect you, to laugh with you and cry with you, and to cherish you for as long as we both shall live."

Josh recited them in a strong voice, wanting everyone to hear.

"Wonderful. Now, it's your turn, Ryan."

Ryan's voice shook and cracked as he repeated the vows. Josh bit his lip, not wanting to cry. He'd shed enough tears that day. It was supposed to be a happy occasion.

"To cherish you..." Ryan paused, regrouped and finished, "...for as long as we both shall live."

"Do you have the rings?"

Bill handed Ryan Josh's ring and Erin slipped Ryan's off her finger to lie in Josh's palm. In turn, they set them on the Bible Rev. Harold held out to them. He blessed them. "May these rings be blessed so that they who give them and wear them may abide in peace and continue in peace until life's end."

"Josh, take Ryan's ring and place it on his finger while repeating after me. With this ring, I thee wed. Wear it as a symbol of our love and commitment."

Josh noted his trembling fingers as he did what the reverend ordered him. He slid the ring halfway down and focused on what the reverend was saying. He repeated them in a shaking voice. After finishing, he pushed the ring all the way on and lifted Ryan's hand to brush a kiss over the ring, sealing his vow.

"Wonderful. Now, Ryan, place Josh's ring on his finger and repeat after me."

When Ryan finished, he kissed Josh's ring and flipping over Josh's hand, he kissed his palm.

Rev. Harold glanced up, including the whole group again with a benevolent expression. "In so much as Joshua and Ryan have consented to life forever together in wedlock, and have witnessed the same before this company, have given and pledged their troth, each to the other, and having declared the same by giving and receiving of rings, I pronounce them husband and husband. You may share a kiss."

They crushed their mouths together, hard enough to split Josh's bottom lip. Relief ripped through Josh. They had made it through a major problem at the beginning of their relationship, proving that as long as they communicated and didn't jump to conclusions, they could weather any kind of storm. The bigger and brighter Ryan's star burned, the more possibilities arose of trouble, but Josh planned on always listening to Ryan.

"All right. You're starting to turn blue, guys."

Bill's comment broke the spell and they eased apart, keeping a hold of each other's hands before turning to face their guests.

"Ladies and gentlemen, I'd like to present Mr. Josh Bauer-Kellar and Mr. Ryan Kellar."

Everyone gasped and Ryan whirled to stare at him. He nodded, knowing what it meant to Ryan. They had discussed whether or not they would change their names. Nothing had been decided, so Josh thought he'd surprise Ryan with the hyphenated name. His career didn't rely on name recognition like Ryan's did. It had been no big deal.

"Three... Two... One."

Screams and yells came from all areas of the resort as everyone counted down to midnight. Horns sounded and Josh grabbed Ryan in his arms, whirling him around as they kissed again, celebrating their marriage and the start of a new year.

"Ryan, I'm sorry to bother you, but I need you two and your witnesses to sign the license." Sam tapped Ryan on the shoulder.

Rounding up Erin and Bill, they went to a corner of the room where Sam produced the license and everyone signed it. When the last signature was signed, the others disappeared, leaving Josh and Ryan standing alone.

"Why change your name?" Ryan pushed into his arms, putting his arms around Josh's waist under his jacket.

He shrugged and cupped Ryan's firm ass, drawing his husband as close as he could with the layers of clothes between them. "I just thought it was fitting. Like a symbolic blending of our lives. Plus you're just getting started in Hollywood, and you can't really be changing your name at this point."

"Thank you," Ryan whispered against his ear.

"You're welcome." He inched away to look into Ryan's eyes. "I love you more than I think you realize, Ryan Kellar. I will do everything in my power to make this marriage work."

"Loving you has opened so many doors for me that I never even knew were there." Ryan's intense focus on him made Josh feel like there was no one else in the room. "I will meet you more than halfway in this marriage to keep our love strong and growing deeper every day."

The kiss they shared this time held promise, love, passion and comfort. There was no fierce urgency, though that would come. It was a kiss between two men who knew they were loved and in a relationship meant to last forever.

About the Author

To learn more about T.A. Chase please visit www.tachase.blogspot.com Send an email to T.A. at chase.ta@gmail.com

GREAT CHEAP FUN

Discover eBooks!

THE FASTEST WAY TO GET THE HOTTEST NAMES

Get your favorite authors on your favorite reader, long before they're
out in print! Ebooks from Samhain go wherever you go, and work with
whatever you carry—Palm, PDF, Mobi, and more.

Samhain
Publishing, Ltd

WWW.SAMHAINPUBLISHING.COM

LaVergne, TN USA
07 November 2010
203868LV00003B/2/P